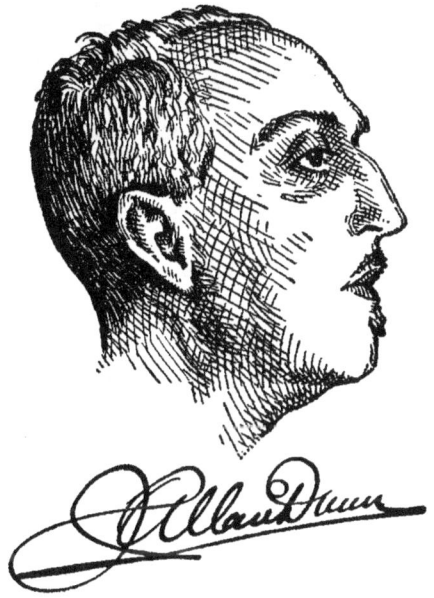

DAY of DOOM

THE COMPLETE BATTLES OF GORDON MANNING & THE GRIFFIN

VOLUME 2

J. ALLAN DUNN

ALTUS PRESS • 2014

EDITED AND DESIGNED BY

Matthew Moring

INTERIOR ILLUSTRATIONS BY

Joseph A. Farren

PUBLISHING HISTORY

"Death's Frozen Finger" originally appeared in the July 18, 1931 issue of *Detective Fiction Weekly* magazine. Copyright 1931 by Popular Publications, Inc. Copyright renewed 1958 and assigned to Steeger Properties, LLC. All Rights Reserved.

"The Menace of the Monster" originally appeared in the August 29, 1931 issue of *Detective Fiction Weekly* magazine. Copyright 1931 by Popular Publications, Inc. Copyright renewed 1958 and assigned to Steeger Properties, LLC. All Rights Reserved.

"The Mottled Monster" originally appeared in the February 27, 1932 issue of *Detective Fiction Weekly* magazine. Copyright 1932 by Popular Publications, Inc. Copyright renewed 1959 and assigned to Steeger Properties, LLC. All Rights Reserved.

"The Way the Wind Blew" originally appeared in the July 2, 1932 issue of *Detective Fiction Weekly* magazine. Copyright 1932 by Popular Publications, Inc. Copyright renewed 1959 and assigned to Steeger Properties, LLC. All Rights Reserved.

"The Dust of Destiny" originally appeared in the July 30, 1932 issue of *Detective Fiction Weekly* magazine. Copyright 1932 by Popular Publications, Inc. Copyright renewed 1959 and assigned to Steeger Properties, LLC. All Rights Reserved.

"Hunch!" originally appeared in the September 24, 1932 issue of *Detective Fiction Weekly* magazine. Copyright 1932 by Popular Publications, Inc. Copyright renewed 1959 and assigned to Steeger Properties, LLC. All Rights Reserved.

"The Unknown Menace" originally appeared in the October 8, 1932 issue of *Detective Fiction Weekly* magazine. Copyright 1932 by Popular Publications, Inc. Copyright renewed 1959 and assigned to Steeger Properties, LLC. All Rights Reserved.

"Death Silent and Invisible" originally appeared in the November 5, 1932 issue of *Detective Fiction Weekly* magazine. Copyright 1932 by Popular Publications, Inc. Copyright renewed 1959 and assigned to Steeger Properties, LLC. All Rights Reserved.

"Day of Doom" originally appeared in the November 19, 1932 issue of *Detective Fiction Weekly* magazine. Copyright 1932 by Popular Publications, Inc. Copyright renewed 1960 and assigned to Steeger Properties, LLC. All Rights Reserved.

"Death in a Leash" originally appeared in the December 21, 1932 issue of *Detective Fiction Weekly* magazine. Copyright 1932 by Popular Publications, Inc. Copyright renewed 1960 and assigned to Steeger Properties, LLC. All Rights Reserved.

THANKS TO

Joel Frieman, Monte Herridge, Everard P. Digges LaTouche, Ray Riethmeier and Jonathan Sweet

TABLE OF CONTENTS

From the Air, Manning Fights the Ferocious
Scheme of His Arch-Enemy, the Griffin

GORDON MANNING usually went for lunch to his favorite down town restaurant. It is open to the public at large, still it is a sort of a club, one of the few places where they still have real waiters who remember the tastes of their customers and know how to cater to them.

The food is excellent, the liquor, if you want it, may be relied upon. It is a true copy of a first-class, old-fashioned English chophouse. There are comfortable stalls where you may enjoy a game pie or a steak and kidney pudding. Manning appreciated good food. He kept himself always in the prime of condition. Now, more than ever, it was necessary to do so.

He was on the trail of the Griffin, the inhuman monster who had terrorized Manhattan, had made his malignant deeds felt throughout the whole United States, with his frightful and deliberate killings of the finest citizens.

Manning, ex-officer of the military Secret Service, had been detailed to succeed where the regular police forces had failed in the apprehension, the elimination, of the Griffin. So far, Manning had also failed. He had grappled with the Griffin's agents, arrested some of them, killed some of them, but he had not succeeded in preventing any one of the crimes that the Griffin so audaciously announced beforehand; nor had he any real clew to the whereabouts of the monster's headquarters.

This arch-fiend, undoubtedly mad, suffering from grandiose dementia, from egomania and homicidal and sadistic impulses, his mentality warped against all that was honorable, against all advancement and achievement, as a demon is warped against all goodness, had adopted as a title the name of the mythical creature, half lion, half eagle, the griffin.

To place emphasis upon his misdeeds, he used a scarlet seal, a flaming oval embossed with the symbol of a griffin's upper body, rampant. The symbol of his own readiness to swoop, to leap, to strike and rend!

Through some mysterious source of knowledge, he had not merely the audacity to congratulate Manning upon his secret appointment, supposedly only known to Manning and the commissioner of police; but he had proclaimed the conflict between them a game.

A contest like that of the chessboard, using living pieces; a game wherein he challenged Manning, reserving for himself the moves of his opening attack, yet boldly giving out not merely the name of his intended victim, but the actual day upon which the tragedy would take place.

Manning sat in his usual seat at the restaurant now, his demitasse of coffee before him. He filled his pipe and lit it, ruminating.

With every thought and energy set upon his task, Manning was so closely attuned to the evil vibrations sent out by the Griffin that he sensed the imminence of the next crime, even as the primitive savage can feel the presence of an enemy hidden in the bush, miles away.

Manning was worn with anxiety. Even his perfect nerves were beginning to feel the constant strain, the heavy responsibility. He had a premonition, a hunch, that the diabolical being had plotted his moves, was ready to commence the play, to open the gambit in the Game of Death. He could not shake it off, and he rose, laid down his always generous tip, picked up the check, paid it to the smiling cashier, got his coat from its peg on the nearby stand, and felt in his pocket for his gloves.

There was a paper that had not been there when he had come

*It was pressed against the panes,
a face—hideous, devilish.*

in! It would not be hard in the busy luncheon hour to thrust a neatly-folded note into the pocket of the hanging garment.

It might be a message from the Griffin!

It was a mystery he deliberately left unsolved until he had returned to his offices, where he practiced as a consulting attorney, doing some legal business despite his tremendous special task.

In his private room that overlooked the towers and spires and set-in buildings reared high against the sky, the monuments of Manhattan, the weblike bridge, and the busy river, Manning unfolded the note.

It was hand-printed with great neatness. Manning read it through three times before he set fire to it and saw it burn in a metal tray to a fragment of carbon which he crushed to ash. Its contents were photographed on his brain.

TO-NIGHT, WHEN YOU DRIVE HOME TO PEL-HAM, FOLLOW THE BLACK CAR WITH GRAY WHEELS, BUICK SEDAN, THAT WILL PICK YOU UP AT MT. VERNON. DO NOT TRAIL TOO OPENLY OR TOO CLOSELY. WE WILL GIVE YOU A LEAD

YOU ARE LOOKING FOR. WE WILL SHOW YOU
WHERE THE MAD DEVIL LIVES. THAT IS AS FAR
AS WE CAN GO. IT MAY MEAN OUR LIVES, BUT,
IF IT MEANS THE DEATH OF THIS FIEND, WE
SHALL BE CONTENT.

Manning walked to the big window and gazed out with
unseeing eyes, considering the communication.

It might be a trap, but, if so, it was a very obvious one; unlike
the Griffin's devious, unexpected methods. Manning had been
indirectly threatened, more than once, when he had run almost
equal risks with some man he was endeavoring to protect. The
Griffin had told him often, by word of mouth over an untraceable telephone wire, through television or radio apparatus, in
letters written in his own bold script—purple ink on heavy gray
paper, sealed always with the scarlet symbol—that, the moment
he failed to amuse the Griffin as an opponent, he would cease
to live.

Though he knew no such thing as fear, physical or mental,
Manning realized that this was a very real danger, hanging
always like the Sword of Damocles upon a thread, a thread that
was the whim of the monster.

He knew also that he was constantly under the observation
of the Griffin's agents. There was a great advantage the Griffin
did not fail to use—his knowledge of Manning's whereabouts,
his home, his offices, his usual haunts.

The agents who had been captured had inevitably refused
under all pressure to give any clew. They were slaves of the
Master, held in bondage by the dread of punishment not only
for themselves, but those they loved.

No doubt they hated him, many of them. There might be a
few of those agents who were of the Griffin's own twisted, evil
kind, but the majority must rebel against their servitude, at the
frightfulness of the deeds which they were forced to commit.

These particular men—there were evidently two or more, as
he understood the note, one the driver of the car and the other

the observer—might well be mutineers, determined to lead Manning to the lair of the master murderer.

He made up his mind swiftly and definitely. He could not afford to overlook any lead. He would trail the sedan, as directed.

I I

FOR SEVERAL hours he worked on the affairs of clients, deciding, dictating, signing papers. He left at his usual hour, getting his powerful roadster from its parking place, driving his ordinary route, sure enough that he was watched. But he saw nothing of the black sedan with the gray wheels until he reached Mount Vernon.

There, true to appointment, it appeared ahead of him, making a right turn, giving him a lead. With his pulse going up a few beats, then settling to normal, but his blood still tingling at the prospect of discovering the aerie of the Griffin, the chance of coming to close quarters with him at last, Manning fell in behind.

He got no more than the barest glimpse of the two men in the sedan; nor had they looked his way. He followed them, through Pelham Manor, his own residential suburb, on to New Rochelle, through Larchmont and Mamaroneck. The steady string of cars had thinned out by now, but there were still plenty of them on the road. Manning kept one or two between his own and the machine he was following.

It was hardly dusk, though some lights were on in the houses, when they headed for Rye. They had kept close to the coast line. Manning had always figured the Griffin would not be far from water, rail, or good roads. He had once used a powerful hydroplane. Doubtless he had calculated on possible getaways. Manning had been pretty close to the Griffin sometimes in their grisly game of tag.

It would not be far now. He felt it in every nerve. Just how close might he get this time?

A long car, powerful, heavy, painted a neutral tint, running silently, swiftly, and so easily as barely to indicate its tremendous speed, passed Manning's roadster as a race horse might pass a farm colt.

Manning was rolling at about forty with plenty of reserve. This car was making eighty.

He had seen it before. Once he had chased it, fruitlessly. Another time it had bested him in pace. He was sure of this car's identity, and was smitten with a sudden sense of failure, of disaster.

It passed the black sedan. Something was tossed from it into, or through, a window of the smaller car. No one would ever tell just what happened. The long car fled with an increased burst of speed. Vanished. Inside the sedan there was a sudden tremendous explosion. Enough force had been released there to have performed a task twenty times as great, and as hideous. A burst of flame, a stench of gases, fragments of wood and metal and of men hurtled far and wide.

Rolling, yellow smoke, as if some terrible jinni had wrought this frightfulness and was escaping in his cloak of vapor, borrowed from hell's own wardrobe!

The car immediately behind the fated sedan was twenty feet away, but it was flung on its side by the force of the explosion; the one back of it swerved to the curb, ran up on the sidewalk, crashing, out of temporary control, into a low stone wall.

Manning had to grip his wheel with all his strength. He set his brakes hard. The impact of the blast had already checked him.

Then he got out, looked at the rough pits torn in the smooth road, at the ghastly scraps that testified to the Griffin's supreme and continuous control over his operatives. It almost seemed to him that, with the terrific trump of the explosion still smashing on his eardrums, he heard also the echo of mocking laughter lingering in the air.

A motorcycle officer came tearing up, intrepid and ready.

Manning halted him with a gesture of authority as he braked to a stop, showed him a badge that brought a swift salute.

"Another racket bump-off," said the cop, conclusively. Manning did not contradict him. There was no evidence. Shreds of human flesh cannot talk. And Manning was not disposed to. Not yet.

I I I

MANNING HAD no appetite for the savory meal his Japanese servants had prepared and served him. He was used to awful sights, to carnage, to dreadful spectacles. It was his soul that had to steady itself in its citadel. There were moments when he almost wondered if the Griffin was really human, not some hideous conjuration of evil, an atrocious creation of a modern Frankenstein made from materials gathered from graveyard and dissecting room. Even a materialization out of hell itself!

He set those fantasies aside, lighting the tobacco in the brier-root bowl. Frankenstein's monster destroyed itself. So it might be with the Griffin.

One failure to make good his predictions, and the man's inflamed brain might well give way like rotten wood at a firm touch.

But he had scored to-night!

There seemed to be a stirring in the air of the room. The logs on the fire fell in, flame leaped and the room grew darker. This was his library. As yet, only one shadowed light suggested the rows of books, the furnishings. Manning himself was deep in a wing-chair that faced the window.

He saw there, pressed against the panes, a face—hideous, devilish. A light from without played on it; its owner was using an electric torch to illuminate it.

There was some sort of close-clinging mask over the high features; nose, cheek bones, eyebrows, chin! The light made the mask look like a leper's countenance, or as if the skin was shedding, as a snake sheds.

Filmy yet close, like goldbeater's skin, the mask clung; revealing but screening, giving suggestions of a hideous, triumphant mirth heightened by eyes that shone like green phosphorescent growths, the cold glow of a firefly, of a fungus, of sea-flame.

Instantly, with a movement too swift to be anything but a blur, Manning snatched the gun he had tucked down beside him in the cushion of the chair, and fired.

Followed the crash of glass, the stillness after the shot, smoke wisping in the room! And, this time, surely there came the sound of a laugh, infinitely disdainful and assured.

The face was gone. Manning, who seldom missed, knew that this time he had not scored. His grounds were inclosed, but there was no sign of intrusion, nothing to show that his alarm was anything but illusion—except for the oval of scarlet paper, like a blotch of bright blood, affixed to the window sill.

The sign of the Griffin. His symbol and unholy seal!

Manning knew well enough that the Griffin always deliberately tried to weaken him, to upset his poise. His nerves seemed sensitive as the shrouds of a ship suddenly plucked by a malignant wind. He forced himself to normal as he waited for the message he knew must surely arrive.

The failure of the little revolt might well hasten the Griffin's next move, or it might not.

The days passed, and no message came. Manning was constantly waiting, half dreading, half welcoming the belated challenge to a test in which he was inevitably handicapped.

Meantime, the Griffin was conducting certain important experiments.

Gordon Manning was right. The Griffin held in subjugation men who served his purposes, carried out the orders of that distorted mentality that still was controlled by the mad will within.

The Griffin imagined himself maltreated by the world. It did not appreciate nor understand him. It had injured him, and he was out for deadly reprisal.

His madness conjured up monstrous things, reacting to what he learned of modern experiments. Whatever science devised and perfected, the Griffin twisted to his own criminal intents, exploiting his slaves to carry out his ideas.

He sat in his thronelike chair back of the massive, carved desk. In front of him swung a suspended disk of bronze upheld between two fluted pillars, each of which was topped by his device of a griffin's head. The symbol was repeated in the inkstand that held purple ink, in a paper weight.

The chamber was circular, seemingly without door or window. The lighting was hidden, the air was kept pure by a ventilating system, though now it was tinged with the fragrance of the tobacco—containing a modicum of hasheesh—that he was smoking through a Turkish hookah pipe.

Hung with golden tapestries, the walls were of steel, fireproof, bulletproof. So were the floors beneath the rich rugs. There was a faint sound of strange, exotic music, in curious rhythm, barbaric and sensuous.

The Griffin was clad in a long gown of black brocade. His features were disguised beneath the thin mask that set off the high-arching nose and cheek bones, the despotic chin. He looked not unlike some mummied priest or monarch of Old Egypt, upon whose face the golden face mask was still undisturbed.

Quantro, the Haitian dwarf, squatted on the floor, grotesque in his vividly hued turban, sash and robe; his arms long as an ape's, his misshapen head too big; a deaf and dumb familiar and bodyguard; perpetually fingering the long blade thrust in his sash, the knife he always longed to use. To him the Griffin was God. A Papa of obi and voodoo.

The music ended. At a sign from the Griffin, Quantro got to his feet with his apish, agile awkwardness, and took the cloth off a wicker cage. In this were two ringdoves. Quantro opened the door, tapped the bars until the doves flew out, circling the room while Quantro squatted again.

The Griffin spoke certain key-syllables at a fixed pitch into the disk of bronze. A low humming commenced, like the sound of a distant dynamo. The doves found no handy perching place. They continued to circle the room. The Griffin watched them with his glittering eyes, hard as onyx orbs.

Suddenly, out of midair, one dove fell lifeless, as if shot, though its feathers were unruffled save where one wing was outspread. The other flew on and then, in turn, tumbled.

The Griffin spoke again. The humming ceased. With a chuckle indescribably fiendish, the Griffin picked up the two dead birds and examined them. Quantro watched with leashed excitement.

"The finger of Death has touched them, Quantro," said the Griffin aloud, while the dwarf tried to lip-read his meaning. "They are quite dead, and the death was swift and merciful. I am always merciful, though I may be dramatic. You, my Quantro, like to mangle and worry and rend. You lack artistry. But I kill instantly and I never repeat the process.

"This is a far different fate from the one that overtook those two foolish, would-be Judases the other day. Them I annihilated. They could not even hold a coroner's inquest, for the lack of remains. It must have been amusing to watch Manning's face. He is not a fool. He is persistent, and, if he comes too close for comfort, he must be eliminated. I may give that task to you, my Quantro. It would be a pretty play to witness."

He broke off, chuckling.

Then he touched a button and entered the lift, whose door suddenly appeared in the curving wall. He was taking the dead birds to his underground laboratories, where his slaves labored for him—men without names, numbered robots. Men of science among them, expert craftsmen.

One was working at a laboratory bench in a chamber of

cement-lined brick. He was once a surgeon, though now he practiced only for the Griffin.

He looked at the doves, ran a long finger almost tenderly over their plumage, touched the rings on their necks, muttering:

"And the voice of the turtle is heard in the land."

"Don't wander, Number Nineteen," said the Griffin sharply. "Dissect these. I want to see what has happened to their vital organs. See if you can tell how they died."

IV

AT LAST the message had arrived. Manning looked at the familiar and ominous envelope, square, of heavy gray paper. His name and office address were written there in bold, characteristic chirography that yet, to an expert, betrayed the unbalanced but powerful mind of the writer.

Manning turned it over, breaking the scarlet cartouche with its embossed symbol. Red as a blot of blood.

"Who now?" he asked himself.

> MY DEAR MANNING:
>
> Once again the board is set, the pieces assembled, and you and I are adversaries. I trust that, by now, you will have recovered from any shock you suffered witnessing the abrupt termination of the lives of my renegade agents. It was foolish of you to think I am so remiss as not to countercheck the moves of those whom I employ.
>
> The next person I shall remove, release from this mortal coil, has annoyed me by his mouthings, his writings, his ultra-altruism.
>
> An old man, but still dangerous. In fact, his powers seem to ripen as his body declines. He has lived too long.
>
> The finger of Death is pointed at him. The stars in their courses decree that celestial protection will be weakest for him on Tuesday next, which will be the seventeenth. On that day the frozen, fatal finger of the Universal Harvester will touch him, unless you, Manning, can usurp the place of the Heavenly Powers, for neither steel nor stone may protect him.

The name is Eric Bannerman.

By the way, Manning, don't try and play the "game" off the board. Though even that effort was amusing. But it cost two lives. That means nothing to me, but you are inclined, it appears, to consider life valuable.

The signature, the Griffin, was appended, with the seal in crimson wax.

Manning felt a wave of revulsion engulf him.

Of all people, Eric Bannerman. Nearing seventy, a singer of the true things of life, of lofty ideals and inspirations. Bannerman, the uplifter, a poet who knew the heart of people and of Nature and reconciled them. A true poet of the people!

And, on the seventeenth, five days away, Eric Bannerman, who lived the simple life and, though close to three-score and ten, had many years of useful, invigorating, enlightenment within him, must die.

By the Griffin's whim, the time for the deed might occur at any moment within midnight of the sixteenth and midnight of the seventeenth. It amused him to keep his victims and their would-be guards on tenterhooks.

Manning had learned by now that most of the Griffin's successes had been consummated through his close attention to the habits of the men he doomed.

Eric Bannerman was wealthy, made so by the will of a spinster admirer who had found in his poetry, his company, and his conversation, an uplift. She had left him, with ample means to support it, her summer place in Connecticut, close to the shore.

There was a group of younger, more or less immature poets, who styled themselves as his "disciples" and called Bannerman "master." Simple as was Bannerman's nature, he had a shrewd faculty of testing others and sifting the fraudulent from the true, unerringly.

He received the homage of his followers with a twinkling eye, alive to their faults and frailties, teaching them much, not merely of poetic technique and license, but of things and thoughts that were clean and beautiful. To him poetry was a supreme art that should never be desecrated and his school was one of direct and lasting benefit.

There were seldom less than a dozen house guests at Windy Ridge, usually twice that number staying in the neighborhood.

Windy Ridge looked south across the Sound to Long Island, east to the broad Atlantic. It was sheltered by trees whose boughs were rocked and tossed by the vigorous sea breezes. The house was commodious and comfortable.

There were terraced lawns, shrubbery, flowers that grew at random in the grass, a rose garden, blossoming bushes. It was a refuge for birds.

On the highest of the terraces, in front of the house, with a magnificent vista spread out before it, was a seat of marble of exquisite proportions, simply but beautifully carved by a sculptor-admirer of the poet. It curved, and the center was deeply recessed and higher backed than the rest, to make a throne.

Here, cushioned and enthroned, Bannerman sat every afternoon when the weather was fine, to sometimes read one of his own poems, or one written by one of the disciples who showed true merit.

His pupils sat on either side of him, or threw themselves on the grass to listen, to hear the master descant on the beauty of poetry, the duties and responsibilities of all true bards.

So Gordon Manning found Eric Bannerman an hour before sunset, surrounded by his court.

Manning had obtained an introduction, but he found there was little formality to Windy Ridge. He stayed back, listening, after he had come to where the Japanese boy showed him the group. It was a simple but dignified and peaceful scene with the bearded poet and his noble face, the rapt pupils.

Save for the modern costumes, it might all have been set in Ancient Rome or Athens upon some verdant hillside.

Bannerman's deep, sonorous voice was declaiming. Manning

caught the lines; a somewhat turgid composition of one of his scholars.

> "…the shouldering seas,
> Shadowed beneath the sweeping argosies of cloud.
> The cliffs, upstanding, arrogant, as they defy
> The steady onslaught till the tide retreats
> In broken, sullen ranks that will reform
> To charge again in the unending conflict
> 'Twixt sea and shore."

Manning introduced himself, as the poem ended. The mutual acquaintance had already communicated with Bannerman, earlier in the day. Bannerman remembered it.

"Ah, yes," he said. "I understand you wish to see me upon business personal and private to myself, business of the utmost importance."

Manning bowed.

"Vital," he said.

"I can imagine nothing more vital or important than a gathering such as this," said the poet, with a wave of his hand.

The clouds were marshaling for sunset in the west, already taking on tinges of the glorious hues they would presently assume. The wind rustled the trees; the Sound was a stretch of sparkling, wrinkled blue; Long Island, twenty miles across the water, seemed ethereal in azure, purple and pearl gleams.

"Unless," said Manning gravely, "it should be the discontinuance of them."

"One may not live forever," smiled Bannerman.

But he was struck by something he saw in Manning's face, in his eyes.

"You will excuse me, all?" he asked. "I must talk with Mr. Manning. We will go into the house."

V

MANNING WENT to the heart of the matter without preamble. To his amazement, Bannerman knew nothing of the Griffin, save as a name vaguely remembered. He listened gravely as Manning enlightened him, recording briefly the Griffin's crimes.

"The man is a homicidal maniac," he concluded. "With a colossal ego. He is in deadly earnest. Your life will be in dire peril from midnight to midnight on the seventeenth. I shall do my utmost to protect you. I believe this, that if the Griffin's plans should once fail, the man would go stark insane, a raving lunatic, unable to plot with his uncanny faculty, to use his immense resources."

"What do you propose to do?" asked Bannerman. "If we can circumvent such a monster, it is surely my duty to place myself in your hands—aside from the fact that I am not at all eager to die. I enjoy life. I believe what there is left of it for me may prove useful."

Manning explained his general plans. Then he showed Bannerman a copy of the letter he had received from the Griffin.

"This time I think he has overreached himself," he said. "I may be mistaken, but I believe he has trusted too much to his own ingenuity and, I hope, underestimated my intelligence. He has had cause to do so, but it is usually a fatal error.

"He talks of the fatal, frozen finger that neither steel nor stone may deflect or keep out. It is my profound conviction that he anticipates using some sort of death ray. He has unquestionably studied your habits. He knows, for instance, of your custom of sitting here on your lawn at a certain hour. I think he intends to project his ray at that time when you would be in plain view to an operator, either through a telescope or closer at hand, perhaps from an airplane."

"I have heard something of these death rays," said Bannerman. "I understood one or more of them were ready, or almost ready, to use in the Great War when the Armistice was signed.

Frightful instruments, and examples of man's inhumanity to man. I had supposed the governments owned them."

"I think they do—the formulae," replied Manning. "I know the United States Government has one, Great Britain another, Germany probably a third. But there has been much experimentation, certain publicity, upon which a clever scientist might follow the trail, repeat the result, even improve upon it. It is certain that the Griffin has such men working for him. He has proved it many times with his diabolically ingenious methods."

"One may not avert one's destiny," said Bannerman. "I am in your hands. You will stay here to-night? Do you think it is advisable to tell the rest? I can trust them all. I think they would risk their lives freely to protect me."

"By all means," Manning agreed. The more protection the better. But he did not intend to go into the means by which he personally hoped to circumvent the cunning of the Griffin. He did not even explain it to Bannerman. For once he intended not to keep in personal touch with the threatened victim.

He had gone deeply, within the past day or so, into the history, as known, of the various death rays; coming finally down to two inventions, the ray invented by H. Grindell Matthews, an Englishman, and the so-called Odic Ray, invented by a Californian, living in Pasadena. At the time, this Odic Ray was investigated by the Mount Wilson Observatory and finally dismissed as negligible, but its possibilities had later been greatly enhanced by its discoverer.

It was highly plausible that the Griffin's captive scientists had even outdone the Californian's results. And it was another name for the Odic Ray that determined Manning on his choice. *The Cold Ray.*

Through his previous connections with the Government Secret Service he was able to learn more about it. The object to its use was the fact that it was impossible to generate sufficient power to enable rays of this nature to wipe out an entire city, as claimed by the discoverers; but Manning was told that it was quite feasible for such a ray to be concentrated, focused upon some definite object, and pass through it, breaking down life, producing death and disintegration at considerable distances.

The Cold Ray seemed a fitting synonym for the Griffin's phrase, "Death's frozen finger."

V I

THE DAY of the seventeenth was passing, to all appearances, as quietly as any other. Morning found Bannerman awakening from sound sleep, eating a hearty breakfast, genial and courageous.

Manning's men, relieving each other in four-hour watches, swarmed in the grounds, were posted in the house. As the morning turned to afternoon, the tension increased with every hour, every minute. How would the Griffin strike, and whence?

No visitors were permitted, no tradesmen. No one left. The poet's disciples had gathered at Windy Ridge the evening before. Few of them had slept.

At his usual hour, Bannerman came out to his seat. He was to read his latest poem. The pupils gathered round. They watched as they listened. Manning's experts were alert. Bannerman had agreed to go inside on request. The terrace was spacious, with its open view of the Sound. Every covert that bordered it was guarded; so was the house behind.

It did not seem credible that such a peaceful scene could become an arena for murder. Its serenity was the same as that of the first afternoon when Manning had visited Windy Ridge. The air was still. The breeze was failing toward sunset. The trees were silent. The Sound looked like a stretch of ribbon, deep blue. The atmosphere was crystalline. Details stood out startlingly on Long Island; houses were distinct. The sky held little vapor.

Bannerman delivered his poem, not reading it, but giving it from memory, his voice like organ tones for depth and strength and clarity. He was, of all of them, serene and unafraid, citing his creed.

> "From the sea we came;
> Clinging and creeping, crawling and inanimate;
> Sexless and formless;
> Knowing not life, nor love.
> Motes on a mote that swung in awful space.
> Atoms of vaguely groping ignorance;
> But quick with cosmic urge,
> Journeying—whither?
> Yet this is known:
> We have that within us is immortal.
> It may not perish...."

A faint and far off drone came out of the sky. It was like the hum of a bee. It came from a speck that soared at a ceiling of five thousand feet, a plane chartered by Manning, in which he sat behind the most expert pilot who had experienced, and survived, the Great War. He was an Ace of Aces who had volunteered with alacrity for the chase of the monster.

It was not Manning's first flight, by a hundred times. The pilot had a machine gun synchronized to his propeller. His ship was fast—faster than anything he had ever flown in France. It could make well over two hundred miles an hour. In Manning's cockpit there were grenades, specially weighted, finned for accurate flight.

Manning could have secured fifty ships, but he feared to arouse the suspicions of the Griffin's agents. Even though they masked their flight by seeming to go through regular maneuvers, the Griffin might defer his attack until after dark. Manning could not tell how far the Griffin's experts might have perfected the Cold Ray. But, with Bannerman in the open, they would strike now; unless Manning's theory was wrong.

And he knew it was not. This time the Griffin would fail—if Manning could find the projector of the Odic Beam.

It was no easy matter, and yet the problem was not too hard.

The Griffin had tipped off his opening moves by his phrasing, his mention of "the frozen finger of Death." Manning's careful survey of the grounds at Windy Ridge had narrowed his search.

The ray might be able to traverse timber, but, unless the wise men in Washington were all wrong and Manning's own deductions and inferences false, the use of the ray was as yet so limited that the object of its destruction must be sighted, must be properly focused.

They had come in the plane from the north, as if a casual air-traveler, making for a Long Island landing. The flight had been timed to fit Bannerman's emergence on the lawn, his reading of the poem. Too premature an appearance would spoil everything.

Manning had glasses of powerful magnification, as he did not doubt the Griffin's fiendish executioners also held. There was no other plane in sight. There were vessels in the Sound, but perfect aim could hardly come from those. He looked to find the base of the Griffin's operations on shore, on the shore of Long Island Sound, at some point nearly opposite Windy Ridge, some place where they could focus Bannerman between the trees. He would make a perfect target. The sprawled disciples in front of him would not be hurt. It was the Griffin's boast to get only his man—with Manning occasionally included.

The plane went swooping down, perfectly flown. Its actions were natural enough, so far.

Beneath them were scattering estates, most of them grouped about havens and inlets. A few abandoned farms not yet sold to the New Yorkers who would make them over into pseudo-Colonial homes. Strips of beach. Hillsides, covered with light growth of trees.

It was these copses that Manning and his pilot watched most carefully, suspecting camouflage. They had only a few precious minutes to find their objective. It was well masked.

It was a desperate hazard. Manning could imagine the Griffin's men hidden below, their powerful generators set up and invisible in some barn or house, or among the woods, sighting the superbly serene Bannerman, concentrating the ray until, like a pencil, like a long finger, it touched that noble heart, passed on and left it still.

Bannerman had said that one might not avert his fate. Perhaps fate would be kind. There was one thing in their favor. A race of sloops was in progress, half a score of dainty yachts tacking, reaching, directly off Windy Ridge and occasionally passing in front of the target. This gave them more time to search.

They saw nothing. Manning spoke through the audiphones and they swung back.

And *then*—

He saw gulls wheeling, skimming, rising and falling in their search for food, their pursuit of a surface school of fish. And even as the test-doves had dropped in the Griffin's secret room, so a gull dropped, wings outspread; then another. They had not been shot. But something had killed them. The ray!

Manning took swift bearings, called through his phone, sighting a glint of metal, something that looked like an averted eye, leveling from the preliminary projection that had killed the gulls.

Out of a barn, half hidden by trees, a long slit cut in the clapboards!

The pilot stepped on his foot controls, thrust his wheel-stick forward, worked his ailerons. They swooped, as a sea-eagle spreads its pinions and swoops to rob a lesser bird. They zoomed in a sharp upcurve not twenty feet above the treetops, seventy above the shingled barn.

There was a futile spatter of shots from flurried men, suddenly aroused and alarmed. They ceased. Manning had flung his bombs in swift succession, winged darts charged with destruction.

The barn fell apart. Plumes of yellow smoke rose, then scarlet streaks of fire.

The pilot swung the plane in a sheer bank. Three men, two of them injured, scurried to a car, got into it and sent it hurtling along a lane. The barn was burning. The infernal projector was destroyed.

"We've got to get those men," said Manning.

The pilot nodded, but misunderstood. He roared down, soared above the car, behind it for the moment. Then he took part in the proceedings with the loosing of his machine gun. The car swerved, lolled into a ditch, lay there, with three dead men inside of it under the riddled top.

"I meant alive," Manning said to himself, but did not speak to the pilot now.

The Griffin had been foiled. Bannerman was saved. And, unless he was mistaken, the already diseased reason of the Griffin would totter on its throne, his colossal ego unable to accept failure.

QUANTRO QUAILED before the frightful fury of his master, for once unmasked, mouthing, frothing at the lips, his eyes aglare with absolute madness as he howled into the brazen disk.

Manning sat in his library, listening, accepting the final challenge, knowing the Griffin utterly insane at last, his powers unhinged.

"Next time I shall not fail, Manning. Luck was on your side. Curse you! I was watching. It was the gulls, the cursed gulls! Now you no longer amuse me. I have upset the board, the men are scattered. It is the end—for you—and for Eleanor!"

A giant hand seemed to constrict Manning's heart. For himself he was not afraid. But for Eleanor, the girl he loved, as the Griffin knew. He blanched.

Then he pulled himself together. Deliberately he set down his telephone, cut off the talk. The Griffin was a raving maniac. Dangerous in purpose, but no longer the supreme antagonist.

Manning had a clew to the whereabouts of his aerie, or his lair. He could take immediate measures to protect Eleanor.

And then?

He took a deep breath. The deeply sunk lines in his face shallowed. Here was the chance of fairly even combat. Once routed, the Griffin, even if he did not realize it, was in retreat, in confusion. Now was the time to strike.

In the Heart of the Madman's Lair Manning
at Last Meets the Griffin Face to Face

A S H E picked up the too familiar gray envelope with the purple script sprawling over the heavy weave, Manning saw that his long held expectation of the Griffin's mania turning to a violent dementia had come to pass.

It showed in the characters of the writing. Once eccentric but firmly shaped, notable to a graphologist for their indications of powerful if unusual mentality, the strokes and curves and crosses now showed an incoherency, an uncertainty, that was clear to Manning.

Beyond question the failure of the Griffin's last attempt at murder, when he had been baffled by Manning's pre-solution of the method to be used, had broken up the peculiar coördination of that brilliant though fiendish brain.

No longer would the plots of the Griffin be laid with the diabolical genius that had hitherto inspired them, that had enabled him to eliminate, in the insane conceit of the monster, a score of the world's greatest men.

It had been grandiose dementia originally with the Griffin. Now it would be nearly a delirium, a frenzy, centered on one object. His whole hate now would be centered on Manning, the man who had finally foiled his machinations, shattered his colossal ego when he had tried to kill America's greatest poet with the Odic Ray.

In his foul aerie, somewhere on the shore line of New York State's mainland, the Griffin still held captive the men who

Manning catapulted forward.

worked out his designs, the slaves of his will, the men of genius whose brains he used to elaborate the satanic schemes hatched in his own perverted mentality. These he could still command in his madness.

Manning had been lucky—and careful. It was different now.

He opened the letter, breaking the seal on the flap, a cartouche of scarlet wax, red as blood, in the oval of which appeared the impression of the Griffin's special device; the design of the heraldic and mythical creature, half lion, half eagle, the Griffin had chosen as his emblem and his name.

Again the letters sprawled, unsymmetrical, out of alignment, the size of the words variant. A madman's letter—but a madman centered on one desperate and devilish design. The usual somewhat pompous style was lacking, with the sardonic sentences. This was an epistle written in such rage that the hand holding the pen had at times trembled, spilled blots of the purple ink.

Meddler:
You amuse me no more. Your fate is sealed with the seal

of the Griffin, the beast that rends and tears, that can swoop and leap and fly. You interfering fool, you have signed your own warrant to a death that will not be pleasant. Nor will it be short.

I shall not tell you when, or how. I have turned the glass of your life's span and the sand is running out. You have dared to balk me, you have presumed to check the revelations and the ordinations of the stars. Your doom is sealed. The Griffin crouches. Soon the Griffin strikes, presumptuous tamperer with Destiny!

For signature the Griffin had drawn, as he had often done before, the upper part of a griffin's body, in the style known to heraldry as issuant. Formerly this had been well done, now it was out of all proportion, certain sign of his agitation.

II

MANNING PUT the letter back into its envelope and filled his pipe. It was a raw night with a mist that was almost rime. He was in his own library at Pelham Manor in front of an open fire that crackled cheerfully. It was in this room that the Griffin himself had once peered in at him through the window.

At least Manning thought it was the Griffin. It might have been an impersonation, but he doubted if the Griffin would let any one assume the yellow mask of something like goldbeater's skin that half hid and half revealed the hawklike features of the monster.

There was a new pane there now to take the place of the one through which Manning had fired—and missed, for once. Involuntarily Manning glanced at the casement and saw nothing but the murk of night. Something, perhaps a scrap of loosened mortar, perhaps a spurt of rain, fell down the chimney and hissed into the fire.

His setter started up, neck hair bristling, uttering a low whine that was half howl, melancholy, portentous. Manning did not move. His pursuit of the Griffin had taken toll of him. He had lost weight, lines had grimly registered in his lean, brown face, and his nerves had begun to get too tense, but now they were unassailable.

The issue was at hand. He would get a chance at the Griffin, face to face. The Griffin would want to taunt him, torture him in his own presence. He would want Manning alive. There was little doubt of that. This insanity would demand a personal vengeance, not a long distance murder.

Manning had not the slightest intention of dodging it. He set the matter of his own risks aside as of no importance compared to this chance to dispose of a creature who was more fiend than man.

He patted the head of the dog as it came close to him. It *did* seem as if the air had grown colder and there was a strange and ghostly suggestion of weird and primitive music in the room. It must come from the radio set. It was the sort of music that came over the telephone when the Griffin used it, employing some synchronizing device to get through and prevent tracing. He would be up to such tricks if they entered his brain, to try and break down Manning's courage.

"There's one thing, Dan," said Manning to the setter. "We don't have to worry about anybody else this time. And I doubt if he has any definite plan, if he is even able to devise one. Our side may win the game and clear the board. We'll do our best."

Dan, the setter, crept closer, shivering a little, whining once more. Manning patted him again. There was a flurry of wind in the breast of the chimney, like a moan, and the fire lifted. A log fell. The setter howled mournfully, low but long, with his neck outstretched until Manning clamped his muzzle and told him to "charge," when the dog lay still, save for shivering.

"Damper needs fixing. Too much draft, Dan boy," said Manning. These sounds were ordinary, stressed by circumstance. The music—that was the Griffin. Static kept it down. A bad night for transmission.

A good night for a murder!

That thought rose unbidden to Manning's mind and he grinned, spoke the next one aloud.

"Good time for a drink. Sorry you don't like Scotch, Dan."

He touched a button, relit his pipe, which had gone out, pressed the ebony disk once more. He had three Japanese servants, all devoted to him. Two of them were away to-night, until midnight, their usual evening off. But Ito, the second boy, should have answered. He set down the button a third time, listening, catching its faint buzz in the distance.

A slight frown came to his face. He rose and slid the automatic that he always kept handy into the side pocket of his smoking jacket.

The pantry was empty. There was cube ice in a brass bowl, a siphon set ready with a tall glass on a serving salver—as if Ito had known what was wanted, started to serve, or had, as he often did, anticipated a call. The ice was slightly melted.

There was a pane of glass inset into the swinging door leading into the kitchen, as also with the pantry door through which Manning had just come. A light in the kitchen. Manning peered through and what he saw made him swing the kitchen door wide with a kick on its brass base plate.

Ito lay on the floor in his white linen clothes, curled up on his side. His knees were drawn up, his hands clenched tight. On his brown, usually impassive face was a look of agony whose distortion death had not yet been able to erase.

All outer doors were locked. On the narrow shelf outside a kitchen cabinet was a dish of Japanese food, a salad of *daikon*, seaweed and bamboo sprouts. It was partly eaten. The fork was on the floor. There was a bottle of soy with which sauce the salad had been seasoned. It was newly opened, used only once, Manning fancied. His boys ordered their own food likings from a Japanese store in New York. It was sent by parcel post. There had been a delivery that afternoon. Yamamoto, his butler, had brought him the bill that came with the goods.

Manning picked up the bottle, sniffed at its sourish contents and set it down. His face was grim. There had been genuine affection between him and Ito, extended to the absent couple.

"Next time I get a shot at you, Griffin, I shan't miss," said Manning. He had no doubt as to who was responsible for this. The means did not immediately matter. And it was an irrational move, the taking of a pawn who was not actually on the board. It was meant, perhaps, to scare Manning, to reveal the Griffin's power, a cat's-paw trick.

Usually the Griffin did not waste life. He liked, he claimed, to do his work neatly, to use no unnecessary moves. But he had struck and he had killed Ito.

"It's my move," said Manning aloud. But it would be a move in the dark. The Griffin knew where he lived, shadowed his movements, and Manning knew only *about* where the Griffin's lair was located.

Manning took a cloth from a drawer and laid it over the corpse of the poisoned Japanese.

He returned to the library and the cowering dog and took up his telephone to call headquarters in New York. It had to be reported. Once more the Griffin had scored and Manning had failed to protect.

"It'll be the last time," he told himself.

Even as he lifted the body of the instrument there came a sound of barbaric music with the well-known voice of the Griffin speaking through it. Manning had always hoped to trace the Griffin some day through that deep and vibrant tone, but it was changed now, changed in pitch and in steadiness. It was the voice of a maniac, close to raving, incoherent, almost unintelligible, uttering dire but vague threats, ending in a burst of uncontrolled laughter that suddenly ceased. The music kept on for a few minutes, then ended abruptly.

Manning got his connection.

"Give me Spring seven—three one hundred," he said in even accents. "In a hurry."

III

QUANTRO, THE Haitian dwarf and mute, bodyguard and familiar of the Griffin, cowered against the
curving wall of the private chamber. He squatted, gibbering
like a baboon, his hands, at the ends of his long, hairy arms,
resting, knuckles down, on the rich rug, his bizarre costume of
turban, robe and sash infinitely grotesque.

He rolled his eyes in terror as he muttered uncouthly, watching his master. The Griffin was to him the Overlord of All
Wizards, greater than any *Papa* of obeah and voodoo, all powerful, all wise. He feared him and he worshiped him, much as
Moloch might have been worshiped.

But now he could not understand. He knew, as a dog might
know, that things were wrong, terribly wrong, with the Griffin,
that his master was in a towering and unreasonable rage that
had lasted for days and might at any moment vent itself upon
Quantro. It had already made victims of certain of the unfor-
tunates, known only by numbers, who were incarcerated in the
subterranean laboratories of the place. They had vanished, and
the rest were uneasy, almost mutinous, broken in spirit though
they were.

The Griffin gave none of them new tasks, did not care for
any inspection or test of the old. The man who cooked their
poor food for them had run short of provisions, and the Griffin
had ignored his request for more supplies. The Griffin himself
had eaten little and slept less, and Quantro, always a glutton,
bewailed that condition.

He hardly ventured to cast a glance at the Griffin, seated
behind his carved desk in the circular room that was concealed
in the midst of the house set on a summit of a wooded hill that
overlooked the sea. To the ordinary observer who might catch
a glimpse of the house when fall stripped the boughs of their
leafy screen it was seemingly an ordinary semicolonial home,
built probably in the late fifties.

It did not look like the house of horror and mystery that it was. It was a small domain, but the Griffin ruled there supreme. In the bowels of the hill were the laboratories, the clammy quarters of the nameless ones who never saw the sunlight. A deep shaft ran from the Griffin's private room, where he made his decisions, worked out his horoscopes against his victims, and studied the details of his murderous plans against them. It was a smooth steel tube and it reached to a natural cavern through which ran a subterranean stream whose existence none even suspected.

A strange chamber, this unholy of unholies, where the Griffin evolved his diabolical schemes. The walls curved in a complete circle that showed no break. They were of steel, covered with gold-woven tapestry; the floor was of steel, fireproof, sound-proof.

The whole was concealed in the middle of the partly dis-mantled house so cleverly as not to be noticed. It was, in fact, built in the well of the original circular staircase of the home, now supplanted by a lift. The chamber had its own elevator to the basement.

There were no windows, but the air was pure. There were no visible means of illumination, but daylight seemed to serenely light the place. In front of the Griffin hung three disks of bronze, the central one the largest. Before him was a sidereal chart, with sheets of horological logarithms, special maps of the zodiacal signs, papers covered with calculations.

He sat there with his yellow mask upon him and, beneath it, veins crawled like worms. His eyes gleamed through the eyeslits like windows through which may be seen darkly the fires of Hades. His mouth worked, his hands clenched and unclenched, and there too the veins stood high and seemed things alive under the skin.

In his fear, Quantro tried to lip-read something of the swift, harsh torrent of words that flowed from the mouth of the Griffin. They were not far from raving, but their threats were still backed by a definite purpose.

In the domed ceiling tiny golden pricks showed as the Griffin touched a button. The belt of the zodiac was limned there in gold, with the signs, the pricks were the assemblies of the important constellations in connection with the pseudo-science that the Griffin implicitly believed in.

He never set the date for a victim's death, never ordained that demise, unless his calculations showed him that the stars in their courses were favorable for his ungodly enterprises.

He glared at his casts and recasts of Manning's horoscope, knowing the day and hour of his birth. The stars mocked him. They showed Manning protected by his stellar destinies.

The faintly intoxicating scent of amber floated through the room. From somewhere came the strains of music that were primitive yet ultra modern; music that seemed to hold the rattle of sistra and the clang of cymbals, the sonorous voice of horns, the boom of mighty drums and the blare of trumpets. Music that embraced and embodied all centuries, all time, from the hollow log, the conch and gourd of the cave dweller to the latest device for stirring the vitals and the spirit of mankind. It was an evil tune. It suggested more than merely evil things. It stirred the blood and roused the pulse to unclean, unhallowed impulses.

But it brought no solution to the Griffin of the manner in which he could desirably wreak his vengeance on Manning. He had struck, once, at the unfortunate Ito more or less blindly. It had not been hard for him, with his connections, to get the poisoned soy into the house. He had hoped to get all three of the servants, but it had been a puerile, unworthy stroke and the knowledge of that intensified his rage. Manning was the one he wanted.

He had cited Manning as having presumed to check the ordinations of the stars and, lo, the stars protected the meddler.

"He is guarded night and day. He is fearful for his life. He dreads my inevitable vengeance," mouthed the Griffin, while Quantro huddled himself closer. "Easy to destroy him, for all

the vigilance of his aides. But not so simple to get him here—
here—alone. It shall be done, it *must* be done. He pit *his* sluggish
wits against mine.

"I challenge the heavens themselves! I will not be denied!"

He rose, pacing up and down while Quantro whimpered like
a cur that fears a kick. He shook his fist at the pictured sky and
stars. His eyes glared as if they were varnished, his mouth
showed flecks of foam. That countenance beneath the clinging,
half-transparent mask was hideously handsome. It was the face
of Lucifer enraged.

The music lessened, came back in stronger waves, died again.
The Griffin almost stumbled over the hunkering dwarf. For a
moment the Griffin's orbs seemed like spangles reflecting
crimson flame and Quantro bowed his head.

The dwarf, for all his misshapen body, was extremely powerful. He had a fearful weapon by his side, a semi-scimitar, keen
as a scalpel; but he never dreamed of protecting himself that
way. Had not the *Papa* blasted him by invisible, paralyzing
forces, merely by pointing his finger at him? If he was to die
he might not prevent it.

But it did not come. The Griffin stood contemplating him,
almost elated.

"It shall be done. We will lure him here, and then you, my
Quantro, shall torture him. Torture him until he screams for
mercy. Treat him as you treat the goat and the white rooster in
the voodoo rites, save that death shall not come so swiftly. But
the warm blood will run and the entrails smoke. You shall make
divination sacrifices of his heart and liver when he can no longer
feel. I will see you do not cut too deep nor mortally at first. The
death of a thousand slices, the Grand Lai Chee of Canton, shall
be a child's game to this. There are other things besides the
knife. Acids, fire, steam, to make a man's soul quake and crave
for respite. You, my Quantro, have the lust for blood and
torment in your veins. A scream is music to you. So, I shall lead
the orchestra and you shall hear your symphony. The harmony
of hate! Ha!"

He stood erect in his gown of black brocade, and Quantro crept out on hands and knees. He had not been able to lip-read the rapid incoherencies of the Griffin's speech, but he sensed that he was to be used, and he was grateful. He took the Griffin's foot and set it on his short and clumsy neck.

The Griffin smiled—if such a grimace engendered of wickedness could be called a smile.

"Sharpen that knife of yours, Quantro," he said. "You will soon be using it. They are searching me out. Manning and his men comb the neighborhood. Well, perhaps I may help Manning to find what he seeks. To come to grips with the Griffin."

He flung back his head and laughed. It was hardly human laughter, nor was it entirely fiendish. It was the sort of cachinnation that echoes through the dreary halls of Bedlam.

IV

IT WAS no mere surmise on the part of the Griffin when he said that he was being searched out. The chase was on in deadly earnest, had been ever since Manning had received a communication from two of the Griffin's unwilling but irrevocable bond-servants that they would lead him to the monster's lair.

The Griffin had blasted them out of existence before Manning's eyes, but they had provided a definite clew, established a scent. On this Manning had concentrated the crack hounds of the law, aiding them with his own deductions.

Somewhere on the coast, beyond Larchmont. Probably in New York State, though it might be in Connecticut. But, in Connecticut, the shore line was more or less public, at least to observation. Shore rights were coveted and limited. Manning sensed some sort of place that had escaped, or defied, the realty developers, kept a fair amount of land.

This was sheer logic, proving itself as the investigation went on. They worked through the local police and fire departments, the real estate layouts, the insurance charts, the tradesmen, particularly those of the last who were ambitious in securing new accounts.

They drew blanks, mostly. Manning analyzed the results. This was a long trail and, while it called for speed lest the Griffin destroy some other useful citizen, he knew it had to be followed carefully. Now, at last, with the conviction that the Griffin wanted him and him alone, it was not so bad until Ito was killed.

He sent Sato and the other Japanese boy to the Bermudas for a holiday and closed up his own house. He provided himself with an escort, though he felt always that the Griffin would want to bring a personal issue into the climax. And Manning was willing to accept that.

It was soon shown that the Griffin did not buy supplies for his household locally. They were almost certainly brought from New York in his own cars. On top of that—connected with that—Manning figured that the goods were delivered, even as the emissaries of the Griffin came and went upon their evil errands, through some method that was cleverly hidden. So hidden, probably, that with its discovery it would appear obvious.

The Griffin might not be the supremist he once was, but in the commencement of his enterprises he had shown all the resources of evil genius.

But the lair of the monster was within a limited area and that was being very thoroughly searched. The hunt discovered speakeasies and liquor landing places—and left them alone. They found many matters that would have delighted the heart and stimulated the activity of tabloid editors, but there were no reporters along. This was anything but a picnic party.

They were on the trail of the Griffin. The hunt was up. The force detectives brought in reports of suspicious places, and while Manning investigated every spot that did not have a clear record, he did not expect to locate the Griffin anywhere that was not, apparently, eminently above suspicion.

Slowly the search narrowed, but the net results included half a hundred homes whose establishment, elaborate or limited, might harbor the Griffin. It was a grisly game of hide-and-seek. The Griffin was resolved to tag Manning. And Manning was willing to let him try, so long as he led him out into the open— or cornered him. His own safety had ceased to concern him.

There had been a time, not very recent, when Manning worried over some one else—the girl whom Manning loved and some day, when the Griffin was eliminated, he hoped to woo and wed.

The Griffin knew her, had even threatened Manning through her and so had made Manning a laggard in love because of his fear that his attentions to her would attract the Griffin. But now Manning was sure that the Griffin, enraged by having been baffled, had forgotten anything but vengeance against the man who had checked him.

It suited Manning well enough.

The Griffin must be destroyed. When that monster swooped and struck he had done so, not merely at an individual who displeased him, but invariably against some one who was a leavening factor in the advance of civilization.

"The best bet is to hoist him through his own petard," he told the police commissioner. "He is like a Chinaman who has lost face. He is centered on getting me out of the way in order to try and gather together the pieces of his own egotism. And our job—my job—is to corral him. To put him where he can do no more mischief."

"In the chair," said the commissioner vindictively. "And that's a death far too good for him."

"Well, this time we'll get him," said Manning confidently. "He used to call our encounters games of chess, but he has lost his ability to look moves ahead. I'm banking on that. We are narrowing down the search for him and I am hoping any day, any hour, to hear he is located."

"There is no sense in your uselessly exposing yourself, Manning," said the other. "You are much too valuable to risk."

"I'm guarded all the time," said Manning. "We've got over two hundred men now in the district where we think he must live. *But,* I'm hoping to catch him at his own game. He figures, I feel certain, that somehow or other he can get me in his clutches. He'd find that a hard job to do by force. We've got too many men who can be swiftly concentrated. And he wants a personal vengeance. I feel a good deal the same way.

"I think he'll try to lure me into his lair. I'm willing. He may use himself as the bait. I'm going to use myself. And the best man wins. I'm up against a madman. I'm sane. I ought to score, other things being equal. To even the score against me. Or against him."

The commissioner had seen many faces grow hard in front of him in his time, but none that set more purposefully than that of Gordon Manning. Many of the Griffin's victims had been Manning's personal friends, others had been men who stood for the same thing that Manning did. And there was Ito, needlessly and wantonly sacrificed.

"You're in charge," the commissioner told him. "Run it your own way. Just the same, don't run too much personal risk. I want you to come back and tell me all about it."

"It's on the knees of the little red gods," said Manning with a grin and a handgrip. "I'm coming back if it's fated so, and if I do, I'm bringing the Griffin with me—dead or alive."

v

MANNING WOULD not have called himself a fatalist, though his extensive travels, often through the Orient, had made him acquainted with strange cults and a witness of if not an actual believer in their marvels. But he did believe that he was going to meet the Griffin at last, face to face, and he had laid his plans accordingly.

Intensive but discreet questioning had been extended to doctors and professional ranks. This was a process of reduction and of elimination. Manning had his suspicions of five places now, one of which was the secluded colonial house on a wooded hill. He had sent men to all of these spots who arrived on various likely errands, as solicitors for various household articles. Two of the five he had discovered, through a lucky capture of a speedboat, had nothing to do with his own investigation, but were linked up with a rum-running syndicate, being cover for their land operations.

The three remaining were all within the length of a mile, in a strip along the shore of the Sound. And they were being watched night and day, though not ostentatiously, from sea and shore. By day Manning commanded what might be termed a flying squadron, a land fleet of motor vehicles manned by picked officers, masquerading as delivery men for stores, some using small trucks and side cars with the names of actual local stores displayed upon them, others in wagons for garbage, in large trucks carrying materials, together with a sprinkling of comparatively obvious detectives.

Manning did not attempt to disguise himself, or his car. He had a simple signal and call system devised by which he could summon a score of his men to his side in less than two minutes at any time, with the balance centering to the alarm at fire engine speed. He was never completely out of sight of at least one man.

The house on the wooded hill, with its screening trees and its acreage, attracted his especial attention because of its special advantages for the purposes of the Griffin. It seemed to be one of the few remaining homes that had once been set along the shore and were now far too valuable, with lots at three or four thousand dollars for a seventy-five foot frontage, to be preserved save by very wealthy families who did not care to sell, by heirs in litigation or disagreement, or by cranks.

Manning looked up the land records and found that the place had been bought ten years before by a man named Taylor. The deed was still in his name. The realtor who had acted as agent was dead; the lead petered out. With the other houses under suspicion he had, besides the agents, employed electricians, telephone operatives and water meter readers. With this house they had their own electric plant and water supply. The hard-featured woman who had answered the door had turned away all others.

"When we want something we send and get it," she told them.

There was a fence round the place that had cost a lot of money, steel posts and wire with an extra overhang. Only in one section it was not used, where there was a sheer wall of dirt, a sort of bluff occurring in a wooded lane that rambled between this and the adjoining property, which was all woodland. The lane led down to the shore.

Manning made a study of the water mains in the neighborhood and discovered that a large artery of the civic supply ran close along the front of the holding. It was easy enough to get the coöperation of any one in the locality, tradesman or corporation, in getting rid of such a fiend as the Griffin. Now a force of men were to start to work excavating along the line of the big pipe. Whether the house was connected or not, Manning meant to have men inside the fence within a few hours, legally or illegally. The grounds were heavily thicketed with laurels, ground pine and artificially planted shrubberies, besides trees. No one had ever been reported seen in these grounds except when passing in or out by way of the main drive, in a car. It screened the house from observation. It would also screen his men, Manning determined.

They would set up a tall fence of vertical boards about their street excavation, as if they expected to build a cement or brick forebay there. And they would work under cover of it, moling through the hill, if necessary, straight to the cellars.

Here, Manning was almost convinced, by reasoning as well as his own hunch, was the likeliest of all places for the Griffin to select. The lane to the sea, a beach with a boathouse and a wharf that looked ancient but needed no repairs. The boathouse had a waterfloor on deep water, doors opening to the Sound, closed tight, padlocked. There were windows, but they were shuttered. The shore end of the wharf joined steps that led down from a gate in the steel fence, exit of a path that was veiled by brush and trees.

The piles of the wharf had been renewed quite recently. Here was either the hideout of a rum-runner or the lair of the Griffin. There would be a fast launch in that boathouse, Manning was sure. Or it might even be an amphibian plane. The Griffin had used one once.

Manning, driving his own roadster, approached the excavation. He had to be careful, for he was working with a wary opponent. But he hoped that the Griffin was still underestimating him, that in his still colossal, if crumbling, egoism, he would not credit Manning with making many elaborate moves out of the usual routine of police investigation, which the Griffin had long laughed at and despised.

Yet it would not do to avoid every caution. By prearrangement, a workman stepped out, carrying a red flag, and halted the car. He seemed to be suggesting that the ground was dangerous and Manning appeared to demur. He wanted to linger as long in the neighborhood as might be discreet, as well as to get a general report.

"We're running in a side tunnel," said the man. "We're going through soft soil, without any bad ledges so far. Mostly loose rocks. We'll go round any obstructions we can. We'll board up as we go. The new dirt-drills chew it up and we are sucking out the loose stuff by pneumatic."

"That's fine, sergeant. Anything else?"

Sergeant Doyle of the Homicide Squad, Manhattan, on special duty. A good man, he looked now like nothing more than what he represented, a somewhat shambling and elderly underling who got three bucks a day to tote a red flag.

"Yes, sir. There's some one up in the cupola, on top the house. You can see it from here if you want to look."

Manning did not look.

"I've got a sort of periscope rigged up back of the boarding and"—he stopped talking for a moment as some one struck with a hammer on the lumber—"some one there now, sir, probably got binoculars, piping you off."

"Right! You get out two trestles and shove your detour barrier board across the road. I'll turn back. If any one asks, you tell them the detour means going around a block uphill. And that I kicked. Said I was going to Larchmont and didn't see the sense of it. Inspector Riverton is tailing me. He's in one of those tricycle vans, painted red, delivering laundry from the Swan Cleanery. If he should say he's lost me, you bust into that house and don't bother to dig a tunnel to it. I'll be there. I've got a tingling in my thumbs, sergeant."

"Me, too, inspector. If we get the word, we'll be on the job, believe me. Good luck, sir."

Manning was slowly turning while Doyle erected the barrier and set up the sign. As he headed back he saw in his mirror that a car was coming down the drive from the house. A car of neutral tint with a long hood that hid a powerful engine. Manning's thumbs tingled again. He was sure he knew that car, had chased it once fruitlessly, had seen it once pass him and annihilate another machine that held two would-be informers.

The hunt was up indeed.

He swung uphill, turned, and the smoke-gray car passed him. It was the Griffin!

V I

NO DOUBT of that. The Griffin, unmasked, but easily recognizable. A face like a hawk, an imperious nose, flat cheek bones and eyes that blazed with insanity. A face that worked with vicious impulse, that leaned forward as if to get a good sight of Manning, but, in reality, to let Manning get a good glimpse of the Griffin.

The lure! Manning had lured the Griffin out of cover. The

Griffin believed that he himself was the lure that Manning would surely follow—to destruction.

Manning played his rôle, pretended not to recognize the Griffin, but braked, slowed, swung about and trailed the smoke-gray car that was traveling at less than a third the speed it could use on occasion.

A red tricycle delivery van stopped at the curb and a man got out with a bundle. Inspector Riverton, inside the van at the wheel. First-grade Detective Halloran playing delivery boy.

They would follow.

The smoke-gray car turned into the wooded lane that ran down to the beach. It had many tire tracks. Bathing and picnic parties used it. The shore sand was firm and they often did not return by the same route.

Manning followed. That steep bank where there was no fence? It had one or two features that had intrigued him. One was that the bluff was covered, almost matted, with ivy. That was not altogether extraordinary, but the ivy was of the evergreen variety. It would screen the bank summer and winter alike. What else might it screen?

It was a rough lane that necessitated slow going, if one regarded car springs. Manning went slowly. He saw the gray car almost stop, saw a tall, lithe figure get out, lean against the verdure-clad bank. It was hidden from view for a moment by the ivy. Then it came forward, or seemed to come forward, stepped into the car again and the car drove on, beachward.

But, to Manning's eyes, the figure was not just that of the first man. Dressed like him, similar in size, but lacking the alert gait, though it imitated it.

He chuckled to himself. There was something back of that ivy.

Did the Griffin think Manning would investigate?

He did.

Manning stopped, locating the spot readily enough by the tire marks that showed where the big car had started up again.

He leaned against the ivy and felt, back of the strands, hard metal.

At the foot of the lane the red delivery van had halted. Halloran, bundle in hand, was arguing with Riverton. All programmed.

Programmed also, Manning told himself, was this heavy, hidden door that slowly yielded to his pressure. The lock had failed to catch?

That did not seem likely, even with the Griffin stark crazy.

Manning remembered a story of the Spanish Inquisition, where a captive found a door ajar and wandered fearfully through corridors, hoping for freedom, shrinking behind a pillar when wandering friars passed by in chat, reaching at last the final gate—and being welcomed by the chief inquisitor with a mock benediction.

Just the sort of devilish device the Griffin would use—in his present state of mind. A door, ajar, for Manning to enter.

But Manning was not an escaping, tortured prisoner. He was armed, he was trained to a hair, and he had allies close at hand.

He pushed back the door and entered.

It clanged instantly behind him.

The tunnel had been cemented. It dripped moisture and it was faintly lighted by electric globes. It showed unbroken sides on to where it turned to the left. He might be trapped, but he was sure it would lead to the Griffin at last. The Griffin wanted to gloat in person over his captive, to twit him, break him down. And Manning was prepared for the ordeal.

He made the left turn and passed through vaulted rooms that were equipped with benches, machines and apparatus, but were empty. And he came at last to one that seemed to be used as a sort of refectory, a table and stools, a stale smell of cooking.

Here a score of gaunt men in overalls were whispering furtively together, men who were stamped with intellect, though bowed by slavery. They looked at Manning with parted lips that showed their teeth. Some almost snarled at him.

The Griffin—if it was the Griffin—had passed on. There was a dark corridor leading from this chamber deeper into the core of the hill, but Manning calculated they should not be far from directly beneath the house.

These wasted men had numbers in brassards on their arms, like convicts.

"I'm not looking for any of *you*," he said. "I am Special Deputy Commissioner Manning of the Manhattan Police Department. I am here—and not alone—to get the man who has held you here. You may be wanted, but not by me. If you can get away, that's your affair."

It was a slim hope enough, for any of them, he thought, but he was willing to give the poor devils a chance. They would be picked up, destitute, wearing what they did. Half starved, at that.

Wolfish eyes gleamed avidly as he showed his badge. Dry tongues licked drier lips. Here was something the Griffin had overlooked, would not have overlooked in former times. He despised these creatures, even as he affected to despise Manning, whom he had tolled within. After all, he had possibly calculated on them. What he wanted most was to get Manning caught in his web.

"You *mean* that?" gasped one man as Manning showed his badge. "You say you're not alone. Then your men'll pick us up if we can get that door open."

"Not this trip. They are not concerned with you. But—I want one thing in return. Where did that insane monster go and how can I follow him?"

He still stood in the passage entrance—exit now—to the refectory, a slightly smiling, efficient, formidable and eloquently official figure. As a few started up, and forward, he shook his head at them and suddenly two guns showed in his hands.

"Play fair," he said.

A man with a gray beard—none of them were lately shaved—cackled.

"Play *fair?* It's a long time since we heard that. You don't get it here. Well, I'll show you where he went, but if you're wise you won't follow him. I've been up there. He's a devil—a devil straight from hell, I tell you. He'll get you and he'll torture you. He'll...."

"Steady."

Manning saw signs of swiftly coming hysteria. He took the elderly man by the elbow.

"Show me where he is: how to get there," he said, "and I'll promise you immunity for whatever you may have done. I'll see you get an ample reward."

The man turned on him, hope in his eyes. Manning saw, with a shock, that, for all his gray beard, he was young.

"I'll give you a note now," Manning went on. "On my card. To the police commissioner."

He wrote rapidly while the others looked on.

> This man is to be taken care of. He has rendered me valu-
> able assistance and I have promised him immunity, no matter
> what happens.
>
> G.M.

"Now," said Manning as he signed his initials and the man put away the card, his eyes glistening with tears and his chin trembling. "Brace yourself. Where did he go?"

VII

MANNING FOUND himself, with his guide, at a corner that curved outward. It looked just like the surrounding cement. But the man grinned at him.

"I saw how Quantro—that's his dwarf and bodyguard—worked it," he said. "You want to be careful of that dwarf. He's strong as a gorilla. Look."

He stood with feet astride a crack in the cement floor that suggested adjoining slabs; then rocked from side to side. The convex corner slid aside and showed the tubular entrance to an elevator.

"There are buttons inside. It's automatic," said the young-old man. "Good luck to you."

"Good luck to *you!*" said Manning, and meant it. No penitentiary could be worse than this underground prison. And that gleam in the man's eyes had seemed to Manning to mean much. Pardon, a fresh start, a reunited family.

He inspected the buttons, touched one, and immediately the curved entrance closed and he shot up—to what?

Manning stepped into the circular chamber. It was filled with the incense of amber and the music he had so often heard over the telephone. He saw the Griffin, unmasked, back of his carved desk, erect, showing above his bronze disks.

"Welcome, Manning. I have been expecting you. Now you are here. I trust you will not disappoint me. As an antagonist, I mean. You cannot win, but...."

Manning had made up his mind just what to do. He was a crack shot, though he had missed the Griffin once, through some chance distortion of a glass window pane. He saw now, out of the side of his eyes, a crouching figure that must be Quantro.

Quantro the dwarf, of whom he must be careful. Crouching like a beast ready to leap. The gleam of a naked knife.

Manning fired pointblank at the Griffin. He wanted his man. He aimed to crack his sternum and his collar bone, to shatter the scapula. The nerve-shock would bring down his quarry. If the dwarf persisted he would get the same medicine—a dose of lead.

The Griffin swayed, caught at the carved edge of his desk, shook his head.

"I am not vulnerable, Manning," he said. "If I was, I would not have let you come here. Hey, Quantro! Up!"

The command was doubtless superfluous and unheard. But obeyed. The dwarf launched himself sidewise at Manning with the shock of a star interferer, interlocking arms about Manning's knees, teeth snatching at cloth and flesh. He had orders not to use his knife—not now.

Manning almost went down. He hesitated to kill the witless moron with a bullet, far more ready to slay the Griffin, though he did not want to. He survived the first shock of the tackle, staggering and raining blows on Quantro's head from the butt of the gun that had proved useless against the Griffin. The dwarf's voluminous turban protected him and masked Manning's objective, which he reached at last, the rocking bone of the cranium. Then Quantro suddenly dropped, nerveless.

Manning pointed the muzzle of his gun at the Griffin, holding it high.

"Wear a steel jacket, do you?" he said a little pantingly. "Well, this is a steel-jacketed bullet that will drill through your head if you are not very careful."

"Manning," said the Griffin, "I have too many headaches recently. For the present, I regret to say that you are safe. The stars protect you. Why, I cannot tell. But they are infallible. I submit."

He held out his wrists. Manning had handcuffs, slender bracelets of chilled steel. The dwarf lay senseless. The Griffin's madness, his paranoia, might well include a sudden surrender. But Manning was still cautious.

He advanced from the edge of the rug toward the desk where the Griffin stood waiting.

It might have been the quick gleam of triumph in the Griffin's eyes, it might have been the quick tremor under his feet; Manning never knew.

But his superb coördination catapulted him in a leap from the diaphragmatic opening of the throat of the death tube, up to the top of the desk, hurling aside the bronze disks, to grapple with the Griffin.

How old the monster was Manning never knew. But he was

supremely virile and in his madness his strength was that of a giant.

It was fortunate for Manning that he knew where and how to strike, how to use the art of jujutsu. Otherwise he would have succumbed instantly. He was fighting a man with the strength of four. It was not a pretty battle. Manning hit shrewdly, wherever he knew he could best sap the other's super-vitality. They rolled from the desk to the floor, barely avoiding the open shaft. They fought round the circle of the wall, and when they came to the slack figure of Quantro there was a struggle to get the knife.

The Griffin was bleeding. His hawklike nose was smashed. One eye was closing, but the superhuman strength of the madman was in his sinews and once, when he got a scissors hold, Manning thought he was gone before he could break it. If the Griffin had known anything about wrestling that might well have ended it.

And, all the time, the Griffin gasped out incoherencies, the slime and smut of many nations, the oaths of the galleys and the ropewalks. He cursed as Manning's thumb drove between the carpal bones of his wrist and released the Griffin's clutch on the knife. Then Manning kicked the weapon into the shaft, where it went tinkling down. And the fight went on.

Soon the dwarf must come back to sense and action.

Again and again Manning applied Oriental holds and could not complete them against the unnatural resistance of the Griffin. Time and time again he got home a blow that should have put out a Goliath, but the Griffin seemed to have the resistance of an octopus.

All the time the barbaric music sounded. The amber incense fumed. And then, dimly, Manning heard a noise of hammering and hacking. His men were on the job.

But they would have to come soon. *Very soon!* Manning knew he was playing out. His lungs could not get air enough. His arms were heavy as lead. He could not easily get at his guns, and he did not want to have to use them.

The Griffin seemed to fail to realize that there was anything to fight with but his own body. He swarmed all over Manning, who, like a clever wrestler, let the other exhaust himself by his own efforts.

Quantro was awakening, crawling toward them. His knife was gone, but his hands opened and shut. He could throttle.

Manning set his knee deep in the Griffin's lean stomach and heaved. He rolled away, got a gun free.

Dead or alive!

They were both tackling him.

He could sight only the dwarf. He got him, through the chest. Quantro curled up and rolled, over and over, to the steel shaft and toppled into it, howling as he fell.

Manning got to his knees, panting, exhausted, his gun hand trembling.

"Put up your hands," he said. "My men are coming."

They were coming. There was no question of that, but they had not arrived.

The Griffin let out a discordant laugh.

"You fool!" he panted croakingly. "Do you think I can be caught?"

He lunged across the room to his desk, slumped over it, badly bruised and beaten, feeling for certain disks.

"We go to hell together!" he cried as Manning fired.

"WELL, YOU landed him, but he's a mess," said the police commissioner. "You got him just in time, nicked him back of the head with your bullet. Same thing they called creasing, out West, when they knocked down the wild broncos. And you surely beat him up. Your second slug went through his lungs, but he had touched that button and if you hadn't had that fake excavating crew on the spot that would have been the grand finish, with the place burning up the way it was."

Manning, stiff and sore and seared, managed a grin.

"I *told* you it was in the lap of the little gods," he said.

"Oh, yeah? Well, you get the credit, Manning. We can't send him to the chair, though I'd like to exhibit him down at the Battery in a steel cage. Swing him there till the gulls pecked him to death. But the law of the land will say he is an incurable lunatic—which I grant—and we'll have to let him live, though why a nut should be allowed to live, after he's done what the Griffin has done, is beyond me. Probably die of T.B. with his punctured lungs, they say. Meantime they want to observe him. I'd like to skin him and set him up in a museum as a horrible example."

"I know how you feel," said Manning. "But we've got him."

"And we'll hold him," said the commissioner.

"Here's hoping," answered Manning. "I did my best."

He surveyed his broken knuckles a bit ruefully. His shots had done the actual trick, but, after all, he relished the memory of the blows he had sent home. It had been a good scrap, man to madman.

"Mind if I use your phone?" he asked the commissioner.

"I might let it go, *this* time. Listen, anything I can get for you?"

"Thanks, but I'm afraid not," returned Manning with a grin the other thoroughly understood. "I'm going to call my girl."

It Was a Fearsome Murder That Had Struck
Two Victims—Murder That Had Come and
Gone a Way Only a Bird Could Follow

THE INSISTENT note of his bedside telephone awakened Gordon Manning. Dawn was not far away, but his sleeping chamber was still dark and the light outside the open windows was a deep purple.

He could afford to sleep with open windows these nights, with the Griffin insane and safely incarcerated. Yet, instantly alert, Manning noted the time, five thirty, on the luminous dial of the clock on his bedside table as he picked up the instrument.

The message was from the chief police commissioner, New York City.

"Manning? This is Melleny speaking. Something strange has happened: a double killing, or at least a double death, on Park Avenue. A local doctor was called in for one—a woman. The precinct captain has been there and two men from the Central Office. I've just got the report. The whole thing is almost incredible. It seems a baffling mystery, especially the cause of death. Manning, if I wasn't sure the Griffin is safely put away—and to make sure he is I just called Dannemora—I'd feel certain that cunning devil was up to his old devices."

For a moment Manning had also wondered whether the Griffin, in some satanic trick, had not got away once more. It had taken him months to capture the arch-fiend whose web of murder and fear had been spread over the whole United States.

"There's only one Griffin, what's left of him," he said to

Melleny. "At that, I'm glad to know he's where we put him. But I need a rest, commissioner."

"And we need you. There's only one Manning. Your commission and authority as special investigator are not revoked. If you'll do me this much of a favor, go there and see what you think of it, then you can say 'no' if there isn't an angle to it that grips you. You'll have full charge. I'll hold everybody until you get there. I'm sending a cartographer and a photographer and a fingerman, though Dr. Henley says there's nothing in it for the last. He told me to say he hopes you'll take the case."

If Henley was puzzled it meant something a long way out of the ordinary. The old lure of adventure, of the mysterious, came back to Manning. He was not as fagged as he had fancied after all. He was still underweight, there were still lines of strain in his hawklike features, but suddenly he was no longer tired.

"I'll come," he said. "Give me the address."

He set it down with pencil and pad, touched a buzzer for Yamata, his Japanese body servant and butler.

"Good man," Melleny replied, and the commissioner's voice showed relief.

Twenty minutes later, having showered and breakfasted, Manning was driving his powerful roadster into the city.

II

THE PRECINCT captain had turned over the police end of it to the Central Office detectives. The three office men had made their maps and pictures, sprayed for prints. But the two detectives of the homicide squad were waiting, and so was Dr. Henley, chief medical examiner. They greeted Manning with eagerness.

It was a modern apartment house, thirty stories high, built in towering setbacks, exclusive and expensive. The woman had been found dead in her suite on the twentieth floor. The man, a well known portrait painter, was discovered on the demi-terrace at the top of the structure below a penthouse. He did

"It was a shape—
crouching—" Power said.

not live there, but had his studio on the floor below. There seemed no reason at present why he should have been on the roof at such an early hour. Both deaths, according to Henley, had occurred about four o'clock. *Rigor mortis* had not set in, but there had been terrible changes in the bodies after death.

"You'll want to look at them before the wagon comes," said Henley. "There will be autopsies, but I'm doubtful about what even they will uncover."

The chief medical examiner was a man well over fifty, experienced in surgery, an expert on criminal matters, whose findings and theories were respected on the Continent as well as in America. He and Manning had worked together before and they appreciated each other's abilities.

They went first in the elevator to the roof, one Central Office man, Sergeant Doherty, with them, the other, Eddy Hanlon, first-grade detective, remaining behind. The husband of the woman who was dead and their maid were being held.

Pelota, the dead Italian artist, whose canvases of society

women had created a furor, lay underneath a blanket. Henley removed it.

Though the sight he uncovered was ghastly it left Henley, used to the dissecting room, and Manning, used to war horrors, unmoved.

The artist's olive skin was the color of old putty. He was clad in pyjamas of an intricate pattern, crimson and gold and purple. The top was open at the throat. Over the pyjamas he wore a sleeveless robe striped in vivid colors, an Arabian *aba*.

The lips had writhed back, showing his teeth. The eyes stared horribly upward. The face was a hideous mask that seemed to register terror. It evidently affected Sergeant Doherty, though Henley and Manning both knew that post-mortem expressions are not to be considered as registrations of mental impression in the fleeting moment of sudden death. They were muscular contractions attributable to other physical causes.

Pelota's whole face was shrunken. So was his body. It was too small for the clothing. The flesh showed waxen and color-less. He had affected a small mustache and imperial, and these stood out from the chin and lip in a strained bristle.

"In life the man weighed about a hundred and fifty pounds," said Henley. "The body has been drained of blood."

Manning agreed with him.

"How?" he asked.

Beneath the collar bone Henley showed two tiny purple punctures. They were so close together as almost to merge.

"They go deep and straight in," said Henley. "That is the only mark upon him, unless I find others in the autopsy. And, believe me, Manning, that is going to be thorough."

Manning looked around. The terrace had a parapet three feet high. It was a platform some twelve feet in setback. There were shrubs and dwarf trees in stoneware vases. The whole terrace was backed by an eight foot wall of sheer cement, faced, and colored a deep green; the base of the penthouse which rose above them. There was no access from terrace to the penthouse.

The only door was the one through which they had come from the main building.

"Who lives up there?" asked Manning.

Sergeant Doherty answered:

"A guy who calls himself Zerah. A Hindu. He's got some sort of a cult. It ain't a fortune telling racket. We've had him looked into long ago. The society dames fall for whatever it is he hands them. His papers are okay, he's got the right backing and he don't charge fees. We've got nothing on him at headquarters. Some sort of a mystic, but we can't touch him. This is a free country—in spots," Doherty finished sarcastically.

Manning looked for clews, for some indication that somebody else but Pelota had been on the terrace at that unreasonable hour. He found none.

"Any suggestions?" he asked Henley.

"The man was strangled to death, I think. His diaphragmatic muscles are rigid. It looks like it might be some kind of poison. Those marks—it might have been a dart, but if it was, it has been taken. And where did his blood go to? I'm saying nothing till I dissect, and I'm not sure I'll find anything. The eyes are dilated, there are baffling superficial symptoms. Damn it, Manning, I don't know! That's why I got the commissioner out of bed and asked for you. But—wait, man, wait till you see the other body!"

III

IT WAS hard to believe that this corpse had once been vital, beautiful, alluring. But Manning had seen pictures of Evelyn Kyrrel Power, aside from the one framed on the dressing table. She had been young, prominent, popular, an acknowledged type of American beauty.

On the bed was a bloated thing that almost made Manning shudder when he saw it revealed. It was shapeless, discolored, monstrous.

Henley pulled up the merciful sheet.

"That staggers me, Manning," he said, "if the two deaths are connected. They may be. Coincidence seems impossible. All the surface veins are broken, burst. Deeper ones may be the same. Tissues are ruptured. I think, but I am not sure, on account of the horrible distension, that there are two marks below the right breast like those on Pelota. I can tell better later. Here is poison again.

"Now, look outside. They have a terrace here. A door opens to it off the dining room. Under this window there's a bed of flowers. There's been no disturbance, unless you can find some trace of it. Supposedly, the window was open. Her husband and the maid say they were always open nights. If this was a dart, tell me what force could send it the distance from another building, even if the target could be seen.

"I'm trespassing on your province, perhaps," he went on, "but this is beyond me. It baffles me. I have thought of a snake, or some poisonous creature, but what beast, bird or reptile has fangs that can strike deep and straight on any one's chest? A serpent must have something within the compass of its jaws to send in its fangs. Even then they are curved, their path is not direct. Neither of them bled. This girl's blood is jellied, the blood vessels are distended.

"Her husband tells, or tried to tell, a weird tale. But he was shocked, incoherent. I gave him a mild sedative. He was talking nightmares.

"I'll leave it to you, Manning, and I trust you find a solution. I may have word for you, after the autopsies."

Manning had made no comment, even when he bade Henley good-by. He searched the room, knowing it had been covered. He looked at the undisturbed flower bed, surveyed the nearest building, two hundred feet away, went out on the terrace and returned.

There was nothing. Only the two bodies, one swollen to the shape of a filled wineskin, the other shrunk like a corpse made ready for the injection of mummifying fluids.

"Where's this maid, and where's Mr. Power?" he asked.

"The maid's in her room. She's the only servant sleeps here. The cook comes later. And the girl's scared stiff. I don't think she knows a thing. I'm not so sure about him. No doubt the doc knew what he was doing, but I'd have let him talk. But Henley said he'd come out of it soon. 'Twas an hour ago he gave him the dose," Doherty said.

MANNING SAW the maid first. It was obvious the girl knew little of the actual tragedy, but she gave enlightening information. Manning asked her to make some strong coffee for her master, and took it in to him himself.

Power was in one of the rooms of the suite. Manning looked at him before he wakened him. The man's face was good-looking but weak, the face of a spoiled boy, not quite grown up. It was haggard with what might be worry, but was certainly part dissipation. He jumped like a landed trout, twitching, when Manning roused him.

"Who are you?" he asked. "Another cop? Who doped me? Why in hell don't you *do* something? Evelyn? Where is she? They haven't—taken her away?"

"You get a grip on yourself and drink this coffee," said Manning. "They had you listed on the All-American team once, Power, didn't they? Then you know how to buck up. If you want us to do something, pull yourself together. My name's Manning. I'm not exactly a cop...."

"Manning? The chap who got the Griffin? Then...."

Power sat up, drank the hot coffee. He gulped at it a bit convulsively and Manning could see the pulses throb in wrists and neck. But he got himself under control.

"I'll talk to you, Manning. The doctor thought I was crazy and the sergeant thought I was lying. I don't blame either of them. I'm not so sure I'm sane myself. I was out all last night, drinking. I suppose May, that's the maid, told you that."

Manning nodded.

"She said you'd been out several times lately, alone. Also that you quarreled with your wife each time before you did go out. You've been played up in the gabby columns, lately, Power. It's hinted that you're more or less of a playboy who has come to the end of his rope. I'm telling you this because I want you to understand you don't have to talk without advice of counsel."

"You think I killed my wife?" asked Power. His nerves were twitching, though he was clearly trying to steady himself.

"I have an open mind, Power," said Manning. "I am an investigator, not a prosecutor, nor a persecutor. You don't have to say anything unless you want to. I won't advise you. It may entangle you and yet not incriminate you. I am out to get the guilty and also to protect an innocent man. You are not in a good position and you may improve it. We know that you have become estranged from your wife, that you have frequently quarreled with her, that she has threatened to leave you, and that you had a violent scene before you went out last night."

"The maid again!" said Power bitterly. "All right, I admit all that. I'll take the blame for the estrangement, if you like, but I'll talk about what happened after I came home, a little before four this morning. I had been drinking, but I was not drunk. If I had been, what I saw would sober any man."

He covered his face with his hands and shuddered. Manning let him recover himself. Power gulped more coffee.

"If I don't tell it to some one who'll listen without showing he thinks I'm crazy, I'll go haywire in earnest. It sounds incredible. I believe, if I thought much more about it, I'd think I had dreamed it in some frightful nightmare, except for Evelyn. It was monstrous."

"I've traveled a lot, Power," Manning said quietly. "I have seen too many strange and monstrous things in Africa, in India, to be a sceptic."

"You've been in India? Then... never mind!"

IV

POWER SHOWED a swift and tremendous excitement. His eyes flamed and then the light went out of them.

"We had been sleeping in separate rooms lately," he went on. "At her request. She—Evelyn—had changed greatly. She used to like society, sports, the theater. She gave them up. She seemed to retire into herself entirely. I have seen her at times when she almost seemed to be in a trance. She disliked to have me even touch her.

"She shrank from me—as if some influence walled her off from me. I've got plenty of weaknesses, but I'm not a rotter. I've tried to patch things up, to bring them back to where we started. But she looked at me now and then as if she hated me.

"Last night, this morning rather, somewhere around four, I came home. I had been to a card club. I had been thinking things over. I wanted a showdown, either to make up with Evelyn, or call it all off. I was willing to make promises, even confessions, to try to win her back. You see, I still loved her.

"I knew she didn't sleep very much, never very heavily. I didn't want to put off the attempt. I was despondent. I have lost a great deal of money, my own and a lot of Evelyn's, the same as a great many other people have. Gambling, in Wall Street. Not losses at cards. And I thought, if Evelyn refused, that the only thing for me to do was to make away with myself. When we married, we each took out a policy for two hundred thousand dollars in the other's favor."

Manning stroked his lean jaw. Power did not see that he was establishing motive for his killing his wife. Two hundred thousand dollars meant a lot to a man who was practically ruined.

"The premiums were fully paid," Power went on. "My contract winnings paid them. It seemed the only honorable thing to do. A bit morbid, perhaps, to you, but here was a total loss ahead, all ways, if I couldn't get through to Evelyn, get her back."

"I can understand it," said Manning. "Go on."

"I let myself in," said Power. "The door of her room—formerly a guest room—was not locked. It was the first time I had intruded on her privacy, but I had to get it over with, one way or the other.

"It was dark. She never used a night light. The window was wide open. I saw the stars shining back of the buildings across the road. I saw the curtains waving in a little wind and then—my God—I saw....

"God or the devil knows *what* I saw, Manning. It was a shape, and it seemed to be crouching. It was furry and spotted, like a leopard in its mottling. Like nothing I knew of in shape. And it stank. It stank horribly, acrid, foul! It was on Evelyn's breast. It had clawed aside the coverings. It was quiet, hideously intent. I thought she had swooned at sight of the horror.

"Then it heard me. It rose, hideous, dreadful. It turned its head toward me. Manning, I saw eyes, not two, but many eyes, there might have been six, perhaps a dozen. I could not tell. I was gripped with some sort of paralysis. The thing reared, the eyes glared crimson and the stench was terrible, ammoniac, blinding, choking. And those eyes! They shifted from crimson to purple, to green, and then I snapped out of it and groped for the switch. I found it. The lamps in her room were all shaded, but I saw the monster leap as if the light scared it. It sprang for the window, through it, without a sound, like some enormous bullet."

MANNING HAD already noticed a persistence of the stench Power had mentioned, when he had looked at the body. It had been vaguely familiar to him at the time. He had hastily connected it with disinfectants Henley might have used. Now he knew it had been something else. Weird as it sounded, he believed much, at least, of Power's story. Power lacked the imagination and the dramatic quality to have evolved and acted out a fantasy of that amazing type.

"I let the thing go—how could I stop it? My first thought

then was for Evelyn. I saw it against the sky, blurred, furry, blotched, and then it was gone.

"And Evelyn was dead. Manning, you've been in Paris? You've seen those optical delusions they show you on Montmartre, where the body of a beautiful girl changes before your eyes into a decomposing corpse. Imagine then! Before my eyes Evelyn was swelling hideously, changing color. She was mottled like the Thing. Her face lost all features. And I—I lost my sanity. I don't know if I've got it back," Power ended wearily. "I only know that she was killed horribly, perhaps before my eyes.

"That terrace garden of ours is private and inclosed. When I reached it, with my gun, there was no trace of the Thing. Not a leaf seemed disturbed. There are no fire escapes. The walls are sheer, up and down. And they were vacant. The Thing had vanished utterly. And my wife lay inside—a revolting sight, even to me, who loved her. I called our doctor with what reason I had left. You know the rest."

"Not all of it," said Manning. "But I hope to. Power, I found this underneath one of your wife's pillows. Do you know anything about it?"

Power stared blankly at the object, an image of brass, female, which had been engraved by hand on the original casting. He shook his head.

"I never saw it before. What is it? Some sort of mascot? It's ugly enough."

"It is an image of Parvati, the wife of Siva the Destroyer, one of the Hindu trinity of Brahma, Vishnu and Siva. Hindu workmanship, unquestionably."

"Hindu? She might have got it from this chap Zerah, who has the penthouse on the roof. He is a swami or a yogi, some sort of mystic or fakir, I suppose. Evelyn and some of her pals used to go to see him, formed some sort of mysterious cult or other. I don't know much about it. Crystal gazing or fortune telling. It was a kind of fad."

Manning said no more, but put the little image in his pocket.

There was no use in telling Power that the Thugs of India robbed and ravished in the name of Parvati, that the Tantrists indulged in wild orgies in her foul honor.

"How big did this Thing seem?" he asked.

"How can I tell? There was a mass, like some crouching body, mottled and furry but not too distinct. It was not less than the size of my head. Then, as I told you, it rose, it swelled, it stunk. There were the eyes! The eyes!"

Manning left Power, with Doherty in charge.

"Don't harry him," he said to the sergeant. "I don't want him to feel he's a prisoner. He's been through hell."

"Yeah," said Doherty stolidly. "I wouldn't wonder. You're a big shot in our game, Mr. Manning, but I can't swallow all that hooey about what he calls the Thing. It ain't human, leastwise I mean it ain't natural, or reasonable."

"Ah!" said Manning. " 'There are more things in heaven and earth, Horatio.' I'll be back presently. I want to find out a few things about Pelota, and then I'm going to pay a visit to Zerah, the Hindu gentleman who lives in the penthouse. Just one thing, Doherty. I want you to come into that bedroom for a minute. Hanlon can keep tabs on Power and the maid, also the cook when she shows up."

v

THEY STOOD in the death chamber. Manning closed the windows where the Thing had disappeared.

"Got a good nose, Doherty?" he asked.

"Not bad. Why?"

"Smell anything unusual? A little like ammonia? It's faint, but I can still detect it."

Doherty enlarged his naturally wide nostrils.

"I noticed that before," he said. "Thought it was disinfectant the doc used."

"So did I," agreed Manning. "Try again, with me."

Doherty sniffed deeply.

"Smells to me like ants," he said. "We had a plague of 'em once, me and the missis, in our little shack on Long Island. They used to swarm in the house and the old lady found a nest. Poured boiling water on it. Killed 'em. But they gave off a smell like this one."

"Ants! Formic acid! Doherty, you've given me a lead. It needs disentangling, but it looks promising. And I won't forget you if it works out."

"You don't mean ants had anything to do with this affair?" asked the bewildered sergeant.

"No. Not at all. Not ants. But the smell, the blistering effect. I'm still groping in the dark, Doherty, but you've shown me a glimmer. Now go back and take care of Power and the others."

Manning was gone, his eyes gleaming. Doherty regarded the closed door confusedly.

"I'd like to know what I tipped him off to," he muttered to himself. "But he's beyond me. And why did he call me Horatio when my name's Patrick Aloysius?"

MANNING GOT off on the top floor. The penthouse had its own automatic elevator for the last flight. But this was where Pelota had his studio, where he painted the flattering portraits of the society women. Pelota whose death seemed due to the same mysterious cause, if Henley's theory was right—twin punctures, driven straight in through the thicker parts of torsos. And the smell of ants.

A woman opened the studio door narrowly, was disposed to close it in an unfamiliar face, but Manning set his foot across the threshold, flashed a small golden badge.

"Police," he said. "Let me in." Then, as the woman's stolid face remained antagonistic, he repeated his words in Italian.

She widened the door, resentfully.

"The maestro is dead," she said in her own tongue. "They

have taken him away. I know nothing. I was not here last night. I clean the studio. I cook also two meals. That is all."

"Perhaps," said Manning. "Have no fear."

The great studio had a high ceiling, a big north window. Its entrance door was close to the one that opened on the terrace. There was no communication from the studio, possibly because of special building changes for the artist's working convenience. But it would have been simple for Pelota to go to the terrace at any hour. Why he had chosen to do so, before dawn, in pyjamas and robe, was still an enigma. Painters did eccentric things, of course, Manning considered.

But the two deaths had been almost simultaneous, the mode of killing, awaiting the report of Henley's autopsies, appeared similar, though the after effects had been so different. It seemed impossible that they were not allied.

Manning got startling confirmation of this idea as he gazed about the studio. Its furnishings were exotic, of many periods and nations, but all blended with an artist's faculty to a superb and striking whole. There were deep couches, rich hangings, marvelous rugs and drapes, ancient armor and weapons, hanging lamps that had once adorned mosques, a magnificently carved fireplace. At one end there was a platform, the sitters' throne. There were two or three big easels, each with a canvas clamped to them.

On one of these the portrait was unfinished. The head and shoulders, Manning fancied, had been completed, but the gown was only rubbed in. The lines of the preliminary drawing showed through here. The paint was entirely dry.

It was the picture of Evelyn Kyrrel Power. It had been painted with fine freedom of color and technique. It was unlike Pelota's usual portraits, smoothly brushed, subtly flattering.

It was unlike the pictures of the woman that Manning had noted from time to time in the rotogravure supplements and social publications. This face was haunting with a mysterious something that was not sadness but suggested an inner brooding. The mouth drooped slightly, the exquisitely shaped nostrils were a little flared and the eyes looked at the observer, through him, with a gaze of mystic expectancy, as if the beautiful woman saw some enthralling vision, awaited a revelation. Yet it was not a saintly look.

And, as if the artist guessed—or knew—Pelota had put into the shadows of the background something that looked like a shape, vague but impressive. By some trick of masterly painting, the effect seemed to come and go.

"When did this lady last sit for her picture?" Manning asked the woman.

"Two weeks ago."

"You know she is dead? Did they see each other often, sometimes when there was no painting?"

The woman flashed scornful eyes.

"Yes. I know that she is dead. I know also that my maestro is dead, but not because of her. She did not like that picture and she said so. I do not blame her, because it is too like her. It shows her soul. Not a good woman, *signore*, but not bad, that way. As for my maestro, what did he care for any of these dolls he painted? He took their money so that, some day, he could be free to paint what pictures he wished, and care not if they were bought. Some day the world would go to them and make reverence. He meant to give them some day to the nations who would understand. But now, they will never be painted. This, the first, will never be finished."

WITH A certain dignity she pulled back a curtain that had screened a shallow recess in the wall. A canvas was shown that was twice the height of Manning.

The woman's protests had not left him assured. He knew the fidelity of her type and doubtless she had looked upon Pelota as little short of a god. Pelota's presence had been constantly sought for, and he had not shown himself averse to the company of fair women who might be also frail. The man was human. He was also a genius, which might well mean a dual nature.

But, as he looked at the great canvas, unfinished but glorious already, Manning was not so sure either of his own ideas. This incomplete achievement might furnish a reason for Pelota's being on the terrace.

The painting was that of a majestic city, mounting to the stars that were paling with a hint of dawn. Mists trailed the sky in forms that suggested vast shapes, even as the background of the portrait had, but these were greater, grander. Mist trailed about the tall buildings, wreathing the spires, the turrets and pinnacles. Here and there a light gleamed in a window, symbol of humanity. It did not need a title to proclaim its meaning. Here was aspiration, inspiration. Man's ambition and achievement, reaching to the stars, to the dawn of newer, nobler eras.

It was a great work. The paint was wet. No great wonder that Pelota, urged by his creative soul, should go to the terrace to wait for the coming of the dawn, to watch the conquest of the night, the twining of the vapors about the tall buildings.

"It is a great work," said Manning.

The proud fire died out of the woman's eyes, drowned by a gush of tears.

"He was my milk-child," she said. "I nursed him when his mother could not, back there in Tuscany. My life was in his. Why should *he* have to die? It was not the hand of the good God struck him down. It was the deed of a devil."

"Why should *she* have had to die?" Manning shot at her. The woman might know something after all.

"She? Why should *she* die?" Her voice was scornful. "I do not know. But, if she was not a wicked woman, she was not a wise one. I have heard things, though I do not know much of the tongue of this cold country. She set aside her husband. She was like many others, all fools, with wealth and idleness to get rid of."

"Just what do you mean by that?" asked Manning.

"I mean nothing, nothing, *signore*. I am only an ignorant old peasant who has talked too much. But, because you have been kind, because you have spoken wisely of his work and because there is talk that my maestro and this woman died after the same fashion, so that, if you find out the murderer of one, you may find out who killed the other, I will tell you this. And I pray to all the Holy Saints, to the Blessed Virgin and her Son, that you find him," she added passionately. "Even as I swear by them that there was nothing guilty between my maestro and her. I speak now—and say no more. No. I go to my grief."

"You have not told me yet," prompted Manning.

She looked at him with her manner almost distraught.

"Go and see the brown man, Zerah," she said.

VI

THERE WAS nothing more to be got out of her, Manning knew. It was not mere stubbornness, it was pride. She would talk no more about her dead maestro.

Manning looked at the door of the private, automatic elevator that led to Zerah's penthouse. There was a speaking tube by the operating button. It was probably controlled from above. That would not stop him from gaining admittance, but he had changed his mind about visiting Zerah immediately. He wanted something more tangible than a little image of Parvati and the fact that the dead woman had been one of the cult, perhaps a disciple.

Zerah would be very, very far from a fool, especially if he was a scoundrel, one of those who deliberately came to America to prey upon the emotions of rich women looking for new thrills, tired of contract, of backgammon, of night clubs and plays, tired of everything that was not new and promising, even if dangerous.

And it was dangerous material Zerah brought to them. For the little statuette Manning had found suggested he was a follower of Siva, and Siva's attributes were many. He was the Destroyer of the Triad, representing the principle of destruction, though destruction in Hindu thought meant restoration. He was god of the arts, especially of dancing. God of a thousand titles.

And Parvati, whom the image had represented, also had many names and many phases. And under her various names she was portrayed as dripping with blood, adorned with skulls, encircled with snakes, worshiped with obscene and bloody rites, with human sacrifice. She was the goddess who presides over life and death, supreme power in the universe, at whose name all India trembled.

Who could tell what Zerah taught his disciples, how he led them on, got them into his power?

He took no fees, Doherty had said. The little brass statue could not speak. And one woman's lips were sealed in horrible death.

Manning wanted another look at the terrace from which the Thing had disappeared. Power was in his own room. Doherty said he was lying down quietly. Manning went outside to the terrace.

There had been certain holes in the flower bed which had appeared natural enough, holes such as might well be made by metal stakes or wires set in the soil to uphold plants. There were some of these stakes still set beside late blossoming dahlias. And there were four holes, equidistant, marking the corners of a curiously exact square, outside the window to the dead woman's bedchamber, the window that had been open.

THEY SEEMED obvious and innocent enough, but Manning carefully measured the distance between them. Then he looked over the parapet, at the sheer wall below. The building was modern. The setbacks were not regularly spaced. They had been designed to conform with the architect's conception of a modernistic exterior. Only the favored and more expensive suites owned a terrace garden.

Manning gazed upward. The wall again was sheer, up to the high pitched, tiled roof of the penthouse, broken only by window casements, flush with the surface of the wall.

It seemed beyond belief that any creature, monster or human, could scale those heights, unless it flew.

Manning had a talk with the maid about the garden. The cook had failed to put in an appearance.

He found out that Power and his wife had formerly slept in the room now used solely by Power. His wife had moved to what had been the guest chamber, a room charming enough, facing the east, getting the early morning sun. But not many women of Evelyn Kyrrel Power's position liked early sunshine. They were apt to sleep until noon.

He saw the superintendent and, through him, the man in charge of the terrace gardens, a highly intelligent Japanese who told him what he wanted.

Now Manning had two more things to do before he called on Zerah. He imagined that the mystic would not hold any class to-day, nor until the funeral of one of his pupils, or disciples, was over. Moreover, he would not be looking for any connection with the story. He was not out for notoriety of that sort. It would ruin him with the social set. Zerah was not going to be easy to see. He might, later, be hard to find. But Manning was not worrying about that.

He wanted to find out what insurance company had issued the two premiums of two hundred thousand dollars each. The fact that Power, hard up, desperate, would profit to the extent of a fifth of a million by his wife's death, about which he told such a fantastic tale, was an important factor. And the papers would make the most of it.

Manning wanted the information first. Power might refuse to give it. Manning believed that Power, now that he had relaxed, would not do any more talking until he saw his lawyer. He would be foolish if he did. The attorney certainly would not talk about the policies.

But the information would not be too hard to get. Manning called up his own down town offices, where he was titled as

Consulting Attorney, and set his staff to work, under his capable secretary.

The second thing was to see Henley. He called first and then drove in his own car to the mortuary where Henley was waiting for him. It was a grim place, smelling of disinfectants, a place where the relics of dead men were dissected, probed into, where the sanctity of the human body gave place to the research of science.

Henley saw Manning in the little office off the autopsy chamber. He was still clad in the grim habiliments of his profession, when in action. He took off the mask through which he had been working and which made him look like some sinister member of the Inquisition, pulled off a pair of rubber gloves, washed his hands and lit a cigar before he sat heavily, wearily, in the chair behind his desk.

"How about it?" asked Manning.

Henley shook his head.

"I'm not quite through, but there's nothing definite as to what killed them. Same in both cases, I believe. I can guess how they were killed. Pretty definite about that, up to a point. They both died of strangulation and coincident syncope. There was a poison injected into them that instantly coagulated the blood stream, paralyzed the main ganglia, clogged the brain. If it's any consolation to the bereaved," he added, somewhat cynically, "I don't believe either of them knew what happened. I don't believe they would have had time to make more than one gasp after they were punctured.

"There might have been some moments of anticipatory horror, if we believe that wild yarn Power told me, or tried to tell."

"He told me *all* of it," said Manning, filling and lighting his pipe. "I'm not so skeptical about it as you seem to be, Henley. He was fairly coherent."

"Mine is an exact science, or supposed to be. You can dally with the riddles," Henley replied. "I'll go ahead. You know enough of medicine and surgery to follow what I'm talking about. Now then.

"There were remarkable changes in the serous albumins and globulins. In Pelota's case the serous fluid was almost all that was left. Yet his blood also had first coagulated—before it was pumped out, or sucked out of him. I found another wound, on his chest. The lips of the lesion were pallid and shrunken, but it was an orifice extending to his pulmonary circulation. The wound was sharply incised as if by a nipping action of sharp blades."

"Steel, teeth, or even a beak?" suggested Manning.

Henley looked at him sharply and nodded.

"I have seen a similar effect made by a vampire bat," he said, "but no bat could take that much blood."

"Their stomachs are small, their bodies only a few inches long," Manning agreed. "Besides, bats fly. This Thing sprang. It did not spread wings."

HENLEY GRUNTED. The talk of Things was not in his province. He continued:

"The heart of Mrs. Power was clogged with viscous blood, both auricles and ventricles. This must have occurred between diastolic and systolic rhythms, in the space of half a heartbeat.

"The poison was extremely swift in action. Those vertical incisions, on her breast, and beneath Pelota's collar bone, penetrated for almost five inches. They were hard to trace in her case because of the breakdown of tissues and blood vessels, but I found them. They were made by some instrument, by duplicate hollow tubes charged with the virus, thrust with violence.

"You know well enough that there are certain poisons, like gelsemin, like the opium alkaloids, that are absorbed swiftly and completely after death and may not be traced, save by the effects they leave behind. This poison had that attribute. I can get no reactions, though, as I said, I'm not quite through. But I might as well be. I'm afraid chemistry isn't going to help you out this time, Manning. Not my branch of it. You'll have to work it out your own way. You know what I have done. What have you got, if it isn't a deep secret?"

Manning chuckled. He knew Henley, realized he was tired, baffled and chagrined.

"It's pretty secret, even to me," he answered. "I've got a glimmer of light, but it's far from brilliant. As to your poison. I don't think it was any vegetable toxin. More likely an active organic secretion. I may know more about it this time to-morrow. I was rather hoping you might have got some trace of formic acid, though I wasn't counting on it."

"Formic acid?" Henley stared at him.

Manning produced the little brass image and set it on the medical examiner's desk.

"I've got this," said Manning. "I may see that you get it for a paperweight later on, Henley. This—and a smell of ants. Doherty is in on that tip."

"You're too mysterious for me," said Henley. "I see the connection between ants and formic acid, of course, but…."

"Mysterious because I have to be," said Manning. "I'm like some one who's picked up two scraps of a jigsaw puzzle. They don't fit, but it's odd they belong to the same answer. I must be going. I'll call my office first, if you don't mind. And I want to get a quantity of buhach, two or three pounds. Where's the best place to get it? Write it down, will you? I'll send out after it."

He picked up the telephone. Henley looked at him, shook his head and wrote down the address of a wholesale supply house for drugs. Manning hung up. He had got the name of the insurance company, also an appointment with its president.

"That secretary of mine is a most efficient girl," he said to Henley. "Homely, positively homely, but clever. If anything ever happens to me, Henley, you grab her, or get some friend of yours to grab her."

"Thinking of making your will?" asked Henley.

Manning grinned at him in friendly fashion.

"Made it, long ago," he said. "I'm not really looking forward to a prompt shuffling off this mortal coil. I weathered the Griffin, you know, but I've got a hunch I might have a close call between now and, let us say, midnight."

He picked up his hat, gloves and the stick he always carried, whether he was driving or walking. It was a steel rod, gold-capped at the head, tapering to a blunt point that served as ferrule. The steel was covered with rings of leather closely shrunk together. The cane was very flexible and it was a danger-ous weapon in the hands of a man who knew how to use it to good effect, whether as a fencer or handling it as a staff or bludgeon.

If the theory that was beginning to slowly evolve a core out of more or less nebulous surroundings proved itself, Manning was going to have need of all his energies, all his resources of mind and body. He would be pitted against forces that could only be surmised until their final revelation, forces bordering on the unreal, malevolent and deadly.

He was going to face them alone, and he went out with a lithe stride to keep the rendezvous with danger.

VII

THERE WAS no answer, by tube or bell, to Manning's summons for admission to Zerah's penthouse. He had not expected there would be, but he was persistent. He had no authority to use force, no warranty, but he meant to stay there until somebody came in, or out. In a way the penthouse was a little stronghold. He imagined there might be some sort of dumb-waiter system for supplies and also meals, since the apart-ment house served them, but that was not the way he wanted to get in, even if it was negotiable. No doubt the superintendent and the engineer had means of releasing the automatic elevator. A man, with means to scale the back wall of the terrace where Pelota had been found, could break in, but this was no time for burglary, for forced entrance.

Finally a foreign voice came down the tube.

"Zerah mus' not be disturb'!" it said. "He will see no one to-day."

Manning's eyes held a twinkle as he thought of the effect his swift Hindustani reply was having on the wallah at the other end of the tube. His sentences were blistering and imperative, those of white master to servant, speech the wallah was used to in India. In the United States he had grown insolent. But Manning brought him to.

"Tell your master," he concluded, "that this is police business and must be attended to. Rung ho!"

A moment later he heard the elevator coming down. Now, when he clicked the latch button, it responded and he entered the private lift, pushing another button that took him up to where it opened again on a foyer. A Hindu servant, in loose tunic, trousers and turban, with a sash and slippers, salaamed profoundly.

Manning's travel and observations placed the wallah as a member of the sudra, or lowest, caste. He wondered whether Zerah was any higher in the Hindu social scale. He thought more likely the man was a clever sharper who might have once carried the begging bowl of a priest and learned many matters he was now putting to use. In his capacity of mystic he did not have to bring references. The sensation-seeking society women swallowed all his specious sayings.

But he had his methods. The foyer wall was paneled with tapestries and paintings of the doings of the Hindu Trinity of Brahma, Vishnu and Siva. Some were mere prints on cotton, others on gold backgrounds. They were impressive, but Manning knew how easily and cheaply they could be purchased in the bazaars of Calcutta or any Hindu city.

At one end of the entrance hall was a stone statue of Brahma, at the other one, carved in gilded wood, of Siva. This showed the god in beneficent aspect, seated on the sacred cow. Bronze braziers gave out incense.

Manning thought about the smell of ants. Nor had he forgot-

ten that checked sentence of Power—*You have been to India—
then*.... Those things were tied up with this visit.

He was ushered into a main room that was clearly the lecture
hall and also the temple of Zerah's cult. Here there were more
incense, more panelings and these pictures were subtly grosser
than those of the hall.

The furniture was of inlaid teak, set with pearl and ivory.
There were many cushions, floor pillows and low lounges. The
lights were dim, showing through globes of pierced brass. At
one end hung drapes of black from ceiling to floor. The windows
were curtained. Behind the black drapes there would be the
altar, the so-called shrine, where Zerah officiated.

"The swami will come, *sahib*, presently," said the wallah, salaamed again and vanished.

MANNING SHIFTED a window curtain, verified the
exposure of the room, generally oriented himself. A gong
sounded, deep and resonant. Then a silver bell chimed. Manning
gazed at one of the picture-panels. He was not surprised to
hear a voice, to see Zerah standing in the middle of the room.
Wherever Manning had happened to stand, he fancied, Zerah
would have come in behind him, unseen, through some trick
panel. It was useless mummery to Manning.

Zerah was in flowing robes of deepest purple, figured in some
small pattern of brocade. His high turban was scarlet. His slippers were scarlet, as was his sash. He had black and piercing
eyes, a nose that was thinly aquiline. A striking figure and, to
Manning, a challenging one. Those dark eyes held cunning and
could hold cruelty, the mouth, half hidden by a carefully
groomed mustache and forked beard, was sensuous, greedy,
dominant.

He gave off a scent of jasmine that made Manning's nose
wrinkle.

"Not much like ants," he told himself.

"You wish to see me?" said Zerah. "I hear you are from the
police. I am in retreat to-day, in deep sorrow because of the

death of one who sat, with me, at the feet of Parvati. It is perhaps, concerning that you come to me?"

"I am *of* the police," Manning corrected. "How did you learn of the death of Mrs. Power, who sat with you at the feet of Kali?"

He saw those black eyes show sudden fires of suspicion, of hatred, then of caution. Zerah was wondering how much Manning knew, this man *of* and not *from* the police. He was appraising his visitor, who knew the difference between Parvati and Kali, who wanted to know how he had learned of the death of the woman who had worshiped there, in the big room with the dim lights.

"I should not have known, but for a friend of hers who called me and thought I had heard the news. One of my pupils. I do not care to give the name. There will be much talk and printings."

"There will be much talk, *and* printings," said Manning. Zerah was on guard. "And you grieve for Mrs. Power? Doubtless she has attained Nirvana, under your teachings. Could you give me any reason for her death, Zerah?"

The glint of hate that had shone when Manning mentioned Nirvana changed again to calculation.

"I should not care to say, save to the police, whom I respect," replied Zerah. Now his tone was slightly mocking. Manning was not inclined for a wordy duel.

"It is as well to always respect the powers of a foreign nation," he said. "What's your idea? Suicide? After all the philosophy you have shown her? You think she may have been despondent, taken poison? Why?"

He saw Zerah's mind grasp the suggestion. It glowed in the look he turned on Manning.

"She had not acquired enough philosophy," he said. "It is hard to teach, to those who are not of my race. But she was not happy."

"With her husband, eh? *He* might have poisoned her?"

He saw Zerah re-rating him, placing him as an obtuse official, the typical policeman.

"It might be," said Zerah. "I cannot say."

"She was insured for two hundred thousand dollars, payable to him," Manning went on. "At the present rate of exchange, that's a lot of money, Zerah. Eight hundred thousand rupees. Eight lacs of rupees. A fortune, in India!"

"Also in America."

"But it seems that her husband is no longer the beneficiary," snapped Manning. "The man who would receive the two hundred thousand dollars, the eight lacs of rupees, according to the records of the insurance company, is *you*."

THE HINDU'S simulation, if it was simulation, was perfect in its amazement.

"I take no fees," he said. "There is a certain voluntary endowment fund, to build a temple. It provides also for my own expenses, but I did not dream of this. It is true that she embraced the Faith, clung to it but that she had willed so much to it was unknown to me.

"That money could not be collected until after her death," said Manning. "Of course, since you did not know of the change of beneficiary, it is quite possible that her husband was also ignorant. But, under the circumstances, you will understand that the question will come up. It establishes what we might call a motive. It does not necessarily implicate you, but you will undoubtedly be asked, in private hearing, to testify. I must ask you not to leave New York, not to change your address until that hearing has been held."

Zerah smiled.

"Of course. I am glad to assist the authorities. After all, how could I leave without their consent? I am an alien, admitted under regulations. My papers are in perfect order, Mr....?"

"The name is Manning."

"Manning? I am glad to have met you. I shall be pleased to assist you. That is all?"

"All, for the present."

Manning bowed and left. The wallah took him down in the elevator. After the door had closed he rang the bell of Pelota's apartment, hoping the woman had not left. If she had, he must make other arrangements. But he had noticed in the studio certain ladders and trestles that Pelota had used in painting his big canvas. They would be convenient for what he had in mind, a private survey and investigation of Zerah's private activities.

Zerah had lied. Manning knew from the insurance company that he had called up, three weeks before, to know how much might be borrowed on the policy by a full beneficiary. No doubt he had been disappointed. The policy was only three years old, the loan value was not very great.

The Italian housekeeper was still there. Her face was wrung with grief.

"I may find the man who killed your maestro," Manning told her. "Will you help me?"

She regarded him earnestly, then caught his hand, and kissed it.

VIII

MANNING STOOD on the top round of the platform he had set up on the terrace and peered through the curtained windows of Zerah's temple. There was light inside and the interior was fairly plain to his view.

The black drapes were drawn. There were crimson lights on and about the altar. On it were images of Siva and Parvati, his wife, in their most diabolical aspects. Two servants knelt, one on either side. Incense smoked. In front of the unhallowed shrine Zerah officiated.

It was plain to Manning that Zerah, as ever, was the dupe of the heathen rituals he practiced. Now he was offering a placation, a sacrifice. He was appealing to the gods he had falsely served to rescue him from the situation, brought about by his own greedy lusts, which now threatened him.

Dimly the sound of a gong came through the window panes. One of the wallahs left and returned with a salver on which was the skinned carcass of some animal. Manning could not see it clearly and it did not matter. It might be dog, rabbit or cat, so long as it was full of blood.

He waited tensely. These were French windows, long, opening inward, but the panes were not large. He had cut a small square in one of them, next to the latch. He had smeared on a section of flypaper to which he had attached a handle of twine with adhesive, long since dried. Now he waited for the chill of the November night to set the gluey surface so that he could snatch the cut segment free—when he was ready.

It was not going to be long. Not after that blood-filled sacrifice, that offering to Kali, had been brought in.

He saw Zerah approach the altar, step on a pedal, saw the top of the altar lower. Then a cage appeared, elevated, resting at last on a level Manning thought was maintained by the re-arising of the altar top. It was square, made of light but strong wiring, about two feet square.

In it squatted a fearsome object. Mottled, crouching. Manning caught the gleam of avid eyes. The Thing was furred. It seemed to bristle at scent of the blood of the flayed offering.

Zerah lifted the front of the cage, stepped back. Manning caught the faint sound of music that grew louder as he yanked free the square of glass, softly set it down and released the latch. Some one was playing on a pipe. The kind of pipe and the sort of music used by the snake charmers. The Thing heard it. It crept out of the cage.

Manning had all he wanted to know. He released the window latch and stepped in and down. Under one arm he carried his steel cane. His right hand was in his side pocket.

Zerah whirled. The Thing was still crawling from its cage, intent upon a feast.

Zerah rapped out a crisp command. He felt in his belt and from it a *tulwar* flashed, a curving knife of steel, inlaid with gold. But he left the first attack to his two servants. Manning had entered through the window. Zerah knew well enough what that meant. His appraisal of Manning was now definite. Here was an enemy—and he meant to destroy him before he himself was destroyed.

THE TWO men leaped simultaneously, weapons snatched from their sashes. Manning struck out twice, right and left, with his cane, left-handed. He hit one man on the shin, midway, and the other just below the knee. They howled with the nerve-shock and his stick swung in the rapid moulinet of a saber expert. The steel tip struck one on the temple, the second on the base of his skull. Both rolled over, no longer howling, and Manning faced Zerah.

The mystic was back of the altar. He had shouted another order. The fluting music changed. It became irritant, high-pitched, and the Thing on the altar gathered itself, lifted, rearing high, and leaped at Manning.

His hand came out of his pocket for the first time. It held something that ended in a tube and jetted out vapor. The terrific, furry monster seemed to crumple in mid-leap. It fell, folding in upon itself, with slender, hairy legs, with eyes that dulled.

Manning swung on Zerah.

"Some of the same?" he asked. "Or this?"

In his right hand was the weapon that ended in a tube. In his left his cane.

For answer Zerah flung his *tulwar* and followed it.

Manning struck the shining steel aside with his cane. As Zerah hurtled forward, he thrust at him, and the mystic yelled with anguish as the rod pierced his body.

Manning surveyed him grimly. The man would not die of that. He had withheld his wrist. Zerah would go to the chair, these other two....

He whirled, just as a cloth flicked about his neck. For a moment he had forgotten the third man, the musician. A Thug, a devotee of Kali! Before the muslin tightened Manning got his hold, beneath the other's thigh, with one arm, while the other hand gripped for a Goorka hold at the spot where the collar bones protect the windpipe.

He was just in time. The Thuggee choker almost had him. But Manning's fingers dug in and shut off his assailant's wind, sent out his tongue between his lips. He collapsed and Manning stepped back.

Now he drew a gun. He surveyed his late opponents. He stepped to the only modern thing in the room—a telephone.

When he hung up he tilted the cage over the crumpled, furry Thing, slid the door beneath its limp body.

"We'll be needing you, later," he said.

IX

CHIEF COMMISSIONER MELLENY and the district attorney sat in conference with Manning. Their eyes were wide.

"I've seen spider's webs in New Guinea," said Manning, "that were used for fishing nets by the natives. They talked of these big insects and I tried to get one. They are nocturnal. Light blinds them, frightens them. When Power turned on the switch this one was scared. They have eight eyes, but they are useful only after dark. Eight legs, also. Tall legs, so that when the thing reared up it looked tremendous. It is tremendous, for a spider. You've got it upstairs. Take a good look at it. Furry, like a tarantula. The natives of New Guinea say it can kill a cassowary, or a tree-wallaby. I agree with them. It killed Mrs. Power—and Pelota."

"How?" asked the district attorney.

"Zerah brought the thing in. He might have thought only to use it as a sort of fetich. You'll never find out, from him. But, in the end, he used it to kill. Got Mrs. Power to shift her bedroom to one that looked east. Probably linked that up with sun worship. But it was right under his own window. He lowered the cage, as soon as he knew she had made over the policy. Lowered it outside the window he knew she always had open—or he told her to keep open—lowered it until its bottom legs hit the flower bed. I've got the measurements to prove that, and the dirt on the bottom of the cage.

"He'd starved it until it was crazy for blood. It had leaped in and out, unsatisfied. He had lifted the lid, raised the cage. Even if they found the thing they couldn't trace it to him, who had brought it over probably as an egg and hatched it out.

"But it was still hungry. When the light startled it, it went up the wall of the house as only a spider can. There was Pelota, on the terrace, underneath the place the thing considered home. He paid the penalty.

"Some spiders have vertical fangs, some have horizontal. This one is of the latter kind. I've got the answer. Henley can prove it. That's why I didn't want to kill the beast."

"But how did you stupefy it?" asked Melleny.

"Buhach! Vaporized it. Got the vapor into a container. Squeeze it, and it emits. Kill off any ordinary insect. Choked this brute. It's recovering slowly. By the way, don't forget to credit Doherty. He mentioned the ants. They give off formic acid. So do other insects. Doherty didn't know that—neither did Henley. But Doherty gave me the tip. And, believe me, that spider stunk of formic acid when I gave it the shot."

There Were Plenty of People Who Hated
Amos Willoughby, but It Took Manning
and Heaven to Unmask the Murderer

"YOU'RE LOOKING fit," said the police commissioner as he accepted appreciatively the imported
cigar offered him in the humidor Manning slid across the table.
He clipped it with an outmoded but eminently practical gold
cigar-cutter, lit it at the standing lighter on the table, and leaned
back in the big club chair with the air of a comparatively casual
and thoroughly contented visitor.

Tanaka, Manning's Japanese butler, entered silently, with ice,
charged water and two kinds of whisky in square decanters.

Belden, the commissioner, selected rye. Manning chose the
Scotch. Highballs were skillfully compounded by Tanaka.

The guest pledged his host.

"Good luck to you! Hope you'll always look as well as you
do now."

"Thanks," Manning answered. "I'm feeling fairly fit, but I'll
be fitter after I've had my vacation. King's invited me for a
Caribbean cruise."

He knew then, in his bones, that the cruise was off, so far as
he was concerned. He knew that the police commissioner had
not come out to Manning's house at Pelham Manor, driving
himself, and using a private car, to make complimentary remarks
about Manning's appearance. There was something in the wind
and it was not an ordinary thing, or the commissioner would
have telephoned. He knew Manning's strictly unlisted number.
But Manning waited for the commissioner to unburden himself.

"Manning," said Belden, "you've got a holiday coming to you, if any man ever had, after your bout with the Griffin. We've got that mad devil out of the way, but there are other things going on that disrupt the public morale almost as much as his crimes. I mean the recent kidnapings and blackmailings."

"The snatch racket," said Manning, beginning to see what was coming. "Who is it now, man, woman or child?"

"It hasn't happened yet," replied Belden. "I want to stop it. I want you to stop it. You're the one man for the job," he added. "Your special commission still stands, Manning. Do this for me and you can turn it in and trade your shield for a gold medal with diamonds in it."

"Thanks," said Manning. "Just what would I do with it? Shoot, Belden. What is it?"

Belden was silent for a few seconds, regarding the lean figure, the tanned, hawklike face of Gordon Manning, ex-Secret Service man with the A.E.F., explorer, scientist, and now, by avowed profession, a consulting attorney. There were fine, deep lines in his face that had not come from the weather or from age. Lines engraved there during Manning's weeks and months of mortal combat against the insane genius and homicide named the Griffin, safely corralled at last in a State institution. Lines that would never entirely disappear.

"YOU KNOW Willoughby? Amos Willoughby the tool manufacturer?" Belden finally asked.

"Know him? I've met him. He's not a friend of mine."

"I doubt very much if he's got a friend," said the commissioner judicially. "And I'm sure he's got plenty of enemies. He's a man who trusts nobody but himself, and he came up fast, from nowhere. His last merger practically gives him complete control of the tool making industry. It's a monopoly, or about to be. 'Ten-Per-Cent' Willoughby, his workers call him, always the first to cut ten per cent off his employee's wages, and the last to restore it. They had another demonstration outside his Erie plant again yesterday. Papers haven't said much about

it—and they won't. He'd make it too interesting for their ad-
vertising departments. But his social side and his business
methods have nothing to do with this. He's a big man and he
rates protection. He's asked for it. He's staying on his place in
Delaware County, where he was born. That's where he goes
when he wants privacy and is planning a new coup."

"Fairtrees," said Manning. "He's invited me up there. Bought
up a whole village and demolished it to include it in his estate,
so that his birthplace is actually inside his own fences though
not the cottage. His father was the village postmaster and ran
a small general store. His mother was a seamstress. He's frank
about those matters, principally because it helps to show what
a big man he is. About the only human thing I know of him is
his hobby for trees. He has transplanted any amount and variety
of them, and they say he has succeeded in developing chestnuts
immune to the blight. If he has, it's the first thing he's ever done
for the cause of humanity.

"I always understood that Fairtrees was always well guarded.
There's a fine trout stream there. He tried to tempt me with it.
He doesn't fish himself, and no one outside his guests are
allowed to. Hence the keepers. Also for preservation of the trees
and shrubbery, and the wild game. The place is a natural preserve. If it belonged to any one else you might call it a Bird and
Deer Sanctuary. With him it's plain selfishness. But he never
struck me as a man to be lightly alarmed."

He lit his pipe, seeing in the smoke the sturdy, dominant
figure of Amos Willoughby, tool magnate, ruthless absorber of
smaller plants, of larger ones also. A shortish man, though he
carried his square, solid body erectly. A man who looked a great
deal like Andrew Carnegie, with trimmed beard that was gray,
like his hair; with gray eyes that were always cold as ice.

"He may be forearmed and now he's forewarned," said the
commissioner, "I don't think he's actually frightened, I don't
believe the man has any more emotions than a shark. You can't
actually scare him, mentally or physically. He's overcome a lot
of stiff opposition in his time. There are still plenty who con-

"I was chancy about getting it out, account the grating was charged."

sider him a menace to general prosperity, but they're leaving him alone. He's the sort of man who battens on depression. He has no more patriotism than a newly landed Armenian immigrant. He doesn't give a whoop in Hades about the common people, but right now he's afraid he may get wiped out."

"By whom?" asked Manning. "The proletariat?"

Belden shrugged his shoulders.

"It's the mystery of it that has got Willoughby's goat," he said. "He has a private wire, an operator in his own house. He lives like a Nabob. But he plugged in himself this time and got through to me. He's been threatened plenty of times, but now he's had three letters, mailed from the General Post Offices in New York, Albany and Philadelphia, all typed on the same machine, with the same ribbon. He checked that up. They all said the same thing. *You've been warned enough. This time you go.* Brief and to the point.

"I don't know if he told me everything, but he believes these communications are authentic and mean business. He wants protection. He's a potentate and I'm a policeman—you, too, Manning. We've got to give protection, or, for one thing, I may lose my job and, for another, if anything breaks like the elimination of Amos Willoughby, right now, people are going to get hysteria."

"Did he ask for me?" suggested Manning. Belden grunted.

"He did," he confessed, "and he gave reasons that are just what I would have advanced. He wants the prevention, the investigation kept perfectly private. He doesn't want a stranger coming to Fairtrees whose presence might be suspected as out of the ordinary. He said he had invited you. You can go fishing. One hint sneaking out that he was taking precautions against kidnaping, or killing, or blackmail, and the place would be surrounded with State Police, County Police, reporters, cameramen, newsreel operators and amateur detectives. You know what they did in the case of Major Olstrom's child. He doesn't want any publicity.

"He doesn't think himself in any immediate danger so long as he is at Fairtrees, but I think he figures that something may start there and be culminated the minute he leaves the place. It's surrounded with steel wire, with barbed slantbacks; steel grids go into the stream bed and it can all be charged with enormous voltage from the power lines. Probably is, nowadays. That fence cost him plenty of money. He wants you to nose out the direction his danger is coming from. Of course, Manning, our appropriations can't begin to pay you your proper fees. You took on the Griffin in a sporting way, largely from a sense of public duty. Willoughby realizes you are not professionally connected with the force. He is willing to pay any amount you care to charge."

"I'll care to charge him plenty," said Manning grimly. "Half of it goes into the Unemployment Fund, a quarter of it to the Police Benefit Association. The rest I'll find use for myself. What did you tell him?"

"I told him I'd see you. Manning, except that the Griffin always named the date on which he meant to kill—and the fact that I called Dannemora this afternoon to find out he was still in the hospital, I'd think he had a finger in the pastry of this pie."

"The Griffin only went after men who were public benefactors," said Manning. "But you're right. And it'll be a public benefit to check anything happening to him. There's been too much of that sort of thing. But I can't go until the day after to-morrow. I have certain matters that must be attended to."

"That's all right," said Belden. "He doesn't seem, as I told you, to worry much, so long as he remains at Fairtrees."

"Then he's a bigger fool than I've ever credited him with being," said Manning. "That's where they strike, these days, unexpectedly, in the place considered the most secure. And get clear on the sheer audacity of it. If it's a racket and the big shots are in it, we're up against brains."

"You don't think it's the communists, then?"

"The proletariats, the underdogs, the downtrodden hoi polloi? My dear Belden, I haven't any opinion on the matter. I'm going into this with an open mind."

"You *are* going into it?"

The commissioner's face was eloquent of relief.

"You can get in touch with Ten-Per-Cent Willoughby and tell him I'll start early in the morning the day after to-morrow, and drive up to Fairtrees with my fishing tackle. I wouldn't wonder if I have to bait this affair. It'll be bottom fishing rather than dry-fly casting, I fancy. Tanaka," he added as the butler glided in, answering the buzzer. "Two more highballs, please."

II

MANNING WAS stopped by closed gates outside the main entrance to Fairtrees. A man came out of a lodge in response to his horn, another drifted into sight from some shrubbery. Both were armed, he noticed. He gave his name and showed credentials, but the house was phoned before he was admitted. Both men were like robots, expressionless, but watchful, suspicious as watchdogs. They wore a compromise between livery and uniform, with shoulder belts and heavy automatics in open holsters. They seemed plain evidence that

Willoughby was taking threats seriously, even at Fairtrees. One of them rode up with Manning to the house in the latter's car.

He noticed other men who seemed comparatively idle as they drove through the grounds. These looked like keepers rather than gardeners in their general attitude. There was no pretense of anything like landscape gardening in the grounds, but the shrubberies and the trees were in magnificent condition. While there were no vistas, everything was given maximum space.

Manning looked with surprise and admiration on the house. It was built entirely of logs, but it had been designed by some notable architect. It had dignity. It looked like some forest fortress of a powerful Fur Company's factor in far western wilds. It fitted its surroundings. Trees grew above it on all sides and cast their shadows over lawns like green velvet carpets, fringed with rhododendron, azalea, laurel and semi-tropical canna and croton. Perfection everywhere. Arboriculture, rather than forestry, was practiced at Fairtrees.

A butler received Manning in the hall, a second man close beside him. They were respectful enough, but plainly vigilant. Manning suspected that both of them were armed. They looked more like the type of guards in a penitentiary than men trained in social service.

The great door of oak and wrought iron reinforcements could hardly have been pierced by machine gun bullets. Fairtrees, Manning fancied, could withstand any ordinary siege, might even have been built with that possibility in mind.

There was a subtle air of preparedness about the whole place. A slightly sinister atmosphere. There were no indoor plants. The walls were hung with great heads and antlers, and with weapons. Manning noticed that, amid the savage spears and clubs and bows, there were modern sporting rifles. If these were kept oiled and loaded there was a very efficient armament ready to hand.

He was ushered up the great stairway, where a third man

awaited him on the landing and walked ahead to the door he held open.

"Mr. Willoughby's secretary, Mr. Everest Mills, will be with you, in a moment, sir," said this third man as he bowed. His accents were crisp, deferential enough, but rough. The butler had remained in the hall downstairs with the second man.

The library was a splendid room with a great stone fireplace, carved and hooded. Books lined the walls from floor to ceiling, save for some paneled spaces where fine paintings hung—all of them of trees, mostly of the Barbizon school.

Everest Mills was sedate, precise and poised, a man of about forty, keen green-hazel eyes, sharp nose, and thin lips. A tall man who moved silently. Without question clever. Manning placed him as one who would serve well, even brilliantly, but might betray a trust. That would not matter to Willoughby, who demanded efficiency and trusted nobody.

Mills greeted Manning gravely. His well kept hands were cold.

"Misfortune has happened," he said, without preamble. "I doubt whether you could have averted it. I trust you can solve the mystery. But Mr. Willoughby has disappeared. Nothing has been seen of him since shortly after three o'clock yesterday afternoon."

"SINCE YESTERDAY?" Manning exclaimed. "You have not reported it. I have called New York twice on my way down."

"To have given out the news might have precipitated a catastrophe," said the secretary. "I am sure that Mr. Willoughby would—as I hope he yet will—approve. News of his disappearance will instantly create tremendous publicity. There will be a great depression on the market of all stocks connected with Willoughby interests. And, as you know, the market is in no condition these days for such startling news. There will be something of a panic. Many investors will lose a lot of money placed because of their confidence in Mr. Willoughby. Some of the mills may have to close down. I do not know all of Mr. Willoughby's affairs. No one did but himself. But I know enough to state that the situation is very serious."

Manning agreed silently. He could visualize headlines. TOOL TRUST TOPPLES AS WILLOUGHBY VAN-ISHES MYSTERIOUSLY. He could foresee the rush of newspapermen.

"You are sure he did not leave of his own accord?" he asked. The secretary shrugged his shoulders.

"His clothes are all here except the suit he wore yesterday, the same as he usually does at Fairtrees. A golfing suit of rough tweed, without a hat. I doubt if he had any money with him. There was a merger pending, important matters for which I had prepared papers, he was to go over last night, before tele-phoning to Detroit. Ever since he received the last threatening letters, the high voltage has been turned on the fence, night and day. He did not pass through any of the three gates. They are kept locked and all have gatekeepers. Extra keepers were brought here last week from the Minneapolis plant. There was no reason for his leaving."

"How do you manage to place the time so exactly?" asked Manning.

"Mr. Willoughby always strolled about the estate after lun-cheon when the weather was fine. He sometimes stayed late. I was not alarmed when he was late for dinner. At nine o'clock I was, and I started an investigation. I found that one man, a tree surgeon named Bailey, had seen and spoken with him close to three o'clock. The man placed the time by the shadow on a tree. He is an expert woodsman and the sun is his clock. He just happened to notice the shadow after Mr. Willoughby left him and walked down along the brook."

"Nobody else see him?"

"Not after he left the house. Bailey was working on a big swamp maple on the bank of Crystal Brook. It was a tree Mr. Willoughby had a strong sentiment for. He has told me how he used to climb into it when he was a poor boy and dream about the career he afterwards accomplished. He does not believe in tree surgery as a rule. A sick tree breeds and distributes decay. It is better felled. But he wanted to preserve this maple, so he sent for Bailey and was very pleased with his work. Bailey states that he had finished and that Mr. Willoughby congratulated him."

"Bailey still here?" asked Manning.

"Yes. He wanted to leave yesterday, before I questioned him. He asked for his check but it was not ready. I did not make the contract with him and I was not sure of the amount. Besides, Mr. Willoughby would have had to sign the check, and would also, I felt sure, want to see him before he left. There were no good train connections for him. So he is still here. By now he knows what has happened, of course. He has been living in the servants' bungalow."

"What else did you do?" Manning inquired.

"I organized a searching party. The estate is far from level in places, the woods are dense. A man might slip, might sprain or even break an ankle. There are over fifteen hundred acres in all. Crystal Brook is deep in places. Land might have caved in on the bank. We searched all night and kept it up until noon. Some men are still out. But we have found no trace of him, dead or alive."

"No signs of intruders?"

"None. They could not have got in, any more than Mr. Willoughby himself could have gone out, without being checked."

"Any trouble with employees?"

"None. Mr. Willoughby was stern, but he was just. There was no motive for anything of that sort."

"Any important legacies to employees?"

Mills drew himself up.

"I do not know the contents of Mr. Willoughby's will, if he has made one," he said stiffly. "You will have to consult his attorneys. It was not a matter he discussed with me."

"How about local hostilities, outside the estate?" probed Manning. He showed no sign of it, but he believed that Everest Mills was pretty certain how he stood in the disposition of Willoughby's post mortem affairs; that he had lied. The attorneys might refuse to consider mere disappearance as an ethical reason for a statement.

III

"WHEN MR. WILLOUGHBY bought up the various holdings in the village of Stone Bridge," Mills went on, "most of the owners were willing to sell, and he was liberal with them. The houses were demolished and the little farms and small acreages and plots merged in the present estate. The last man to come to any terms was a saddler named Friel. His place was mortgaged, and finally Mr. Willoughby bought the mortgage from the bank and foreclosed, but gave Friel a bonus. Friel was a surly, drinking type, and he made threats at the time because he was dispossessed.

"The people are scattered. Friel also left. There are rumors— there were rumors—that he has been seen lately in the neighborhood though I have not confirmed them. He was an illiterate man. I doubt if he would send typewritten letters. He would have acted, if he still felt a grudge. But he could not have got in."

"I'd like to see those letters presently," said Manning. "Meantime I'd like to see this Bailey."

Mills talked through a house phone. Then he got the threatening letters from a safe hidden by paneling. Manning glanced through them, returned them as the tree surgeon was shown in.

He was an elderly man with stooped shoulders and bowed legs, walking with a slight limp. He was clean shaven but his hair, almost entirely gray, was still plentiful and hung untrimmed to the collar of his coat of ill-fitting tweed. A man who did not care for appearances, evidently. An eccentric. He wore round, thick-lensed glasses and he kept his hands, which Manning noticed were none too clean, folded behind his back as he faced them. He had his dignity. He was not subservient. Diffident, rather than respectful. He had the air of a man who was self-sufficient, master of his trade, and he seemed annoyed by his detention.

Mills introduced Manning as investigating the disappearance.

"I've heard of ye," said Bailey drily, in a nasal twang. "You caught the Griffin. I'm fearful I can't help ye much. And I'd like to get away. I work by myself, mostly. I've other things waiting me. This was a special job. The bill can wait. And I don't like to get mixed up in things."

"Just a few questions," said Manning mildly.

Bailey answered readily enough, though it was clear he had distaste for the proceedings. Willoughby had met him three years before; Bailey had been working on a private estate in the Berkshires. He had talked with Bailey about the matter of native chestnuts becoming resistant to the blight, about pine rust and beetles. But he had said nothing of the old maple at the time. He had impressed Bailey with the idea that he was set against tree surgery. But evidently Bailey had impressed him with his craftsmanship, so that when the big maple showed signs of swift decay Willoughby had sent for him.

"The last I saw of him," Bailey ended, "was going down the brook, like he always did. I saw the shadow on a big dogwood, and though I didn't look at my watch I knew pretty close to the time. I just noted it incidental. Mr. Willoughby was a fine man. He liked trees and knew a lot about 'em. He ain't the kind things happen to. That's all I know. The job's finished, I'm all packed and I reckon there's nothing to detain me. As I said, the bill can wait, though I'm not a rich man. It ain't as if he'd been killed, and I doubt then if you'd have any right to hold me."

He exhibited doggedness and a little rancor towards the end

of the questioning. Manning gathered he had been persuaded to stay this long against his will. As Mills had said, it was hard for anyone to leave Fairtrees without authority.

Bailey seemed well within his rights. The house phone rang and Mills answered it, frowning as he listened. For a moment he covered the mouthpiece as he spoke to Manning.

"The news leaked, inevitably," he said. "The sheriff is here with Lieutenant Carey of the State Police. What shall I do?"

"You can't do anything but let them in," said Manning.

The thing had to happen and presently there would be a besieging mob of writers and cameramen. If they were kept outside they would fly over the place. There would be an army of curiosity mongers, professional and amateur. He was none too pleased that the search had taken place before he got there. It was natural enough, but the odds were that all clews were long ago destroyed. And there must be clews. Willoughby was not taken out by secret plane; not if there was a merger forward. He would not have left in such clothes. He had hardly been abducted, for Manning figured it would be hard for even an autogyro to take off from the wooded estate, even if it had achieved landing. And escaped observation.

THE SHERIFF was, palpably, more politician than criminal investigator. He looked always to see which way the cat would jump. Willoughby, to him, was his supreme patron.

Lieutenant Carey was different. Manning heartily approved of him. Carey gave him a salute when Mills disclosed his identity.

"Glad to work under you, Major Manning," said Carey, while the sheriff looked askance, like an old dog fox. Carey knew that, during his search for the Griffin, Manning had been given a special commission by the governor that had probably not been revoked, since Manning was again in the field.

"I'm observing privately, on a request by Mr. Willoughby himself," said Manning. "I'm not interfering with local rights."

The sheriff grunted, eying Bailey.

"I suppose your nephew told you, sheriff," said Mills. "If he did he loses his job."

"Never mind how I learned about it," retorted the sheriff. "You should have reported it yourself. I understand this here freeman knows something about it." He jerked his head at Bailey, who blinked back through his heavy lenses. "I called in the State Police because I ain't got no efficient force to handle a case like this. There'll be hundreds camping round here, inside here, like enough, inside twenty-four hours. Mr. Willoughby was a big man. This case'll kick up a rumpus. I'm holding this Bailey, to begin with. He's a material witness. Yes, sir. I'm taking him to the county seat and holding him."

"You can't hold me," Bailey protested. "There has been no crime committed."

"That's as how it turns out," the sheriff replied. "It ain't no ordinary affair. Millions in it. I've got the authority. Judge Smalley'll back it. He was a close friend of Willoughby. So was the County District Attorney. If Willoughby ain't dead, where is he? Dead, or kidnaped. He ain't the sort to drop out of sight. And here's the last one to see him alive. I'm holding him, first and last, unless he puts up bail and that'll be plenty, if I know the Court."

"I've got no funds for bail," said Bailey, glowering and angry. "I'm a poor man. I'm supporting five people. You can't hold me. I'll get out on a writ of habeas corpus as soon as I get in touch with an attorney."

"Try it," snapped the sheriff.

Manning said nothing. He knew how county politics and court procedures worked. His sympathy was with the tree surgeon and he did not think the latter would have much trouble in getting away after a little.

"We'll examine everyone on the place," the sheriff went on. "And me and the lieutenant, and Mr. Manning, if he wants to," he added grudgingly, "I'll search the whole place. I ain't going to have it said there was a leaf or a stone left unturned."

His anxiety to protect his own position was almost pitiful. It was clear that he believed that if the mystery was unsolved he would be held responsible for it when it came to reëlection—or if Willoughby reappeared and thought he had been derelict—though, on the other hand, Willoughby might deem him too officious, Manning reflected.

"We'll have the house servants in here first, if you please, Mr. Mills," said the sheriff with growing importance. "Check 'em all over as to their occupation and whereabouts yesterday afternoon. Take the outside men later. I suppose you can testify to where you were, Mr. Mills," he went on with a chuckle that was not entirely convincing. The man would have arrested his own father if he thought it politic, Manning believed.

"There's no evidence of foul play, so far," the sheriff went on. "But that don't...."

A knock on the door checked him and he stared at the entrance. Mills called out, "Come in."

The sudden knock had struck them all as intensely dramatic, almost as prophetic, Manning thought, as the knocking on the gate in Macbeth. They were startled, and not calmed when a houseman ushered in a keeper whose coat sleeves were soaked below the elbows, the cuffs, and his hands, that carried something wrapped in a blue bird's-eye bandanna handkerchief, were smeared with green weeds. Water dripped a little from the object he held so carefully.

His face was twitching a little with excitement. It was a dramatic incident, an entrance that seemed timed with almost the precision of a play.

"What is it, Curtis?" asked Mills.

The man looked at the sheriff, at the uniformed lieutenant, at Gordon Manning and then his glance rested on Bailey and stayed there.

"You can tell *me*," the sheriff broke in.

So far, like Manning, the lieutenant had not interfered. He was a well balanced officer, controlled of judgment and action.

"I was looking down along the brook," said the newcomer, "along where they say Mr. Willoughby was going time he was last seen. I went clear down to where it runs under the fence. There's a grating there, a sort of grid that fits the bed of the stream. Ain't room for even a mink to get under it, I reckon. Fence crosses on top of it. It's all choked with weeds, leaves and rubbish, but I saw something there that looked different.

"I was chancy about getting it out, account the grating was charged like the fence. But I fished it out with a stick I cut to a forked end—and here it is."

I V

"IT" WAS a tool with a crescent blade thickest in the center, that was twin-edged, inset in a brass socket at the head of a thick wooden handle. The edges had evidently been frequently ground, and they were sharp as razor blades. The amount of steel had plainly so balanced the flotation power of the handle as to act as a keel, insufficient to sink it, sufficient to carry it along the surface of the brook without being totally submerged until it brought up at the grid and was found by the keeper. A sort of knife that was a lethal weapon, that could inflict a frightful, fatal wound at one stroke.

Its owner, forgetting to take into account the many honings that had reduced the weight of the blade with its size, might have tossed it into a deep pool in the brook, believing it would sink, or he might have flung it away in the swift revulsion of a murderer.

They examined it as the keeper exhibited it. Manning picked it up carefully by the tip of the steel blade, which was broken. It looked like a recent fracture. He could see no sign of bloodstains, no evidence of finger-prints; but the immersion in swift water for hours, the chafing against the slime and rubbish of the grid might destroy those. Manning said so. Bailey looked at it stolidly. Mills was greatly disturbed. The sheriff was triumphant.

"I suppose you'll say this ain't one of your tools for scraping rotten wood or cutting it out," he gloated. "Well, we'll hold you now. You might as well confess, Bailey. That knife'll put you in the chair, anyway."

"It looks a bit serious," Carey suggested to Manning as the sheriff brought out a pair of handcuffs, intent upon making an arrest.

"There's no body, as yet," said Manning. "That might be a skiver, a knife leather workers use for thinning, or skiving, leather. The sort of knife a tree surgeon might use, but so also might a saddler, for instance. I've heard of a man named Friel who was once a saddler here and held a grudge against Willoughby. There are rumors he was round here lately. I can see no motive for Bailey's supposed crime. And, as I said, the corpus delicti is the vital factor."

"You don't think the tree man did it, then?"

"I'm hardly down to the reasoning point," Manning told him. "But I don't believe Bailey killed Willoughby. I'm not at all sure Willoughby is dead."

Bailey was talking now, aroused.

"That's not my tool," he said. "I'll come with you and I don't need handcuffs. It will be wiser for you not to put them on. I wouldn't get out on bond now if I could. I'll go to prison until you have to release me, and then, by God, I'll sue the county and the estate for false imprisonment. I'll make you pay for this, all of ye."

Mills tried to quiet him.

"I don't think you're guilty," said the secretary. "I think Sheriff Horton is being hasty."

The sheriff merely grinned. Bailey waved his arms wildly.

"You say that so I'll not sue the estate," he cried. "But I will. This is an outrage."

"You'll come with me," said the sheriff. "Lieutenant, I'll leave further examination to you and Mr. Manning. If you find anything important you can let me know."

"If we run across anything more important than Horton we'll have a worthwhile find," said Carey, under his breath. "I hope you're right, sheriff," he said aloud.

"I know doggone well I am," replied the other triumphantly. "Come on, Bailey. I'll leave the cuffs off, seeing you're so willing. Will you phone the gate to let us out, Mr. Mills?"

THE EXAMINATION of employees and the search of the grounds produced little of importance, but Manning was not satisfied. The ground all about the swamp maple, especially, was trodden down. It was plainly high time the maple was treated to preserve it. Even now it did not look over sturdy to Manning. Its trunk must have been more or less a shell before the expert doctored it, and parts of its roots protruded through the bank of the brook beside which it stood. Looking for prints, marks of a struggle, proved fruitless. They raked up the ground to find the broken tip of the knife, or tool, without success, and though Manning submitted the soil for analysis he had faint hope of finding blood traces that would prove anything.

One thing he did observe, that it might be possible for a passage to be made *above* the charged wire at certain places where heavy tree limbs stretched almost horizontally and sometimes overlapped. But he could not see a man like Willoughby, warned, taking precautions, being ambushed, snatched away in such fashion.

The army of newsmen and the morbid arrived and were kept outside the estate, much to their indignation. They assailed everyone who emerged or entered. Mills' prophecy of dire depression in certain stocks was justified.

All Willoughby holdings made a new low and still descended, together with the holdings of all companies and organizations in any way affiliated with him, or suspected to be. It was a three-days wonder that lasted for another three on the front pages. The police worked hard on the case.

Bailey remained in the county jail. He was fed from outside by funds provided by Mills, who seemed concerned for his comfort. He was permitted to shave, to exercise frequently, to have the usual privileges of a material witness, since they could not prove him more in fact. To the sheriff he was the prime suspect.

Manning visited him from time to time and did not change his opinion. This man had not killed Willoughby. Manning secured, partly from Mills and partly from the County Surveyor, maps and descriptions from which he reconstructed the village as it was before Willoughby absorbed it.

The State Police ran down Friel. He admitted he had been in the neighborhood, fishing, taking delight in getting trout, with which Willoughby had stocked Crystal Brook. But he had a perfect alibi for two days ahead of and after Willoughby's disappearance. He would have poached, he said, but he had learned the fence was charged.

Manning still studied the grounds and made a few excursions of his own, tracing the old inhabitants. The furore about the mystery died down gradually. Congress was in the throes of balancing the budget, presidential candidates were flinging their hats in the ring.

Bailey, in jail and morose, began to clamor for release. He had been there three weeks and had lost weight and money, he alleged, still set to sue for damages, surly even to Mills.

The affected shares reached their final bottom, stemmed at last by bulls who bucked the short market in the conviction that the price was absurdly low, and, slowly, Willoughby holdings and their affiliations began to rise.

V

IT WAS the twenty-second day after the disappearance, with Manning in the library, going over some notes; when Mills came in excitedly. His calm demeanor was fled, his slick hair was rumpled.

"I've heard from Mr. Willoughby," he cried. "He spoke to me over the telephone. Long-distance. Completely identified himself, and his voice is unmistakable. He has been held, presumably by racketeers who worked for a syndicate that wanted to depreciate Willoughby stocks and then buy in to obtain control and make enormous profits. A shrewd scheme. They dropped on him from the trees, he told me, drugged him, carried him off. He'll be released in a few days. I am giving out statements to the papers."

"How about one to the sheriff?" asked Manning drily. "This lets Bailey out."

"Of course. But I'll attend to the press first. After I've called Mr. Willoughby's attorneys. An hour or so more won't affect Bailey. We'll make it up to him."

"It seems a shame to hold him any longer than necessary," said Manning. "Suppose I drive in with the news? The sheriff can call you, just to check up."

"That's good of you," said Mills. "I'll appreciate that."

There were some scattering, sanguine news-gatherers still about, most of them free lancers. To them Manning gave the news as he drove through the gate, and left them jubilant, with the scoop, racing to query editors how much they might send.

Manning stopped at a filling station and phoned to Lieutenant Carey.

"Thought you'd like to be in at the death," he said. "Meet me at the county jail."

"A death but no funeral?" Carey commented. "You were right about Bailey after all. He didn't kill Willoughby."

"No. He had no motive. Like to meet you, just the same, Carey."

"I'll be there, Major."

Manning liked the lieutenant, and Carey admired Manning. He felt there was some reason for Manning asking him to be present, perhaps to share in the downfall of the cocksure sheriff.

Willoughby's attorneys had been more revealing than Manning had expected. Aside from certain not too liberal bequests, the Tool King had left his estate to found an institution of Arboriculture and Forestry that would supplement the work of the Federal Service, conduct experimental plantations for the introduction of new trees, and support a laboratory for the investigation of tree diseases. Mills had been left ten thousand dollars. Other employees in lessening sums. The trees had the best of it. It was a curious fad, but a useful one.

The weather changed as Manning drove to the county seat. The blue sky clouded and a strong wind rose in the north and east. It was sturdy enough to buck his car on certain roads. When he reached the jail, to find Carey waiting there, the heavens were black and thunderous and it was blowing a steady gale.

"Looks like the Day of Judgment," Carey observed with a laugh.

"Quite the correct setting," said Manning. "Let's see the sheriff."

That somewhat disgruntled officer was stubborn. He telephoned Mills, two judges, and the County Prosecutor's office, with cross-checkings, before he was convinced he could no longer hold his prisoner. A writ of release was issued and on the way. Manning sat with Carey in the sheriff's office while he fussed. They had not yet seen Bailey. At last the order came and the sheriff summoned them.

"I'll turn him over to you," he said, "since you seem so all-fired interested in him. I'll have my deputy get his things."

Bailey seemed incredulous. He came out almost unwillingly.

"I ain't through with this," he said. "You can't hoodwink me with last minute kindness."

"We're not trying to," said Manning. "But we'll take you in my car, if you want to come."

"I want to go to the depot," said Bailey. "I'm going back to Massachusetts. Mills gave me my money and I'll pay my way. But I'm not through."

There was thunder muttering now in earnest. It was mid-afternoon, but it was almost as dark as night. Lightning stabbed swollen masses of vapor, or edged them luridly. As yet there was no rain. And the wind was almost a hurricane for such northern latitudes.

"This will test some of your best jobs, Bailey," said Manning.

"What do you mean?" asked Bailey. "Is this the road to the depot?"

"I mean you're not through yet, Bailey," answered Manning. "And this is the road to Fairtrees. We're going back to see Mills, and take a look at that maple."

The tree man scowled at him. He sat beside Manning in the latter's car. Lieutenant Carey sat behind, vigilant.

"You see," Manning went on, "there are some things about this case that got overlooked. In the first place, Mr. Willoughby never played in that swamp maple. He never had a chance. It grew in the grounds of Simon Marsh, who had no use for small boys or any trespassers. He swears that Willoughby was never on his premises before he bought them. Then it seemed curious that Mr. Willoughby should choose a tree surgeon from Massachusetts when his own State is full of them. No doubt he had a reason for it. And I think I've found it."

THE WIND fairly rocked them as they came to an exposed place.

Javelins of forked lightning changed the blackness to a vivid glare of lavender. Bailey shifted in his seat.

"Sit still," said Carey from the back seat, and set a gun between Bailey's shoulder blades. "You might not get killed if you jumped, but you'd sure be crippled. We want you sound."

"That wasn't a skiver's tool," Manning went on. "It was unlucky for you it didn't sink."

The man beside him stared at him through the thick lenses, uttered something guttural and inarticulate, and subsided.

At the gate of Fairtrees they were challenged. Carey, in uniform, jumped from the car, his gun covering the gatekeeper.

"You'll open up, in the name of the law," he said, "or you'll never turn another key. Never mind the telephone."

Manning shoved his own gun into the ribs of the man beside him, who tried to leap from the car.

They drove through the gates and on towards the house, after Manning had dismantled the telephone.

"You'll stay out of this," he said to the gatekeeper and another man who appeared; "if you want to stay out of jail. You get Mills, Carey, and bring him along to the tree. I'll drive as close to it as I can."

Bedlam broke loose in the woods as Manning drove one-handed, his gun still in Bailey's ribs. Then they got out and plodded through rain and wind along the brook. Broken twigs and boughs strewed their way. Here and there a tree was up-rooted. The brook was high. Rain had fallen in the hills already.

"This may save some ax work," said Manning grimly. "Don't try to bolt. Carey said this looked like the Day of Judgment. He was right. *I thought so!*"

They had come in sight of the swamp maple. It was down. The current had washed out more roots. The gale had clutched its crown and torn up the hollow bole.

It lay on its side. The iron bands bolted about it still held, but the cement that filled its hollow, Bailey's handiwork, had cracked. The rotten shell of the trunk had split, revealing a gruesome sight.

The body of a man, in golf clothes, stuffed into the hollow, partly decomposed but recognizable.

A bolt of lightning made everything livid. Manning, alert, swung his gun to club the man, who suddenly grappled with him, desperate with maniacal strength, kicking, biting. The muzzle sight of the gun slashed his scalp, half stunned him, but he fought on, clutching for Manning's throat.

Carey came charging through the woods. He stared at the fallen, twitching body.

"A wig!" he said. "And the other's Bailey?"

"Willoughby was hard-pressed," said Manning, "short of cash to swing his deals and keep things running. He might have had this in mind for a long time, seeing how things went. He chose Bailey, because they were about the same size. He waited until the last minute and killed him, changed clothes, shaved himself, put on the wig, stuffed Bailey in the trunk and cemented him up. He knew how to do it. He was actor enough to play the part of Bailey, who kept to himself. He figured to disappear, as Bailey, and then presently to come back as Willoughby with his cock-and-bull story of abduction. His idea was to run those shares down to the limit, then buy in, get control of the industry, gain ready money as well. Mills was in with him. Mills is clever, but he wrote those notes on his own typewriter. Mills professed sympathy for Bailey in jail, saw he was as comfortable as possible, saw that he kept clean shaven. But he forgot about his wig. A wig doesn't grow. Willoughby, as Bailey, was three weeks in jail and his hair didn't grow. What did you do with Mills, Carey?"

"I arrested him, as you said. I locked him up, handcuffed, in the cellar. I've got the keys. He's safe. He crumpled. My men are there by now. You're a marvel, Manning. I don't see—"

"It looked phoney," said Manning. "I never liked Willoughby. Nor Mills, when I met him. The depression makes men desperate. Willoughby might have gone in for trees, but that yarn about his sentimental affection for one because he'd dreamed in it seemed fishy. It turned out to be. His New England accent as Bailey wasn't too good. There was no evidence he was dead or even kidnaped. The evidence the other way was too strong. Bailey's record was excellent. A man who doctors trees doesn't go around killing the one who gives him a job. Mills worked the market. Got instructions when he visited the jail. But they both overlooked the fact that *wigs don't grow*. He's coming round. Needs a few stitches. It's your arrest, Carey. You handle the case. I want to get away on a vacation."

Gordon Manning, Conqueror of The
Griffin, Probes the Mystery of the Man
Killed by a "Bolt from the Blue"

I T   W A S   one of the narrower, one-way streets in Greenwich Village, about as wide as the colloquial "biscuit toss." Many of its ancient houses had been converted into studio apartments with patio gardens; nearly all the remainder harbored at least as many families as there were floors. One exception was the residence of Morton Hyde, well known amateur physicist and delver into the laws of gravitation and electrodynamics and magnetism. One of the few men recognized by Einstein as capable of sympathy and comprehension of the latter's theories.

Morton Hyde, once a wide traveler and explorer, was still hale and hearty, but he had grown stout in the years beyond sixty, and his life was largely sedentary. The house had come to him several years ago in an inheritance. He had remodeled its interior and changed its roof.

The ground floor had been made into one large apartment, the rear of which took up the full height of the original building and was roofed by a skylight, used as library and museum, filled with the gatherings of Hyde's travels. It had a large open fireplace and was comfortably furnished. The front half of the same floor was both dining and living room, its height unraised. Above it were the bedrooms and bathrooms.

There was a perfectly equipped kitchen in the basement where Hyde often performed culinary miracles for his chosen guests, or was served by his one factotum, Bino, a Filipino of uncertain age but certain fealty and service. A dumb-waiter connected kitchen and dining room. Bino slept in the rear of the basement with his own lavatory arrangements.

The small garden space was enclosed in glass. By an ingenious arrangement of heating pipes Hyde had turned it into a place where strange and spiny growths flourished, brought from deserts on four continents; while rare and curious tropical fishes found themselves quite at home in a great octagonal tank, set amid bristling aloes and agaves. The glass was unbreakable and had been treated with acid to destroy transparency.

On the roof Hyde had made a terrace, its floor of Moorish tiles, awninged with striped canvas beneath painted metal, to protect from the fire of casual cigarettes, cigar ends and smouldering matches sometimes tossed carelessly from the apartment buildings. There were grass mattings for rugs, bamboo lounging furniture, cushions, a low parapet in front.

Hyde did not entertain very frequently. Whenever the capricious New York climate permitted, he spent hours on his terrace in a deep Badak chair with a high back, lounging in meditation, watching the sky in a mood absorbed by his theories; sometimes reading, sometimes smoking a Turkish hookah.

A self-contained man with a brilliant mind, somewhat of a recluse.

His awnings gave him seclusion. The house directly opposite had been unoccupied for two years. Its windows were without blinds or curtains, grimed with the dust of a dozen seasons. Its ownership was tied up in involved litigation. Hyde had tried to buy it so that there would be no observers of his sessions or siestas, but he could not, though he had obtained an option for a first bid from the lawyers of the controversial heirs.

Hyde had been honored by scientific societies throughout the world. He still contributed papers and pamphlets that were invariably received with great respect by the learned bodies.

ONE LATE afternoon, August, the eighteenth, he lounged in his Badak chair with considerable satisfaction. He had read once, and meant to read again, the announcement that amount-

Manning ran his car close to the wall,
using it as an aid to reach the top.

ed to an acknowledgment of the correctness of his belief that space was infinite and actually increasing; the subject of his only controversy with the great German-Swiss scientist.

Occasionally, as reflected, he glanced at certain paragraphs through his thick-lensed glasses. His sight was beginning to fail him, with his hearing; the results of severe malarial fevers contracted on his travels. Otherwise he was in full possession of his faculties, his mind was still brilliant.

It was growing dusk and he was thinking of going in. He straightened a little, preparing to close the bulletin of the Astronomical Society, which had contained the satisfying news.

His action ended abruptly, his head jerked suddenly. A dark spot appeared in the center of his forehead, exactly above the bow of his spectacles, the base of his nose.

A crimson bubble rose there, broke, and scarlet rain dripped down upon the printed page, that rustled for a moment in his quivering hands and then slid to the floor. The body of the scientist relaxed utterly. He lay still in the Badak chair, staring upwards at the sky.

There had been no sound to disturb the street. A slight thud as the missile bored into his skull, a low twang. That was all.

He had been dead for half an hour when Bino came to remind him he had guests for dinner.

The Medical Examiner, on his arrival, set the time at approximately two hours before, which coincided with Bino's statement. The detectives proclaimed it murder and commenced their fruitless search for clews, taking Bino away to be held as material witness, unable to secure bail, under suspicion of the crime, when it was found that he was beneficiary under Hyde's will for five thousand dollars. There were a few other personal bequests, none of them large. The residue, and bulk, of the estate, was left to the Society for Cosmic Research.

The autopsy disclosed that the missile was a curious pellet about the size of a shrapnel bullet, or a marble. It was even suggested that it was a marble, though not of a sort known to any of the dealers in those playthings. The papers made the most of it, especially the tabloids.

It was heavy and of a streaky green. Too heavy for glass, though it resembled it. It was not exactly spherical. Part of it was covered with a thin film of fused crust. In analysis it proved crystalline; it reacted to tests of metallic iron, and of nickel. It baffled the experts of the Crime Scientific Investigation Bureau. It was something new in the annals of crime and it seemed untraceable.

The house across the street was searched. The detectives found everywhere a coating of soft dust on the floors, the stairs, the stair rails; dust, undisturbed, from cellar to garret. Empty, silent as the grave, with not even the track of mouse or rat to disturb the dust in that inhospitable mansion. Cobwebs and dust and silence.

Such a missile, it was pointed out, must have been discharged from a smoothbore, hand-loaded. It had not formed part of a cartridge. It was too large for the bore of the old type Kentucky or pea rifle, but there were guns made for trade with natives that might fill the bill. Weapons like these were used sometimes for ornament, they could be bought at a Broadway store. It might have been an ancient pistol. But there had been no report heard. It was a quiet street but there had been passers-by at that hour. Of course a muffler blow-out might have covered it, but as Hyde sat in his chair (as the probe of the wound showed) that shot must have come from across the street if it had not been fired at close quarters, on the terrace.

The bullet, if it might be truly styled a bullet, had not penetrated the back of the cranium. There were no powder marks.

Bino swore no one had been in the house but himself. The guests, both well known scientists, had arrived later, to be shocked by the news. It could not have been an air rifle, the commissioner pointed out. The diameter and the weight of the missile precluded the use of such mechanism.

And there was no weapon, no lightest imprint in the house across the street.

The press called it *The Marble Mystery*, and rode the police.

11

THE POLICE COMMISSIONER held appointment in his private office with Gordon Manning, specialist in crime, late Investigation Officer in the A.E.F., renowned traveler and explorer; the man called in to run down the madman known as the Griffin, who selected prominent people for horrible deaths and dared to announce the date of his crime. His special commission, signed both by the commissioner and governor, was still in effect.

The commissioner showed the lean, tanned specialist a

moulage cast of the missile, colored in facsimile, together with what the analysts had left of the original after their pestles and acids had failed of a solution.

Manning examined the cast, touched a portion of the pellet to his tongue, and produced a pocket magnascope through which he inspected it closely for a few minutes.

"It is, it was, a meteorite," he said. "What is known as a chondrule. A cosmic granule with traces of nickel but consisting in the main of chrysolite, which is magnesium iron silicate, found in certain igneous and metamorphic rocks, in masses or grains. When it occurs in transparent crystals it is called olivine, or peridot, a semiprecious stone of a yellowish emerald color much used by jewelers for inexpensive ornaments. I've picked up olivines by the quart on volcanic slopes in the South Seas."

"Good God!" cried the commissioner. "You mean to say Hyde was killed by a gem?"

"Without question, but this one came from space. No doubt of that, that fused film-crust proves it. They are common enough. The Moros call them sky-stones. They are carried as amulets. I've known Arabs to use them as bullets to kill enemies supposed to be protected by magic. There are plenty of them in the museums, in private collections, or sold for charms and cure-alls. Almost every desert prospector has one for a mascot. I shouldn't be in the least surprised if Hyde himself had several in that museum room of his. He was interested in anything connected with space that might tend to prove or disprove cosmic theory. He wouldn't value them, probably forgot he had them."

"Wait a minute," said the commissioner. "I'm sending Hogan down there now. Bino cleaned the place."

"As I remember it from the time I once dined there," said Manning, "the top shelves were pretty dusty. Hyde said so himself and apologized for not getting down some Indian drums. You haven't got anything out of Bino, Commissioner?"

"Nothing. He pretends we've scared his knowledge of English

out of him. He's stubborn as a mule. Just the same, there was five thousand dollars coming to him on Hyde's death. That's a lot of money for a Filipino. He might have got tired waiting for it. But there isn't a thing to pin on him except motive. He called the police and he didn't leave the house. We'll hold him until he comes through."

"I'll have a talk with him," said Manning. "I can talk his lingo well enough. I know the five main dialects. The language is based on Malay. I'll drop down to the house myself—to both the houses. Hyde's and the one across the street."

"If you find anything but dust in the latter I'll eat it. The dust."

Manning grinned.

"I don't want to make you eat dirt, Commissioner," he said as he filled his pipe. "By the way, have you called up Dannemora lately?"

The commissioner flushed slightly.

"I did," he answered. "And the Griffin is still getting hospital treatment in the insane ward. Why?"

"This case has some of the earmarks of the Griffin's modus operandi. Bizarre and ingenious…. Though The Griffin was sporting enough to announce the date of his crimes. I trust he never makes a break from Dannemora, for all our sakes. By the way, it would be wisest, I think, not to give out anything about meteorites, either in connection with my statement or anything Hogan may find."

"It'll be hard to keep it from the news sharks," growled the commissioner. "They smell out such things. And we've got between three and four hundred police at headquarters who are clerks and operators. The place leaks like a sieve. I'll do my piece. You've got a good reason for it."

Manning nodded as he stood up to leave.

"Quite a good reason. I don't want the chap warned that we have any kind of a clew at all. If you don't mind taking another suggestion, don't bully Bino too much. He might go *juramentado*."

"Whatever that is." It was clear that the commissioner believed the Filipino guilty.

"Mata glap, they call it in Java," Manning said. "It is a curious state of the Malayan mind when they think they are being accused unjustly, or insulted. They run amok, or amuck, as some call it."

"He'll not run amuck where we've got him."

"He may have the brainstorm, just the same. I'd like to see him first."

IT LEAKED, as Manning knew it would, as important news leaks from headquarters on all occasions, despite discipline and the fine morale of the majority of the force.

An exultant press and avid public got vicarious thrills out of the theories and suggestions put forward by the ingenious writers.

Gordon Manning, the capturer of the Griffin, had been called in. And reporters made trips to Dannemora to make certain that maniac was still behind bars. The star men put out their best efforts. The worst one was a suggestion that the shot might have been fired from a passing airplane. It took the over-credulous to support the idea.

But—the body had been found gazing into the firmament.

He was a delver into the laws of the infinite.

The missile came from space. Manning's statement was confirmed by experts on meteorology. It was a bolt of Jove sped with terrible accuracy that had sped the cosmic projectile to still the brain of the man who had presumed to probe the secrets of the universe.

It was as if indignant gods had rebuked him, destroyed this too daring mortal.

Meteorites, it was pointed out, could fall by day and might

well travel unnoticed, not flaming spheroids that showed plainly after dark.

Such things were eerie, gripping the imagination of both the superstitious and the stolid.

A famous meteorologist pointed out that these chondrules did not fall singly. That they were sprayed from the exploding mass like shrapnel bullets. No more had been found in the neighborhood. Twenty years before fourteen thousand had fallen at Holbrook, Arizona. He cited other instances. Reports and opinions came from England, from Germany, France, Holland and Japan. But they were not played up.

The theory of the avenging *"Bullet from the Blue"* was much too fascinating.

One thing did not break. Hogan kept his mouth shut. Manning got to the house before the find was made. A dozen similar pellets with other odds and ends of celestial origin. They were on a high shelf in a carved ceremonial bowl from African Congo, which was split with age, stained black by sacrificial blood. But the contents lay under dust and under spider webs closely woven, which themselves were filmed.

"Just like the house opposite," said Hogan. "I was over there. If there was any one there, the dust gives him a perfect alibi. He must have floated."

"There's no such thing as a perfect alibi," said Manning. "Or a perfect crime, though I wouldn't wonder if the chap back of this imagines it one."

" 'Tis beyond me," said Hogan. "Will I go on looking?"

"Carry on," said Manning, "though I'm afraid you won't find anything." Nor did he.

Nor did Manning find anything in the house across the way—but dust.

It had been trodden in by the sturdy feet of exploring detectives, but even they had early seen the folly of trampling all over a house that eminently proclaimed its long desertion. Manning saw their blurred footprints on the stairs and the planking of the rooms. He confined his own search largely to the floor that was on the level with the terrace, and to the stairways, aside from a trip to the basement.

The fine dust made him sneeze, as it must have the police. They had gone to the windows, by their tracks, and looked out through the dirty panes to where the murdered man had sat. Manning was willing enough to take the commissioner's word, backed by that of the sharp observer, Hogan, that there had been only the filmed floors when they searched; that the tracks now there were of the police.

Manning tried the front windows. Both were locked and the catches were gray with the silt of old houses, the silt of the street, that had sifted in. The right-hand window slid up easily and he looked across the narrow way, trying to reëstablish what might have happened. It was uncanny. One writer had brought in a harrowing touch, in his search for something different; and suggested a spook, that used a phantom weapon and a bullet from another world.

Did a ghost kill Morton Hyde? had been the heading to his contribution.

Manning had seen many strange things in the far places, things that seemed to insist upon a supernatural origin. He believed in psychic affairs but, when it came to criminal investigation, he insisted upon physical foundations.

If the meteorite had been discharged from this house, as seemed certain, the killer *must* have left traces, though they might be as impalpable as the dust that rose about Manning as he left the place.

There was still Bino. Lately, there had been several killings by Oriental servants of their white employers. There was a prejudice against them that boded Bino little good. The average jury would believe that he would murder for far less than the sum he would inherit. The evidence might not send him to the chair, but the motive would go far in the hands of a clever prosecutor. It would mean penal servitude. And an out for the police.

III

H E F O U N D the Filipino despondent in his cell, broken
down, miserable, and weak. He had no visible marks
upon him, but Manning imagined that he might have been
introduced to the "goldfish"; made to sit under a terrific light,
thirsty and sleepless, while dicks questioned him. That sort of
thing might go for a Manhattan gangster. It would not answer
with Bino.

Manning spoke to him first in Tagalog and got only a wild
stare. Then in Bisayan, and Bino, haggard and glaring, gave a
hectic greeting. Manning had him out of his cell, gave him
cigarettes and told him he was his friend, showed him he knew
his country, his own district; spoke of men Bino knew and
respected.

"Why do they keep me here?" he demanded. "I have done
no wrong. I would have given my life for the *tuan*. Once he
saved mine. I am a son of Islam, I am not a lying dog. I have
made the trip to Mecca, I am hajj'. I have kissed the Black Stone
and I have seven times circled the Kaabah. *Tuan*, I swear to
you, by the beard of the Prophet, by my hope of Paradise, that
I have done nothing but my duty. Bring me a copy of the Koran
and I will swear upon it. But these infidels think that a follower of Muhammad is an outcast. They laugh at me when I
perform my devotions. They offer me beans, with *pork*. To *me*,
who may wear the green turban."

Manning soothed him as best he could. He promised him
that he should be placed where he would not be ridiculed, where,
when he praised Allah four times a day, he should be given a
chance to observe his rites. Also he said he would arrange that
suitable food should be brought in. He had the authority and
they were willing enough in the Tombs to cater to the conqueror of the Griffin.

Bino had been kept without news. He could read a little
English, but he had not been given the papers. He had been
urged to confess that, in some way, he had fired a stone into his

tuan's brain, and he was bewildered. Manning's visit saved his
sanity and aroused his gratitude. He remembered Manning as
having once been a guest of Hyde's and did not connect him
with the police, but accepted him as a protector.

"How well do you remember the men who came to your
tuan's house?" asked Manning.

"I should know them all," said Bino. There might be a means
here, Manning thought. A long way round, unless some short-
cut showed. He did not press the matter. He explained to Bino
about the stone that had killed Hyde and saw the Filipino's
face go suddenly blank, his dark eyes lose their luster. The commissioner had sworn that Bino was holding out information.
It looked like it.

"There were more of these sky-stones in the carved bowl on
the top shelf, Bino," said Manning. "But the bowl has not been
touched for a long, long time. Many people think those stones
are magic. Did the *tuan* ever give you one?"

Minutes passed and Bino stayed remote. Manning knew he
could not be forced. At last the Filipino spoke.

"There were three prophets to whom God revealed himself,"
he said. "To Moses he gave the Taurat, which is the Law. To
Jesus the Injil, which is the Gospel. To Muhammad the Qu'ran
(Koran). Muhammad is the seal, and the Last of the Prophets.
There is no God but God, and He is Allah, the Just and Merciful! I speak under the Seal of Muhammad. What I speak is
truth, but, unless you swear to me, by Taurat, by Injil and the
Qu'ran, that you will keep it secret, I shall be dumb, as if they
tore out my tongue."

He meant it. He had made the hajj', the pilgrimage to Mecca.
He was assured of Paradise if he did not forswear sacred vows.
It was not a matter to be explained or considered in an American courtroom, any more than the admission of medical science
as opposed to common law.

But Manning had a free hand. He felt that here was a vital
clew. He took the triple oath.

"I had one of the sky-stones," said Bino. "The *tuan* gave it to me long ago as a luck charm. They are star-dust. Aguinaldo had one, or he would not now be alive. And I lost it. There is an Arab in this city who is a cunning workman in gold and silver, and he made me an open cage of silver for it, so it would hang from my watch chain, as an amulet. But I lost it and, with the loss, came ill fortune to me—worse to my *tuan*."

"Know when you lost it?" asked Manning.

"It was at a dinner that the *tuan* gave. There were five there, three women and two men, beside the *tuan*. That night he made a salmi...."

"Go on," said Manning. The more details Bino remembered, the better. It looked like a definite clew. It might not go far but it would serve, it might be a bit of a jigsaw puzzle that he could solve, putting it together and suddenly sensing the whole in a flash of inspiration, as he had suddenly lit upon the solution to wartime secret ciphers, after weeks of patient work. "Did you show anyone the sky-stone that night?"

"My *tuan* noticed it. It was the first time I had worn it. They all looked at it and I told them about Aguinaldo. They smiled. I did not miss it until I went to bed. It had been wrenched loose. It might have caught in a chair. I searched everywhere, but I could not find it. I feared it had fallen while I was cleaning up, fallen into the rubbish and gone into the incinerator. The *tuan* wished to give me another, but I explained that one may not bring back luck that way. I did not suspect any of the honorable guests of finding it, and keeping it."

"Can you remember those guests ?"

"By sight, yes. By name, no. Perhaps one or two. One was bald, I think, but I am not sure. *Tuan,* I have not eaten, I have not slept. It is hard to think."

"You try, Bino. Sleep first. Eat, perform your devotions. Rest. Remember I am your friend. *Salaam aleikum!*"

HE LEFT the Tombs tingling inwardly. If Bino could remember.... A long, long way from proof, from conviction. But, like a hunting dog, Manning faintly winded the early scent. He was a thoroughbred; he would not turn aside for lesser game. If only the scent lasted!

Meantime, he borrowed the use of the Department's fluoroscope and made an interesting discovery that set his eyes glowing with an inner fire. The quarry was not yet in sight, but he knew he had picked up the trail.

He drove home in his powerful roadster to his own house at Pelham Manor, and was greeted by his Japanese servants.

There was mail awaiting him. He reserved one envelope, addressed in unfamiliar writing, to the last. Ito, his butler, had brought him a highball, he was slippered, his pipe drew well and his dog was at his feet. Manning chuckled as he read. It was like old times—with the Griffin. He had told himself he needed a long vacation from the wear of that affair, but now the zest of the chase rose within him.

The epistle was written on a sheet of thick paper of the type known as vellum finish, without a watermark, easy to procure at any drugstore. The envelope was of the same material, mailed at the Grand Central Station post office during the morning rush hours marked 8:45. The ink seemed ordinary writing fluid. The writing was characteristic, distinct and scholarly. The letter had none of the Griffin's arrogant showing of gray paper and purple ink, of scarlet seal and griffin's head for signature. This was unsigned. Yet it was somewhat patterned on the Griffin's methods.

> Dear Manning:
> It is an honor to have you assigned to the affair of the Bullet from the Blue, as the papers so euphoniously describe it. If it had not been for you, I doubt whether they would ever have known the bullet was a meteorite. You must make the most of it. I really had nothing against Hyde. He was a man of parts, though he was ridiculous in his efforts to bring cosmos out of chaos by mathematical calculus.
> The sky-stone seemed an apt vehicle for the demise of a man who prided himself upon his knowledge of the Universe. He realizes his ignorance now. I could have used something

else, but this fitted in and it is a hobby of mine to produce a crime at once original and perfect. It is the process, I enjoy, the resultant exultation, far more than the demolition of the individual. He is only the end to my means, if you will pardon the paraphrase.

I think you will find this case a little hard for even you, the demolisher of the Griffin, to solve. I am willing to pit my liberty, perhaps my life, against your ability and undoubted reputation.

It may interest you to know that I am working on another problem. These things suggest themselves. But I shall not, like the Griffin, give out warning. He is now in Dannemora because he was too generous.

Some day I may devise a perfect crime in which you, my dear Manning, will be the principal. I consider you a worthy subject.

For a few moments Manning considered the calligraphy. In one respect, the writer had divulged identity. He had called the meteorite a sky-stone. That was a phrase he must have heard at Hyde's own house. A phrase general to Tagalogs, Moros, Bisayans, but not elsewhere outside the Philippines. A phrase Bino had used.

It was another spoormark on the trail. It seemed as if the killer *must* have been at the dinner when Bino lost his talisman.

Still a long way to go. A long, long way. But Manning began to see a dim horizon, a vague dawn. There was still dust in his eyes.

He opened a steel file and took out the "Lee and Abbey" chart for calligraphic tests. The writing of the unknown, but acknowledged killer, fell into Class Three.

It displayed skill. The small letters were apt to be disconnected, as in Greek script. The shadings were fairly heavy. There was some embellishment indicating vanity. The movement was forearm and showed vigor, speed, freedom and originality of purpose. The terminal strokes inclined downwards, and the general degree of slant was over eighty degrees. It was the

THE DUST OF DESTINY

writing of an educated man, a monomaniac and something of a sadist, undoubtedly; but a clever villain.

He tested it for finger-prints and found none. Most likely the writer had used collodioned fingers.

"You are clever, my friend," thought Manning, as he ran his fingers through the rough hide of his dog, "but you are not so clever as the Griffin. You may be dangerous. I rather hope you are. But, with all your cleverness, you give me some ideas and a few definite clews. I rather think *you'll* eat dirt instead of the commissioner, and there may be lime in it. It depends, a bit, on Bino's memory.

I V

"THE MAN," said Manning to the Commissioner of Police, "is a monomaniac. His mania may be concentrated on the development of a perfect crime, but I would not be surprised if the core of it was envy. Jealousy of Hyde, for instance. The peculiarity of his type—a cultured one, mark you, very likely inbred and mentally perverted—is, that, having committed one perfect crime, or one he thinks is perfect, he will proceed to others.

"I have a literary friend who prowls New York, looking for situations that may stimulate his imagination for the mystery stories he develops. He gazes out of the windows of elevated trains, seeking combinations of buildings, of gardens, of ways of entry and escape that suggest what he emits, harmlessly, in a yarn. He studies unusual people. I have an idea it may be much the same with the man who killed Hyde. I don't know now what his motive was, for certain, but I know he was not sane. He is like the jungle tiger who eventually kills human meat and becomes a man-eater. In the letter to me, he shows his quirk. Dislike of Hyde, ordinarily smothered by polite conventions and breedings, may have let loose his murderous idiosyncrasy. Once released, you cannot determine its limits. Aside from this crime, he is a menace to society. We'll run him down."

The commissioner regarded a list of five names that Manning had given him. The list of the people dining with Hyde on the night Bino had lost his sky-stone.

"It looks to me as if you are facing a stone wall," he said. "These people are all responsible people. We'll have to prove this thing. I don't want to discount your record, but it looks to me as if Bino handed you something."

"I think he did," Manning agreed. "The East is East, and West is West, but *sometimes* the twain *do* meet, Commissioner. Christianity and Islam have points of similarity."

"What has religion got to do with this case?" growled the commissioner.

"More than you'd think," said Manning. "Mind letting me see what you've got on those five guests of Hyde's?"

The commissioner shoved the report across the desk. He had not lost faith in Manning. He had come up from the ranks himself and he knew that he lacked education, but he felt he knew human nature. East or West. Those five names were all in the Social Register. Manning did not care for such things. The commissioner had to. There must be proof, overwhelming proof, to combat the assembled defense that would be made. Defense, backed by money and position, not only social but political. A stand the papers would be swift to take up as vital news. If he went into court he must be impregnable. Manning's reputation was strong, but the commissioner had to show positive evidence.

He watched the crime specialist's face and felt some relief at the grin he saw.

"Commissioner," said Manning, "we won't start reaping until we're sure the wheat is ripe. So, hold your horses. Did you ever read the book by Rosamond Lehmann?"

"I don't read many books," said the commissioner. "Who is she, and what's the book about?"

"It's not so much the book, as the title," said Manning. "The book is called 'The Dusty Answer.' I'll explain that to you in a day or so."

"You'll be explaining it to a new commissioner if you don't hurry. Election's ten days from now. There may be a new Mayor and, if there is, there'll be a new commissioner, particularly if this case is still unsolved."

"The Mayor seems fairly well set, even for a third term," said Manning. "And I'll give you your dusty answer before Election Day. And you will get all the glory."

"If you solve the case," returned the commissioner, "you are welcome to the glory. All I want is not to get run out of my job."

"All I want," said Manning, "is a vacation. And I'm going to get it."

The commissioner grunted in his non-committal fashion. He was not so incredulous as he appeared. He could see no positive solution to the case, but he held faith in Manning and he was cheered by the farewell grin Manning bestowed upon him as he left with the police report of the five names remembered by Bino as guests of Morton Hyde on the evening when Bino lost his sky-stone.

There was only one name Manning considered. The other four were coupled, married attachés of two big museums. Manning had met them all, more or less casually and he dismissed them from the case.

The fifth name and record he pondered very carefully.

KUYPER. JOHN KUYPER, descendant of the original Jan Kuyper who was contemporary with Stuyvesant; a trader who had sold turnip seed to the Indians for gunpowder, both because it was profitable and safer than letting them have the genuine article. Jan had grown to be a merchant, a power in Manhattan, the family successfully hanging on to their holdings through all phases of politics and revolutionary wars. They had become wealthy aristocrats. They had invested wisely and secured their interests. They had been careful also about their breeding, as a result of which the Kuyper family had run some-what to seed.

The present John had been stodgy in his student days. He had not achieved greatness in class or field or track. He was not a social favorite, except where newspapers flattered him in their social columns or mothers cultivated him for their daughter's sake. He became a fraternity man by force rather than favor. Before he graduated he had inherited the Kuyper millions, was fat and already inclined to be bald. Lonely, no doubt, for all his position.

He had, it appeared, shown more interest in astronomy than anything else. There was a professor who felt that this vague trend toward science might be cultivated, that the Kuyper heir might endow an observatory that would outshine all others, bring fame to the university and opportunity to the professor.

It is hard to believe that an astronomer would stoop to earthly affairs and motives, but it was noticed that his daughter took a special interest in young Kuyper, that she assisted her father in certain observations, when Kuyper would act also as her aide in the hours spent after dark in the dim observatory while transits were observed and spectra noted.

The university got its new observatory. It was called by Kuyper's name. It gave him some sort of scientific kudos that might have compensated for the sad fact that, once the endow-ment fund had passed over, Kuyper got, not the stratosphere of celestial bliss he had hoped from the lady, but what is known as "the air."

He soured. He withdrew into himself and became somewhat of a misanthrope with a vast sense of his own unacknowledged importance. He mooned about at scientific meetings, contrib-uted to the funds for celestial exploration. It was in such a manner that he met Morton Hyde. Kuyper might not supply ideas and theories, but he was a patron who could be depend-ed upon for expenses.

Such a man, self-centered, inclined to be morose, might,

Manning believed, have killed Hyde, have contrived the murder with considerable ingenuity and pride himself upon the achievement. The world might think him dull, but he would demonstrate that he was a genius. He could not proclaim it, but he could not resist writing to Manning. And Manning, if his theories evolved properly, was willing to give him credit for a devilish ingenuity.

But there had to be utter proof and Manning's first attempt met with staggering and disheartening failure.

The old Kuyper home was on Staten Island, the estate diminished in acreage by the increased values of real estate which could not be overlooked. But there were still spacious grounds, trees and a garden behind high walls; it would have been a showplace if visitors were permitted. Kuyper had lived there in the summer, but this spring he had closed it up and stayed in town. He lived at his club. Manning had a decoy letter written there that suggested Kuyper's coöperation in an expedition to a crater in Central Africa for the purpose of observing the transit of Venus. Kuyper would achieve certain honor as sponsor.

The reply came promptly, on club paper, written by hand, as Manning had hoped. And the handwriting did not resemble in the slightest degree that of the one sent to Manning.

There were plausible enough explanations. Either the letter from the club had been written by somebody else, which was hardly likely, but possible, or the one received by Manning which he had classified as Three by the calligraphic chart, had been dictated. That, however, would mean a confidant. The third suggestion was that Kuyper had deliberately cultivated two styles of writing. The fourth that he was innocent.

Manning lost no time in making his next move. He was going to visit the house on Staten Island, without invitation and without warrant. The latter would not be issued, even to Gordon Manning, lacking all legal cause. It would be a burglarious entrance. If Kuyper should surprise him there and killed him, Kuyper would only have to claim that he did not recognize him but thought he was a thief.

Kuyper, Manning believed, had made at least one trip to Staten Island since the house was closed. He might make another. But with this visit of Manning's the crime specialist's theory, so far as proof was concerned, must sink or swim.

IT WAS early in the morning when Manning's roadster was braked in the wooded lane that ran back of the Kuyper mansion. Here were great wooden gates in the high brick wall whence had issued, in earlier days, the horsedrawn vehicles of the family.

Manning had taken the first ferry from New York. At this hour none of the inhabitants of the section near the Kuyper house was abroad. Manning ran his car close to the wall, using it as an aid to reach the top. Manning kept always physically fit and he made it without difficulty, dropping down into a paved court on which faced the stables. There was a bar across the big gates, which he removed, replacing it after he had driven his car inside. The buildings here were all locked and he did not bother with them. He carried with him two packages and a black bag, with certain apparatus in it designed for general analysis. Manning was a fair chemist, but it did not need any extraordinary skill in that line to do what he proposed to do, to find what he hoped to find. He had determined to make his tests on the spot as he might have to undertake several of them from various samples.

He was armed. It was not improbable that Kuyper might have been watching him, or having his movements reported. Kuyper might have repented sending that bragging letter, and, in that revulsion, wondered whether Manning could suspect.

Getting into the main house was not difficult. The basement windows were barred and those on the ground floor shuttered, but Manning became a porch climber and deftly opened a fastening on the window that gave upon it. He closed it, unlocked a rear door, retrieved his packages and his bag.

He had a powerful electric lantern with him, but he hoped

to find that the electricity had not been disconnected. He tested a switch and found it was still on. From this moment fortune seemed to favor him. The house had been modernized. As he went through it he saw an incinerator and what suited his purpose far better, a connection for a vacuum cleaner that carried all the dust removed to a container in the basement. The container was of considerable size. It had not been emptied and was a third full of dust.

Manning had brought a vacuum cleaner of his own, and also a carpet sweeper, but now the way seemed open, the trail was clear, the scent strong.

He set up his little laboratory in the library. Magnascopes, an instrument for use of the fluoroscopic ray, vials, test tubes and other paraphernalia. He brought up from the container in the basement a liberal portion of the dust it held. One of his packages contained dust from the house across the street from Morton Hyde's residence. Dust from the top floor that was level with Hyde's roof terrace, from the front room where the window had slid up noiselessly. Dust from the treads of the stairways and the halls and passages. Dust from other floors.

He had already determined their analysis. The dust on the floor of the top floor room differed prodigiously from that of the lower floors. Under the magic black ray it had shone with opposing hues. Analysis of the dust confirmed the fluoroscope, which could not play him false. The dust from the stairways and halls was more or less of a blend between the two.

The dust on the lower floors showed the grit of New York, soot from soft coal, from carbon dioxide. It was the dust of the street, the city street.

On the upper floor it was the dust of the country, almost gritless, dried garden soil, desiccated mould high in percentage of vegetation. It was imported dust. It showed difference even to the trained eye, it smelled different. Under the tests the result was amazing.

Manning worked fast but carefully, concentrated on his

search, in his belief that swiftly grew to surety that he was right. There was no doubt of it.

He was so intense that he did not know that the front door had been opened after a car had rolled silently up the drive from the main gates. He looked up from a delicate reaction only when the door swung back and he saw Kuyper standing there.

KUYPER'S OUTER appearance was phlegmatic, but his Dutch blue eyes were blazing, though his voice was under control.

"Most interesting," he said. "May I ask why you are here and what you are doing, unbidden, in my house ? You broke in, of course. And what is all this foolishness?"

He picked up a graduated receptacle of earthenware, now partly filled with mud. And he did it with his left hand. Manning knew that ordinarily he acted normally. But he was ambidextrous. He could write with either hand, and produce two different styles of script.

"I got a letter, Kuyper," answered Manning, "from the man who claimed he killed Morton Hyde. That letter was a challenge to me which I have answered. You wrote that letter, right or left-handed. You knew Hyde's habits and they intrigued you into this grim murder game of yours.

"It was easy enough for you to get into the house across the way. You can enter from the patio court after dark in the rear without any difficulty. The lock on that door is a very ordinary one. I think you were clever enough to figure out beforehand that the place would be extremely dusty. It would inevitably show tracks.

"Therefore you took up to town dust from this house, the same I have taken from your cellar. You may have used compressed air, or you may have only used the tool gardeners use for spraying dry arsenates on plants. The idea may have come to you from seeing your own man at work. It was most ingenious, the covering up of your tracks in that fashion. But you overlooked analysis. These dust samples are going to put you in the prisoner's dock, Kuyper, they will send you to the chair."

Still Kuyper's expression did not change. His face was like a mask.

"You are evidently a man of resource, Manning," he said. "Might I suggest, however, that someone else may have taken similar soil? Have you found the weapon? Even your genius cannot link this with me, I think."

"I know where you got the missile," said Manning. "Bino lost it the night you dined with Morton Hyde, with Mr. and Mrs. Buxton and Mr. and Mrs. Woodward."

"Ah!" Kuyper sighed softly. "Nevertheless, Manning, if you will come with me into the next room I can show you that you are mistaken. It is a small snuggery and I have some brandy there that I should relish."

The snuggery was little more than a butler's pantry. There was a small table and two settles much like a modern breakfast nook save that the wood and workmanship were old, as was the paneling of the walls. There was one window of leaded diamond-shaped panes of stained glass. Kuyper slid back the door of a cupboard and brought out a decanter and two glasses.

Manning, alert, took the seat opposite Kuyper after the latter had sat down heavily. He again refused the brandy. Kuyper poured out a brimming wineglass, drained it, and repeated the drink.

"We Kuypers," he said, "do not go to trial. You win a hollow victory, Manning. I have taken a poison that has no antidote, even by stomach pump. It gives me no uneasiness and allows me several minutes to live. I acknowledge your genius. It seemed a perfect crime. A most entertaining problem.

"The missile was chosen because of its aptness. The newspaper accounts have all seen that point. Hyde was old and getting smug, damned smug and patronizing.

"The dusting was eminently successful until you came into it. As for the weapon, I thought of several. It must be silent and efficient. An air gun of sufficient bore and power could not be procured. It would be absurd to have one manufactured. I wanted to use that sky-stone, as Bino called it. Bino literally dropped it into my lap that night. I made the weapon myself. It was the same idea as the slung shots the children use, or used to use. A forked frame and rubber bands. I improved upon it. I used springs. I practiced with it here in my own garden, unseen, of course. I could bring down birds with it and never miss. I tested its range, its power. It could be held in the hand, either left or right, with me, and discharged with the other. Or it might be fixed, the frame held rigid, and then…."

Manning, watching, saw his pupils contract to pinpoints. The irises were pools of blue flame. The whites were bloodshot. The masklike face was breaking up. Kuyper's mouth twitched and twisted.

Automatically Manning ducked, thrusting his hand into his right-hand pocket for his gun.

There was a click, a twang, and a bullet this time of lead, sped across the room, through the space where Manning's head had been. It struck the paneling and exploded. If it had hit Manning it would have killed him.

He clutched his gun and then, swift as a striking snake, Kuyper snatched up the decanter and brought it down on Manning's head. The heavy cut glass broke. Half stunned, blood flowing, blinding him as he wiped it from his eyes, Manning leveled his gun while the madman stabbed at him with the jagged neck of the decanter.

"We Kuypers do not go to trial!" he cried. Then he collapsed as Manning's snapshot smashed his right shoulder. He lost his glass dagger, but he fought desperately as Manning grappled with him, mastered him at last and got the handcuffs on him.

The weapon that had killed Hyde showed where a panel had shifted at a touch from Kuyper on some hidden catch. There was a space where it had been firmly set, loaded with the explosive bullet, and the strong springs extended. It was doubtless the perfect crime that Kuyper had devised for Manning, as mentioned in the letter, rigged in the belief that he could lure the detective there.

There had been no poison in the brandy, but Kuyper secured some in prison, or smuggled it there. He was the last of his family and "the Kuypers did not go to trial!"

The Young Man's Story Sounded Like Merely a Lover's Problem, but Manning's Instinct Leads Him into a Deadly Mystery

GORDON MANNING pushed forward two open boxes towards his visitor. One was of silver, wrought with writhing dragons in high relief, containing cigarettes. The other was carved in Polynesian tapa design from golden Hawaiian koa. He suggested a drink as he took out the letter of introduction from the unsealed envelope.

John Stanhope refused all three. He was wrought up, nervous as he pushed back a forelock of black hair from his bronzed forehead. Nervous, imaginative and demonstrative. Capable and determined. So Manning appraised.

The introduction bore a signature that was a compelling one for Manning. The writer was not one to ask favors for himself or others. Beyond question he considered Stanhope worthy of assistance.

"Where did you meet the colonel?" Manning asked, lighting his pipe.

"Pahang, Malay Peninsula. Four years ago. I was after tin. He smoothed the path for me. I hardly know why, except he seemed to take a fancy to me."

Manning nodded. He could understand that. There was something compelling about his visitor's ego. Manning had known the colonel in Johore. He was the sort to help younger men accomplish what he might no longer attempt himself.

"I don't want to waste your time, Mr. Manning," said Stanhope, his fists clenched, the fire of emotion and purpose in his dark eyes. "I know it's valuable. I think you are the only man who can help me, though I did not expect to ask for that when I presented that letter. Four years ago I was in love with Alice Minturn. She lives now not far from you, in Pelham Manor, at a house called The Lilacs, with Elmer Brent and his sister, who are distant relatives. When I first knew her she was in college at Northampton and I was finishing at Princeton. She was also in love with me."

He was clearly under great stress and Manning admired the succinct way in which he came to the point, stated his case.

"I found out that she was an heiress, very wealthy in her own right. An orphan. I had a few thousands. We had talked of marriage, but I told her I would not marry a rich girl while I was poor. I stuck to it, though it was hard to resist her.

"I had specialized in mineralogy at college. I got interested in the tin mines of the Malay Peninsula, perhaps, because it was so far away from Alice. She told me she would wait for me, forever. I made my pile. I sold out certain interests and retained others. I am a rich man. But now"—the light died out of his eyes, his fists opened—"everything has gone wrong."

Manning sent up a ring of smoke to the ceiling. He knew the house called The Lilacs and he knew something of Elmer Brent, who was a sculptor. In a general way he knew they were the friendly guardians of a sick relation, a girl, but he did not recall her name.

"Go on," he said.

"I am staying at the Brummell Apartments," Stanhope continued. "I started to call on Alice day before yesterday, in the afternoon. The house is fairly close to the road with a brick wall in front of it. The grounds are at the rear. I just happened to look up. I saw Alice sitting at the window on the second story. She looked at me and she did not know me. She waved her hand to some school children who were passing, but she did not recognize me. Her face was pale and sad. It looked as if she

Manning's steel-cored cane flicked like a whiplash.
Twice it struck bone on shin and arm.

had been ill. We had not written each other since I left. I did not tell her where I was going."

Manning puffed another smoke ring. It seemed commonplace enough, for all Stanhope's suppressed, but visible, emotion.

"I rang the bell. A Japanese answered. Mr. Manning, I know the Orient fairly well, though, of course, nothing compared with you. That man was not merely hideous, he was evil. He hissed at me and said he would see Mr. Burton. He showed me in to a sort of reception room, and locked me in. Rather, it was a spring lock set to open only on the outside. I heard it click and I tried it.

"Burton came in wearing flannels. He said he had been playing tennis with his sister. I told him who I was and he said he knew about me from Alice. Then his sister came in. I think she is older than he is. She's red-headed, and she wasn't over amiable. To make a long story short, they told me I could not see Alice unless I got permission from her doctor—Dr. Thorndyke of Larchmont. The sister said that Alice was not at all well—confined to her room, and in a wheelchair. She seemed to blame the illness on me. Said Alice had gone into a decline after I went away, hinted that she was not expected to live long. I told her that if my love had harmed her it could also cure her, but they wouldn't let me see her. She wasn't at the window when I went away."

IT SEEMED to Manning that Stanhope was too much wrought up with the shock of finding the girl seriously ill; of her not having recognized him after four years—bronzed as he was. He fancied Stanhope inclined toward tragedy.

"I called up Dr. Thorndyke," Stanhope went on. "He was out. I wrote him and I got an answer. He regretted that he could not consent to any interview that would, in his opinion, be extremely detrimental to his patient, who was high strung and in a precarious state of health; a condition that appeared to have been primarily evoked by a shock to a nature, peculiarly sensitive, that might not survive a second."

Stanhope spoke scornfully, evidently quoting the letter whose sentences had bitten into his brain as if they had been etched there by acid.

"I don't see what can be done," said Manning. "Thorndyke is a reputable physician. A specialist, by the way, in psychiatry. I've heard of him. Burton is a reputable sculptor. You can't very well force your way to her against the advice of a doctor and the consent of those who take care of her. That she failed to recognize you after four years is not so surprising. Also Thorndyke suggests that a visit from you might be detrimental. A decline, in medicine, means two or three things. One of those is the expression for a general deterioration of mental and physical health. You would not forgive yourself easily if you injured her. I am not a detective...."

"I realize that," Stanhope broke in. "I tried to see you in New York before I learned you lived here, within a stone's throw of where this thing is happening. You are a consulting attorney, but, just the same, you solved the mystery of the Griffin when the police failed. You're famous. I haven't told you all. Burton's red-headed sister acted as if she had no use for me, but Burton was grinning up his sleeve. I knew it then and I knew it for certain yesterday. I was outside the house at the same time. Alice was there, waving at the kids coming from school again. She saw me. I saw her eyes shift. And then she pulled down the blind. And, as I passed the gate, I saw Burton picking a flower for his buttonhole. He stood back of the hedge and grinned like a wolf. Thought I didn't see him.

"I had a hard time finding Alice at all. Finally I learned she was living with her cousins—with the Burtons. And I found out something about Burton. He's not selling, these days; he hasn't exhibited for three years. He has an apartment in town and a studio. I went to both of them. The studio was closed. A man who runs a store across the street told me Burton hadn't been there for months. The apartment is a penthouse that costs him a big rental, aside from the parties he pulls there. Parties that the columnists wise-crack about. He has a Jap there, too, and he sold me the information about Burton living here— when he isn't raising Cain in his penthouse. Where does he get his money from? I'd give a lot of mine, to find out. I'm going to. You don't see it the way I do, but I'm telling you there's something devilish going on. They've done something to Alice. And I'm going to do something about it. I'm obliged to you for the interview."

He rose and Manning touched a bell. His own Japanese butler came, showed the ruffled Stanhope out.

Manning tapped out his pipe, ran a fresh cleaner into it and put it in a rack. He was sorry for Stanhope, sorry for the girl. He trusted Stanhope would do nothing rash. He regretted he had been unable to serve him and their mutual friend. He read the letter of introduction over again.

"There are all the makings," Manning told himself. "I've got a hunch there might be something to it."

He summoned Takayama again.

"There is a Japanese who works for Mr. Burton, at 'The

Lilacs,' close by," said Manning. "I am interested in a young girl who lives there. It seems hard to get information about her."

He did not have to say more to Takayama. He and the other servant of Manning, also Japanese, were devoted to him. There were a number of Japanese servants in Pelham Manor.

"That Japanese at that place name Ito," replied the butler. "He not very good. Other Japanese boys not like Ito. I don't think he speak along of me. But I try."

A note came in the morning mail from Stanhope, written on the heavy paper of the Brummell Apartments. Its tone lacked courtesy.

> ...Some day—it ended—you will find out that I am right. In the meantime, since you won't help me, I shall do the best I can by myself.

I T W A S clear that Stanhope was convinced there was something unnatural in his reception. Clear also that he was going into unadvised action.

Takayama made his report as he served Manning his melon, omelette and coffee. He had compiled it over night, as Manning expected.

"Young lady that house very sick. Doctor come one time a week. Nobody else see her except Missy Burton and Mister Burton. Maybe Ito see some time. Nobody outside. All time she stay in room, big room upstairs. Missy Burton stay home all time and take care of young lady. Mister Burton he go New York plenty time. Play tennis with Missy Burton plenty time. Young lady she very fond of children. She give plenty present to school for them. All time she like to wave to them and they wave back every day when they go along to school. They say her face never smile. She very sad."

Manning did not feel he had learned very much, save that Stanhope's opinion of the Japanese Ito seemed to be well founded, that Miss Burton devoted herself to the sick girl and was fond of playing tennis with her brother who, it appeared, was content to exercise with her as an opponent. Nothing else new except the reason for the hand waving.

Yet that strange phenomenon called, for want of a better term, a hunch, seemed to flourish on these items.

As a dog knows of the existence of a buried bone in a strange yard, so Manning was sensing that there was something rotten here, something that needed the light.

His special commissions from the New York Commissioner of Police and the Governor of the State had never been revoked. The police were still grateful for Manning's detection and defeat of the maniac known as the Griffin, homicide extraordinary, now in Dannemora. He got the commissioner personally on his private wire and asked for a service which was promptly granted. Burton was being investigated by men more competent in such matters than Stanhope.

Twice during the day he called up Stanhope, but found him out. He held no offense against Stanhope for his letter. He was willing to aid him, because of his hunch, not because of any definite suggestions or clews.

At midnight Stanhope had not returned to his apartment. In the morning there was a registered letter from him. A legal looking document was enclosed which Manning set aside for the moment. He read the letter twice. Its contents struck him as illogical, considered in the light of the previous note, which had been almost insulting.

> DEAR MR. MANNING:
> By the time you receive this I shall have gone away—not to return. My plans are not entirely definite, but I am leaving for the Orient.
> I have seen Alice at last, through the courtesy of Dr. Thorndyke and Miss Burton. She does not love me, she does not ever want to see me again; it was very evident that my visit was painful to her, and may have been harmful.
> It smashes things up for me. I shall always love her. I have made a will, a copy of which I enclose, leaving her everything. To offset legal complications I have provided that, if I should

be missing for the space of one year, the estate shall pass to her.

I have taken the liberty of naming you an executor, together with Dr. Thorndyke and I use this opportunity of thanking you for your patience and courtesy in my behalf.

Very truly yours,
JOHN HARTLEY STANHOPE.

The legal document was typed. The letter hand-written. Manning compared it closely with the shorter note. It seemed authentic, but its wording did not ring true. Stanhope, after writing the first note, would not be the kind to ask so great a favor.

He took the letter up to his private laboratory in the attic of his house and made some curious discoveries. Under enlargement the second letter stood up with the first. The words showed no signs of patching. There were some slight discrepancies, but none that might not occur in the ordinary course of writing. Checked by the Lee and Abbey analysis chart, both classified alike. Yet Manning was assured that the letter appointing him executor was a forgery, though it might be hard to prove, except for one thing. Even that, handled by a clever lawyer, could be discounted.

There were no finger-prints either on the letter or the copy of the will, except those made by Manning himself in perusing them. The person writing it must have taken extraordinary precautions, using very thin silk gloves or gloves with the ends removed and his fingertips collodioned. It seemed impossible for a person to write a letter without leaving finger-prints

THERE WAS one other matter. Testing by fluorescent ray, showed that the two letters had been written with different ink, It seemed significant to Manning.

His next move was to get Dr. Thorndyke on the telephone. They were both named as executors. This gave Manning the entrée he was glad to take advantage of. He lived quietly enough in Pelham Manor, but undoubtedly every other inhabitant knew of his fame in connection with the Griffin. If there was anything wrong, any interest he might show in the case would put people on their guard.

Thorndyke was cordial. He made an appointment for nine o'clock that evening. He seemed to have been expecting the call.

Manning filled his pipe, tucked his pouch in his pocket, took his favorite cane and went for a stroll before dinner. The cane was also a weapon.

It was a slender rod of flexible steel, one end forming the slender ferrule, the other set into a gold head. Over the core hundreds of leather rings had been set and shrunk, then varnished so that their joints were not discernible. It was light, and strong. In the hands of an expert, it was a good weapon indeed.

Children were coming home from school as he passed The Lilacs. Near the window on the second floor, he saw the girl seated there, her chin resting on one hand. Black tresses framed the exquisite oval of her face. Her hair was drawn back in a snood. A face of haunting beauty, but of great pathos. A face that never smiled. The sadness seemed graven there from suffering. That face, Manning thought, was surely meant to laugh, to show the flush of health, of varying emotions, but it hardly seemed to be alive; save for the eyes that showed light between long lashes, eyes shadowed in deep orbits, with hollows beneath them. The girl seemed unconscious of her surroundings.

Her eyes shifted and she waved a hand as two young girls came running past, calling up a greeting to the closed window. It seemed, to Manning, little short of tragic; the children, happy and carefree, waving a more or less perfunctory salute to the imprisoned girl.

Stanhope had hinted that she was held by more than illness. Manning's hunch proclaimed anew, that here was danger, sinister and deadly. It gave Manning the same feeling he had experienced in the dense jungle when savages crept menacingly toward him.

Something sinister seemed to draw his eyes to the window of The Lilacs. He took care not to glance more than casually at the girl. He felt that she regarded him intently. He could see no one else.

He passed on, noting that the next house was For Sale; a legend frequently displayed these times. He fixed the name of the agent in his mind.

He called at the Brummell Apartments, not surprised to find that the manager recognized him. Manning explained that Stanhope had written him he was leaving hastily, but that he had hoped he might intercept him or at least get a forwarding address.

Stanhope had left none, the manager told Manning. He spoke of him as a "very pleasant gentleman, though he seemed a bit down in the mouth." But he had "cheered up" and was "in very good spirits when he checked out."

There was a doorman who took the numbers of cabs, but not of private cars. Stanhope had tipped him liberally and left in a Lincoln sedan whose driver was a Japanese.

It was getting on towards dusk when Manning again neared the vicinity of The Lilacs. He had with him a key to the neighboring property, entrusted to him overnight by the real estate agent. Manning passed swiftly between shrubbery of the garden and entered the empty house. Upstairs he could overlook the rear premises of The Lilacs. The window was shaded with Venetian blinds and he shifted the slats with the utmost caution.

He saw strips of lawn, flower beds, shade trees and long shadows of twilight stretching across the space and checkering a tennis court on which two players moved. One was Burton, the other his sister. The leveling rays of the sun made her uncovered hair flame. They were finishing a set. Burton was by far the better player, though his sister was agile and graceful enough. Manning, handball expert, wondered at the fraternal spirit that sought such feeble opposition. But he wondered still more why Burton played on such a court.

It was of cement. The cement had heaved and cracked, scaled and pitted. Accurate play was impossible. They went at it mechanically, as if the exercise were a tiresome duty.

THE WOMAN double-faulted in play, tripped, but recovered herself. She shook her head and walked off the court towards the house. Burton shrugged his broad shoulders and followed.

Manning took a window seat to smoke a pipeful before he let himself out at the rear, to depart out through the garden entrance where there were big gates leading to a garage and a hedge.

It was quite dark when Manning stirred. Street lamps were lit, but trees broke up their light, making flickering screens of shadow.

Something moved in that shadow, something shifted stealthily in the laurel hedge that bordered the rear of The Lilacs. Leaves shifted uncertainly in the vague-light, and they shifted to the height of a stooping man. A form evolved itself. It was in black, amorphous, crouching. There was the glint of steel, gone, shown again in swift, offensive movement.

Manning's steel-cored cane flicked like a whiplash, like a Toledo blade—twice. Twice it struck bone on shin and arm, and he heard a queer, guttural yelp of muffled agony as the leaves swerved and a dark figure darted away. A knife dropped at Manning's feet. He kicked it to one side before he picked it up. Whoever that lurking assassin might be he was marked. His shin was notched, his elbow cracked.

Manning did not follow. He was not ready to bring the issue to a close. He had a fancy that this attack was individual, not planned by the master minds of the plot he was now certain existed—and which he meant to unmask.

That letter—the second one—which Stanhope had not written, had been a direct challenge from those who sought to blindfold him.

Stanhope had vanished. Manning had put in a call to headquarters that automatically started a checkup of railroads, steamers and ticket bureaus of the United States and Canada. Manning did not expect much more from this than corroboration of his own belief that Stanhope was within a twenty-five mile radius of the Empire State Building—and was in jeopardy. As for Alice Minturn, he had begun to fear he was too late to save her.

The knife that had been dropped at his feet was of the sort sold in so-called Oriental bazaars. A bone handle coarsely carved, a long crude blade with Japanese characters upon it that denoted its factory. The sort of thing a tourist buys for a paperknife, but nevertheless an excellent weapon.

Manning ate dinner leisurely. He had had a busy day, and he expected a busy night. To-morrow might prove even more crowded and more exciting.

At eight o'clock the man he had borrowed from headquarters drove up in a private car, a first-grade detective named Doherty.

"This guy Burton," said Doherty, "throws some fancy parties in this penthouse of his. Nothing to crash in about, so far, but something hot might break there any dawning, take it from me! He has plenty cuties and he gives them plenty hooch. One of 'em may make a dive over his parapet some morning, though they ain't the type to do it to save their virtue. His babies ain't got any. It's just hot-cha-cha, but it costs him pe-lenty. Here's a list of some of his guests. Them marked ones are regulars."

Manning glanced over the names.

"That's fine, thanks," he said. "You'll have another drink, and a fresh cigar? Now, what is the address, and does Burton lease the place?"

"He leases it and pays the rent regular, which is why he can do what he pleases. I wrote the address down on this card."

Manning saw that Burton's penthouse was on the roof of the building in which Thorndyke had his offices, which might, or might not, be pure coincidence, viewed in the light of the fact that Dr. Thorndyke's name was on the list as a regular guest at Burton's revels.

"HE'S PULLING one of these parties to-night," Doherty went on. "They don't start until round one or two o'clock. I got a line on Burton's income. If he's earned enough in the last two years to pay three months' rent on that penthouse, I'm a China-man. To say nothing of what his chow and alky sets him back. He's had one job in the last twelve months for a theatrical outfit. The show flopped and he didn't get paid. But he sure lives high in town. I'm telling you that if he sculps in the nude, he gets plenty inspiration, from what the lad who runs the all-night elevator that goes to the roof tells me. It was him I got the list from. He wants to be a detective. Can you beat it?"

"That's just what I wanted to know, Doherty," said Manning. "I'm going to make a call presently. I wish you'd stay here and make yourself comfortable. You and I may drive into the city later. I'd like to get a peep at that party, if it can be arranged."

"Duck soup," said Doherty. What between panatelas, pinch-bottle Scotch and a lounge chair in Manning's library he foresaw a pleasant hour or so ahead of him.

Soon afterwards Manning drove off to Larchmont in his own car to keep his appointment with Dr. Thorndyke. As he went he considered the clause in Stanhope's will that provided for his estate to be turned over to the girl if he should be found missing for over a year. He doubted whether that was legal. It was the sort of thing a quixotic lover might insert, but the outstanding fact was that the sooner Stanhope died, the sooner the girl would acquire his estate. In view of her own fortune she would hardly need it. But others might.

Thorndyke was more or less the usual type of successful physician—in his thirties, well set up and handsome in a way that would, Manning considered, make him attractive to many women. His features were aquiline. His mustache and pointed beard, together with his dark hair that grew to a peak on his forehead and was silvered at the temples, and upward curving eyebrows gave him a satanic cast of countenance. His dress was immaculate, though a trifle foppish. He was in dinner clothes, as was Manning, and he received the investigator affably, offering refreshment, which Manning declined. He would never have cared to accept the doctor's hospitality. The man was plausible, cultured, but he suggested secret dissipations.

Manning came promptly to the point, speaking of his having received the letter and the copy of the will. He did not mention the first letter. He was pretty certain the doctor did not know of its existence; he fancied that, in that unwitting omission, Thorndyke had made a mistake. He, or Burton, or both.

"Before I decide whether to accept or decline the responsibility of being Stanhope's joint executor with you," said Manning, "I should like, at least, to see Miss Minturn. Stanhope brought me a letter of personal introduction from a mutual friend in the Orient that gives him a claim on my offices. He was in a morbid mood when he wrote that letter and made that will. I hardly set him down as a suicidal type, though inclined to be rash. He may have exaggerated conditions."

"I don't quite agree with you, speaking as a psychiatrist," said Thorndyke, stroking his torpedo beard. "Even today there are plenty of the Romeo type, killing themselves on the bier of a dead love. Otherwise normal. I think Stanhope might make away with himself. The case is unfortunate. When he returned he found Miss Minturn suffering from partial amnesia, induced by a shock to her amatory emotions, induced by young Stanhope's refusal to marry her, his departure and silence. This upset her sex reflexes, it has put her on the borderline between sanity and insanity at certain periods. It produced in her, at first, lack of recognition of her lover, later, a revulsion that wounded him to the quick, that upset his own normality. It may seem involved to a layman, not to an alienist."

Manning had himself studied medicine, but he did not mention it. He knew that Thorndyke had been called in as expert in several prominent trials where good fees resulted and the alienists on either side invariably disagreed. He had his own opinion of such testimony.

"You think her condition will improve?" he asked.

"I trust so. I sincerely hope so and believe that with the proper treatment it will. She has suffered a second shock, a renewal of the bruise. She is now too readily excited, her cerebral tissues too readily inflamed.

"As to your seeing her," Thorndyke continued, "that can be arranged. I should, however, have to be present, out of mere medical precaution. I am going out, presently, on an important call. So, let us make it to-morrow evening at, say this time. She is usually calmer at that hour, more rational in her behavior."

"We will consider it an engagement, then," said Manning as he took his leave. He was aware that his dislike towards Thorndyke was fully reciprocated. It was a mutual mistrust, as sincere and natural as that of the trained dog for vermin, the mongoose for the cobra. He also gathered that Thorndyke in no way considered himself inferior.

THE PENTHOUSE was not set exactly in the middle of the roof of the building. On one side there were two shallow terraces with steps joining them. These were set with lawns, flowers and shrubbery with dwarf trees of weeping willow reflected in twin pools where water lilies floated, and Midas fishes swam, fat and golden. Lanterns of fretted metal-work were suspended everywhere, giving broken spots of color, amber and crimson and emerald. More light filtered through from the windows of the penthouse that faced this hanging garden of Manhattan, windows shuttered with Venetian blinds. Casements were up to offset the warmth of the summer night.

Through the windows came the sound of laughter, of gay voices, the clink of glasses, a babble of revelry that sounded a little forced, a trifle boisterous. Now and then there were exclamations, false protests, little bursts of applause.

The party had only just commenced, according to the elevator lad, but seemingly all had arrived well primed. And everyone was there. Burton himself had told the operator that there would be no more.

"He told me not to let no one crash the party," said the lad.

"We're not crashing it," said Doherty. "We ain't going to make any trouble for you, kid. All we want is a looksee and then you can forget it."

The operator showed them where a narrower terrace ran at the back of the penthouse, little more than a pathway of brick with a hip-high parapet, on which evergreens in stone tubs were set at regular intervals. This walk surrounded the penthouse on three sides. In the rear it passed unscreened windows that threw out bright light and from which came the voices of servants.

"Japanese?" asked Manning, remembering the oriental chauffeur of the car that had called for Stanhope.

"Yep," whispered the elevator lad; "two of 'em. One lives here, the other comes in from out of town with Mr. Burton. He drives his car."

"Lincoln?" queried Manning.

The operator nodded. Something in Manning's authoritative query made the lad look at him more closely as they stood in the private entry that led from the elevator to the roof. He drew in his breath.

"Gee," he said in an awed voice, "ain't you Gordon Manning, the guy that copped the Griffin? I saw your picture in the papers," he added as he regarded Manning's lean, bronzed and hawklike features.

"That's him, kid," said Doherty. "Now scram. Keep your trap closed. We'll ring when we want you."

The two of them stepped out of the entry to the bricked walk. The penthouse was entirely detached; its front door opened onto the lawns and garden. Manning and Doherty stood in dense shadow. A bright moon soared over Manhattan. It turned the falling spray of a fountain to an iridescent shower.

One of the Japanese was singing a curious, broken air in a

high-pitched voice. He broke off to speak to his fellow. The odor of spicy cooking came out of the kitchen and pantry windows, along with the click of dishes.

If one of these men had driven the Lincoln he could be identified by the houseman at the Brummell, but that would only prove what Burton might not care to deny; that Burton had used his own car to take Stanhope to the depot. Questioning a Jap was a pretty hopeless task.

Suddenly, as they looked between the shrubs, that masked them perfectly, Manning saw a broad sweep of light as the main door was flying open. There was a burst of strange music, pipes shrilling and drums beating, in a wild rhythm that stirred the blood. There was the plucking of strings; the wail of violins, but the syncopated drumming dominated everything. It might have been the orchestra of a camp in Tatary or Cathay or musicians in the kalang of a Javanese sultan. It was as weird as the eerie crowd of creatures that came gamboling out, capering about the terraces, posturing, dancing, as the lanterns winked out and spotlights rayed in crossing beams of orange and purple and green.

Mythical beings they seemed, half men, half beasts. Men and women alike, scantily attired in breadths of skin, in wisps of tissue with the gleam of metal and of jewels. Bizarre, incredible as a nightmare, a phantasmagoria such as Doré sometimes drew.

Griffins, cockatrices, phoenixes, dragons! Medusa and Gorgon heads, shriveled mummy faces, skulls, birds and brutes; faces of supreme beauty, faces that were frozen into types of sin and hate and cruelty. Emblazoned creatures of heraldry; fiends, harpies, sirens. Succubus, witch, virgin and harlot. Ape, warrior, hermit and troglodyte.

ALL THESE were masks, supremely wrought. Many of them covered the head as entirely as a helmet with lowered visor. They were masterpieces and those who wore them seemed to have become imbued with the attributes of the creatures they represented. Burton's party seemed destined to become an orgy.

"That was his last job—making masks for that stage flop. 'Manhattan Nights,' they were going to call it," whispered Doherty.

Manning nodded. He was beginning to see things more clearly. Masks for stage work had been a vogue, now fading. The effect was startling, but illuminating. But unless they unmasked, which did not seem likely for a while, with the saturnalia just beginning, recognition would be impossible. They knew Burton was there and Thorndyke. The elevator boy had brought them up, knowing them well.

"I've seen all I want," Manning said. Doherty was surprised, but said nothing, warned by the ring in Manning's voice that a lukewarm trail had suddenly become hot. They went down in the elevator and into the street.

"Let's take a look at the studio," said Manning.

The studio stood back a little from the street; with a courtyard in front, and double gates which were closed, but had a little grille through which Manning looked at the place. It had a high-pitched skylight, large, barred windows in front. Once it had been a stable. There was no light. It appeared deserted, neglected.

Manning stood in the empty street, scanning the general surroundings.

"I'm leaving you in town," he said to Doherty. "Find out whether anyone has seen anybody come in here. Make a thorough job of it. Come down to Pelham to-morrow night. Come in time to have dinner with me. We've got an engagement afterwards that may prove important."

Doherty saluted, proud of the invitation, and Manning got into his roadster and drove rapidly north through the almost silent streets.

Manning rose late. There was, after all, only one thing for him to do that evening before he kept his appointment with

Dr. Thorndyke, to see Alice Minturn. It was to call on a builder and contractor who referred him to another in the same line of business. This did not take long and the call proved satisfactory.

Manning's face did not reflect his mental grimness as he rang the bell at The Lilacs at nine o'clock. It was answered by the Japanese Ito, who was not liked by other Japanese. The man was a mixed Malayan type. He had bowed legs and long arms. He was dressed in semi-livery of black alpaca with a low-cut vest. It was hard to tell if he actually limped.

He placed Manning's card on a silver tray and carried it stiffly ahead, after he had taken Manning's hat and cane. Manning watched him sharply as he hefted the latter, but the man's face betrayed nothing.

Thorndyke was with Burton in the library, both in dinner dress. They made a strong combination, for certain purposes, Manning thought; Thorndyke the plotter, likely to be an extremist; clever as the devil. Burton bluff, burly, none too intellectual, easily dominated, but dogged.

Katherine Burton came in silently. She was in black, her skin was white and smooth as ivory, her hair magnificent. Several rings gleamed on her slender fingers and there was a square-cut emerald pendant at her throat, which was apparently flawless—extremely valuable. Manning fancied all the gems were unusual. Her otherwise simple tastes seemed to permit jewels. And then Manning saw her eyes, as they looked at Thorndyke, and the jewels were dull glass in contrast.

She was infatuated with the doctor. Her gaze betrayed her to an observer like Manning. She would have followed Thorndyke barefoot over lava wastes, through cactus thickets, adoring and serving him, fired with the flame of a superlative and starved passion; a flame fanned the more by the cold airs of the physician's demeanor toward her.

THE ROOM was momentarily electric with a current that somehow lacked a spark. It flowed from the woman and was received by the man with a certain insolence, a disdain; much as an age-old idol might receive incense.

As for Burton, Manning doubted if he realized the situation, patent as it was.

She gave Manning a ring-clustered hand. He held it a moment, admiring the star sapphire that showed its mystic and elusive fire.

"They say in Borneo, where they find a lot of those gems," he said, "that the star is the imprisoned spirit of a woman who loved, but who died without having her love returned. That is a very beautiful stone."

Her manner was not cordial as he released her hand. The light had gone out of her eyes. Suddenly she looked plain, old and tired.

"I will get Alice ready," she said. "I have not told her she was to have a visitor. We were afraid it would disturb her. Do you want me in the room, doctor?" she asked Thorndyke.

"I think not. The less the better. Just Mr. Manning and myself," he answered.

The big double chamber was dim with shaded lights. The bed, curtained and canopied, was in a recess that seemed to have been added to the original room. It would not accommodate the wheel-chair that stood at the foot of the bed; mute evidence of the helplessness of its occupant.

"We built out a solarium," said Thorndyke, "so that when the sun shone its rays might help her. The panes are crystal. It cost a lot, but she could afford it and while the rays have not seemed to help her, one cannot say how they may have retarded disease."

He spoke in a low voice before they moved towards the bed. There Manning saw, sunk amid soft pillows, the sorrowful, beautiful but inanimate, face he had glimpsed at the front window.

One arm was outside the coverlet, ringless. The nails had been tinted. The lips were rouged. Some feminine impulses and vanities apparently remained in her.

"This is Mr. Manning, Alice," said Thorndyke. "A friend of mine, and of yours."

The girl showed scant interest. Her fingers stirred, balling up the silken coverlet.

Manning had agreed to mention nothing that would link him with Stanhope.

"I represent the Seminary, Miss Minturn," said Manning. "They appreciate so much what you have done for them. Especially for your gift of books for their library. They want a bust of you to set there. Mr. Burton, your cousin, will make it, of course, but we want your consent and, perhaps, a few words from you, over a microphone, set up here, in your room, without any outside people, just yourself, talking to them."

The quiet, lovely face on the pillow showed no change of expression, but Thorndyke made a sound and took a step, as if he meant to interfere. Manning had startled him. There had been a gift of books in the name of Alice Minturn, but the rest was cut out of whole cloth. Manning had explained that the reason for his seeking an interview was to assure himself of the girl's sanity. He could not, he told Thorndyke, assume executorship in a will that enriched or might enrich anyone whose reason did not seem to him, at the time, sound.

"There have been rumors, as there always are," he assured Thorndyke. "I do not subscribe to them. This is merely a matter of form, for my own comfort."

"You've overdone things," Thorndyke said, and his low tones were suddenly menacing.

"No," said Manning calmly. "Not I, Thorndyke. You! And overlooked things, also. I am surprised that Burton as an artist, did not catch it, but I suppose he left the staging to you?"

"Just what do you mean?" demanded Thorndyke. He stood with his hands in the side pockets of his dinner-jacket. "Just what the devil *do* you mean, Manning? Are you over infatuated with your own reputation? Look here...."

"No. Look *there*," Manning replied quietly. "I admired Miss

Burton's ring a little while ago. I also admired her hands. Criminal science observes finger-prints closely. It has not yet advanced to the study of fingers. No two hands are alike, digitally. The palmists will tell you that. They ascribe various influences to the shape of fingers. I don't, but I *do* know that Miss Burton's thumbs are unusual. They extend between the first and second knuckles of her forefinger. She should not have left her hand outside the quilt. Otherwise, the illusion is excellent."

He leaped forward into the narrow space at the side of the bed. The couched figure rose with a gasping protest as Manning tore off a mask, the pate of which was wigged with black tresses; surrounding the skull like a helmet. Its removal exposed flaming hair—and the face of Katherine Burton, deadly pale.

MANNING STOOD sidewise to the bed. He had used his left hand for the dramatic disclosure. His right gripped a flat automatic. Thorndyke took the warning and backed to the wall.

"I want to know where the girl is," said Manning. "Burton has been forging her signature to receive her income and pay it out, just as he forged the letter Stanhope is supposed to have sent me—forged Stanhope's signature to the will. An excellent forgery, but a forgery none the less, as I can prove. I want to know where Stanhope is. They may both be dead. If so, you'll burn for it, you and Burton and Burton's sister, masquerading in the bed now, and in the window every day as Alice Minturn—when she isn't playing on that cracked up tennis court. Stanhope may be still alive, but he won't be long, left to you. You're the boss devil in this conspiracy, Thorndyke. You cooked up this scheme to replenish the funds you've spent—giving this woman's jewels as a sop—and wasting the rest on the orgies in the penthouse Burton leases. I was there last night, Thorndyke and I saw."

There came a gasp from the woman on the bed. Manning had scant pity for her.

"You love Thorndyke," he said, without taking his eyes off the doctor. "If you had seen him last night...."

She broke into uncontrolled sobbing. A hundred happenings flashed back to her, confirming doubts she had fought against. She wrung the hands from which she had removed the gems of deception.

"That tennis court of yours aroused my curiosity," said Manning. "You seem fond of playing on it. The man who laid the cement for it tells me he warned you to put a foundation of cinders under the cement, but that at the last moment you told him to go ahead without it, after you had held up the job for three days. I want to know why? I think I can guess, but I'm going to find out."

The woman collapsed. Thorndyke advanced, his hands up.

"You win, Manning," he said. "I never dreamed you'd come into this. The luck ran against me. But they're both alive. My gun is in my right-hand pocket. It's the only one I have. I should have known better than try to hoodwink you."

Manning took his weapon, but he did not turn his back on the bed. This surrender, sensible as it was, came too pat. Then he saw the doctor's hand go to his mouth. His features writhed and he fell. It looked like cyanide; but his arms wrapped themselves about Manning's legs like twin pythons as the door burst open and Burton, with the Japanese back of him leaped into the room.

Manning, half off his balance, swung his gun. He clubbed Thorndyke behind his ear and saw bright blood spurt where the gun-sight broke the skin, opened veins, and stunned the doctor.

A shot rang out and he felt the sting and sear of hot lead in his left shoulder. That arm was out of commission as he kicked free from Thorndyke's relaxed grip and threw a light chair at the Japanese who was crouched for a spring, knife in hand.

The bullet had shattered bone and Manning fought off the nerve-shock as he dropped to one knee while Burton's second shot roared out. The missile tore the air just above his head. Manning fired from his hip and Burton spun about, falling with a yell, his hip smashed.

The Japanese shouted. Katherine Burton huddled under the sheets. From outside Doherty crashed the rear door with his hurled weight and raced up the stairs. He threw himself upon the Jap who landed on his shoulders, his knife driven through the thick rug into the floor.

Burton was writhing; Thorndyke lay prone. Doherty struggled for a moment with the Jap and finally clicked the handcuffs on him.

"Try your damned jujutsu with me, will you?" he panted. "Howd'ye like the Kilkenny clutch? You're hurt," he said to Manning.

"We'll fix that," said Manning. "Call up the local station and tell them to bring a surgeon. We've got to find that girl."

THE SHEETED huddle in the bed stirred. Katherine Burton spoke in a harsh voice.

"I'll tell you where she is," she said. "But she's dead, and buried under the tennis court, though I don't see how you knew that. But we didn't kill her. If anyone did it was Stanhope; going away and not saying where. She was a romantic sort and she didn't care what happened to her. She came to us. We were hard up. We'd lost all we had. There were no commissions for my brother. Alice let us handle her money. Thorndyke attended her. He was hard up, too. Now I can guess where some of his income went. He made a fool out of me. Now I'm fooling him. Alice died one night when he was here. It was her heart. It meant the end of the money. She had left us some, but she had made a crazy will with all sorts of bequests. My brother owed Thorndyke money, or so he claimed. Well, the ground was cleared and leveled for the court. Soft dirt, rolled. It wasn't much of a job to bury her and roll the dirt again. But it rained the next two days and I suppose we all got nervous. Ito had seen us and he wanted to know what we had hidden away. Elmer got the

contractor to leave out the cinders and finish the thing in a
hurry. It's haunted us ever since. We've played on it to lay the
ghost, Elmer and I. Thorndyke doesn't play tennis, but he took
his share of the income. It didn't last long. They didn't tell me
where it all went.

"I didn't know about the penthouse," she continued with the
hellish fury of a scorned woman. "Then Stanhope came. He
had money. He wanted to see Alice. So…."

"I know the rest," said Manning. "I hope, for your sake, they
haven't made away with Stanhope."

"Try and find him," snarled Thorndyke. "You can't prove
anything without a body, Manning: When you disinter the one
under the tennis court you'll only uncover natural causes."

"Aside from murder; forgery and kidnaping, fraud and a few
other matters may be found interesting," Manning answered.
"I'm going to search Burton's studio. Then I'll turn the affair
over to the police. After all, I am not a professional detective."

"Damn you amateurs," gritted Thorndyke and Manning
laughed at him.

"That was *your* trouble, doctor," he said. "You went outside
your own profession."

"IT WAS a good guess, and a lucky one," Manning told the
commissioner, "looking for Stanhope in the studio. They'd have
taken him for a ride before long. It doesn't look as if we could
pin murder on them, but there's plenty beside that. The case is
cleared."

"Thanks to you," said the commissioner. "There's one thing
not quite clear. You claim the letter that came with the will was
a forgery. Our man says it isn't. So does another expert."

Manning chuckled.

"It was because the letter was forged that I got busy," he said.
"The trouble is with a good many criminal detective scientists
that they can't see the wood for the trees. They rely too much
on modern inventions, micro-photography and black rays. I'll

show you something. Mind writing your name on a sheet of paper?"

The commissioner obeyed.

"I want an ordinary sheet of glass," said Manning. "The glass out of a picture frame will do. Or what they use downstairs for mixing finger-print ink."

It was not hard to secure. Manning placed the paper with the commissioner's signature to the left, another blank sheet to the right.

"Nothing magical or complicated about this," he said. "I used it as a kid to help me learn drawing. Hold that glass upright, will you?"

With suddenly revived recollection the commissioner obeyed, nodding as the image of his writing was refracted accurately on the blank sheet.

"Did it myself once," he said while Manning traced the image over with a pen.

"Pretty good job," Manning remarked. "For an artist with a free hand, like Burton, it would be duck soup, to quote Doherty."

The commissioner nodded.

"It'll make the experts sit up," he said. "Knowing this method and finding no finger-prints tipped you off, then?"

"That—plus a first class hunch," said Manning.

THE UNKNOWN MENACE

Seemed to Gordon Manning, as He Clung
Desperately to His Dead Companion,
That a Strange New Monster Had
Risen in the Underworld

THE OLD trainer of the private gymnasium that catered to those of the business men of lower Manhattan who cared about their physical condition, looked approvingly at Gordon Manning as he came naked from the needle shower, after having taken on and defeated the younger professional at handball.

Manning was fit. There was not an ounce of superfluous flesh on his body, which was as coppery as a Carib Indian's, neither was he too finely drawn. The lines that had been graven indelibly in his face by menace and suspense, by mental strain and physical stress, were barely visible. He was "in the pink" and the trainer told him so with both pride and affection in his voice.

He loved this efficient ex-major of Military Intelligence, world-wide traveler and explorer, recent conqueror of the most malicious and crafty of all murderers, the evil genius of the twentieth century.

"It's the vacation," said Manning. "I managed to wangle it at last. I'm feeling great."

"I didn't like the way you looked just before you ran down that devil who called himself the Griffin," said the trainer. "I hope they keep him safe in Dannemora."

"It's not an easy place to get out of," returned Manning with a laugh that, like the chime of a bronze bell, proclaimed the perfect coalition of healthy mind and body. "If he does we'll have to put him back again, that's all."

*Deliberately he
fired two shots.*

At the moment, as he toweled himself, he took the grim suggestion lightly. Yet the chase and capture of the Griffin, after that madman had mockingly proclaimed and executed the death of a score of the world's most brilliant and useful citizens, had almost made an old man of Manning before his time; had plunged society, science and commerce into turmoil; had terrorized New York and horrified the whole of America.

That was over now. The insane but brilliant being, whose distorted mind conceived the most diabolical exploits, was safe in Dannemora. He had suffered physically in his final encounter with the law and from that he had been reported slowly recovering. But his mind showed the effect of the moment when his supreme conceit had been broken by Gordon Manning, when his egomaniacal belief in his supremacy had been challenged and shattered. He was said to have alternate moods of homicidal rage and deep depression when, like Giant Despair, he would sit biting his nails and glowering with eyes in which the fires of Hades seemed to flicker.

Manning dressed and started to walk the few blocks to his offices where, as proclaimed upon the outer door, he practised as Counselor at Law and Consulting Attorney. When he got restive he disappeared and club members wondered what distant, unknown trail Manning might be following; hobnobbing with South Sea kahunas or Aleutian shamans, guest of a Tibetan Lhamasery or deciphering the runes of a pro-Toltec steles and pyramids?

Many looked at his keen, hawkish face with its beaky nose, clean-cut jaw, and his eyes at once serene and questing, without knowing who he was, but recognizing his distinction. Others were glad to nod to him, to call him by name as he strode swiftly south and east; hatless, carrying his favorite weapon, a cane—a steel rod covered with shrunken leather rings. In the hands of Manning it was as efficient as a rapier; it could flick shin or knee or elbow with a painful precision that was disabling. It had beaten many an attempted gundraw or slungshot blow.

There was mail waiting for him. All of it save that marked "Personal" had been opened by his efficient secretary. She laid one letter, typed perfectly but curiously on an imprinted sheet of heavy bond, on the top of the sheaf of correspondence where he would see it first. She was a pretty, red-headed girl, extremely capable, and devoted to Manning. She had intuition allied with brains and he saw now that she attached some special significance to this communication. He read it through—once. There was no need to do so again. The whole page was imprinted upon his mind as if it had been photographed there.

There was no address, extremely wide margins, single spacing.

> Gordon Manning, Esq.,
> Consulting Attorney,
> 79 Wall Street,
> New York City.
>
> Dear Sir:
> As you have been interested from time to time in similar happenings, it may now interest you to learn that a plan has been made to end the life of Joseph Curran. There may be others of that name, but there is only one Big Joe. The attack will take place within the next forty-eight hours. If you should

decide to try and protect him you will undoubtedly run grave
risk of sharing death with him.

    Sincerely yours,
    Well Wisher.

WITH THE typed letter in his hand, Manning stared out
of the window, seeing, without registering, the towers of Manhattan, the spidering of the great bridge.

The anonymous writer was correct. There *was* only one "Big
Joe."

Joseph Curran, ex-contractor, now a man whose millions
seemed to have weathered even the depression, was a power in
the land. He wielded more power than any one in the State,
though it was a power that never appeared in public, that dis-
claimed all authority.

"I have nothing to do with politics," Big Joe said, time and
time again, when he gave out interviews. "I am naturally interested in the welfare of the community, selfishly first, perhaps,
and then, let us hope, more altruistically."

But it was significant that those in the seats of the mighty
took counsel with Big Joe; that professional politicians weighed
the words of one who styled himself an amateur. Whoever Big
Joe championed, openly or secretly, was ninety per cent sure to
win. Equally those whom Big Joe did not approve went down
to obscurity and oblivion.

The sort of man who has many friends—and many enemies.

Reporters wrote down what he permitted them to say with
their tongues in their cheeks. If he had been the back number
he professed to be editors would not have sent reporters to
interview him.

He had been in politics when he was a contractor, no doubt
about that. And the political leopard does not change his spots.

Not that Big Joe was essentially a leopard. He was undoubtedly fearless and aggressive, though his movements were
masked, but he was faithful to his associates so long as they
were staunch to principles. No one was more charitable than

Big Joe Curran and, in his charities, more often than not, his right hand did not know when his left hand gave alms. The field of charity was the only one into which politics did not enter with Curran.

A big man, physically and mentally. A man who knew men. A bigger man than the Mayor of Manhattan, than the Governor of the State, than the State representatives and senators rolled into one. His influence was felt at the White House.

Some crank, Manning was convinced; some fancied victim of slight or injury, one of the hundreds to whom Curran was forced to deny or withdraw favors, meant to kill him—and might accomplish it.

There was never a bad man of any renown, whether he came from the Badlands of Wyoming or the slums of Hell's Kitchen, New York, who does not have imitators. Crime in Manhattan, as published in the lurid columns and pictures of the tabloids, has egged on many a man whose mind was evil, but did not otherwise have the courage to emulate Billy the Kid or Gyp the Blood when he began to figure out his own private vendetta.

As for the warning, it could have come from the would-be killer himself. Then, too, the killer might have boasted of his intended plans to someone who hoped to nip them in the bud.

Cranks were strange people, their motives as eccentric as their actions. Manning had known men who confessed to murders they had never committed; men who denounced themselves as kidnapers. Some strange wish to get into the limelight might actuate most of them, but Manning believed that there was some deep motive back of this new warning. Politics breeds not only strange bedfellows, but brings in sinister creatures. Jackals become ravening lions when denied a share of spoils they believe due them. Julius Cæsar was neither the first nor the last man to die of Politicalitis.

Manning resolved to turn the letter over to the Commissioner of Police, but he meant to do so with a comment that

he himself took the matter seriously. No doubt the commissioner would, also. Big Joe was his patron saint. If anything that
the police might have prevented happened to Curran, it was
going to be just too bad for the head of the Department.

Curran was not going to be too easy to protect. As all the
world that read the papers knew, Big Joe lived through the
summer at his residence on Long Island, known as Blue Bay
Lodge. He was unmarried. Blue Bay Lodge was Bachelors' Hall
for those lucky enough to be its guests.

There he grew roses for diversion, yachted, lived the life of
a country squire, to all appearances. But big men with high
ambitions went there and asked favors or received instructions.
So did office holders. The week-end parties there often held far
more significance than a political rally or convention.

It was quite likely that Big Joe had personal guards, more
likely that his menservants, house, garage, stables and yacht
were chosen with a dual purpose in mind. In any event he would
guffaw at the idea that he would be bumped off by an unknown.
In his time, Big Joe had made waste paper of thousands of
anonymous letters. He might be hated—doubtless was—but
he was also feared and even loved.

MANNING HAD met him. Big Joe belonged to two of
Manning's clubs. They had met at banquets. They had discussed
many things, but not politics. Politics was outside Manning's
life; but he knew the quality of Big Joe. He was a modern
Warwick, a king-maker.

That Big Joe knew his own realm Manning granted, but
there was more than a chance that some obscure underling,
working up a minor grievance that darkened his very reason,
might be the one to make an attack. Some brooding man, especially in these times, when depression stalked the land with
its grim retinue of hunger, homelessness, destitution and death,
was likely to be dangerous. Cranks have killed presidents, started
a world war, assassinated kings. It might be a humble ditch-
digger, denied a job, half mad from seeing his family suffer,

determined to wipe out the man at the head of the party in control. Or it might be a discharged clerk or secretary. Somebody who knew that Big Joe's assertions of having nothing to do with politics was a myth.

Manning believed in hunches; in his subconscious mind, his trained powers of observation and his experience; in his tremendous coördination. Hunches had become part of his metabolism; the automatic chemistry of his body. Hunches seemed to ring alarms that geared him to high tension, making him supremely receptive to evil vibrations. Such hunches had saved him from the savage rush of a man-eating beast, from creeping head-hunters in the bush, from modern killers of the metropolis.

He believed that this crank, whether or not he was the actual writer of the note, was not merely blowing off steam in his threats.

He set aside the pile of work that cried for his personal attention, put in a call to Centre Street, and drove there, to be instantly closeted with the commissioner, to whom he showed the letter.

The commissioner frowned as he perused it.

"Funny it should be sent to you," he said. "Still, you have been in the public eye lately. I've got a duplicate of it myself. A crank, of course. I hadn't decided what to do about it. No sense in bothering Big Joe. He wouldn't pay any attention to it, or thank me for showing it to him. How does it strike you?"

The commissioner knew that Manning considered it seriously or he would not have asked for the interview.

"Got a hunch, Manning?" he inquired.

Manning nodded.

"Call it a crank," he said. "It wouldn't be any member of a mob or a gangster. They wouldn't dare, any of them. This man may not be a criminal with a record, but, to my mind, Commissioner, he may be a potential criminal and a very dangerous one. The mere fact that he is an amateur is likely to give him a tremendous advantage. I have seen an unskilled fighter break through a professional's guard more than once, both that of a boxer and a sabreur. It might be some crank who would be cunning enough to show up at Blue Bay Lodge with an unimportant excuse and get through to Curran by his mere appearance of harmlessness. I suppose Curran is guarded there, but I imagine he'd be more or less careless himself in the country."

"You're right, Manning," said the commissioner. "In the first place, I've got a deep respect for your hunches. In the second place, I can't take any chances with Big Joe. If some crank only *tried* to pull something and it got out, it might mean my job. I'll send some men over there. He'd raise merry hell if he knew. He laughs at this sort of thing, and he's probably right. He's been threatened enough and yet, in most ways, he's the best protected man in the U.S.A."

Manning nodded.

"I've got to get back to work," he said. "The look of your desk after you get back, takes all the joy out of a vacation. If you send men down there, Commissioner, remember the three elements. The danger might come from sea or land or the crank may be some chap who can fly and wants Big Joe to have a certain type of plane used by the City, the Army and the Navy."

"There's no bigger crank than an inventor," said the commissioner. "Thank you, Manning. Now you go along and do your homework. I'll attend to this. Curran may scrap anonymous letters, but I don't scrap your hunches."

MANNING TOOK work home with him that night after he had stayed late at the office. It was early morning before he got to bed and then sleep evaded him. His hunch annoyed him like a conscience, like an ulcerated tooth. He could not rid himself of the idea that Big Joe Curran was in deadly danger; that the commissioner's precautions might not prove sufficient. If the matter had been left entirely up to Manning's private soul, he might have dismissed the matter. But he could not evade this inner suggestion that murder was forward, that this crank was one of those creatures who, like the rabbit, once in a thousand years, bites a dog.

The world might get along without Big Joe and be the better for it, but his killing in this fashion would be murder. Moreover, the anonymous writer had been correct. The possible peril, the mystery *were* incentives that challenged Manning.

Nine o'clock found him in his roadster, crossing Queensboro Bridge on his way to the northeastern shore of Long Island, on the road to Blue Bay Lodge. And the hunch rode with him. Its warming tingle spread through his veins, promising adventure; the old thrill that yet was ever new, and welcome. He drove faster and faster. If he was checked he had means of dismissing this trouble. His special commissions, issued by the commissioner and also by the governor, were still in effect. They had never been revoked.

He had promised himself that he would get them cancelled, that for a while, at least, he would devote himself to his legal business, but the fascination of baffling crime had gripped him once again.

As Manning came to a gap among the trees that crowned the hill and lined the highway, he saw below him the outspread estate of Joseph Curran, lying in a saucer of land with its northern border tilting to the cobalt waters of the bay that had given the place its name, Blue Bay. There were other houses nearby, and a yacht club.

The harbor was shaped generally like a horseshoe, notched irregularly here and there. It was a good anchorage and had ample room for protected cruising, if the Sound proved too boisterous. Manning had secured a description of Curran's house and had no trouble in recognizing it, built of brick in Colonial style, stately, with its pillared portico and finely placed windows—one of them a beautiful Palladian above the portal. Garage and stables were subordinated, vine-covered and almost hidden by trees, of which many fine specimens were set about the spacious grounds—terraced lawns and walks, shrubberies and Curran's famous rose gardens, whose blooms had often captured prizes and disproved a popular fallacy that roses, except for the coarser varieties, could not be successfully grown on Long Island soil.

Manning knew that Big Joe had been an athlete in his younger days, he was still a sportsman in his sixth decade, playing a consistent eighty-four at golf, skipper of his own yacht, driving his own car and riding spirited horses. With his fixed determinations, his enormous prestige, he would be impatient of any idea that he had to be protected.

But Manning trusted that he would be able to get in personal touch with him. By appealing to Curran's hospitality, he could be assured of being close to him for several hours with an opportunity for deciding whether this threat was or was not the act of a crank. He could also prepare special precautions for protecting him without the latter's knowledge. This would be in addition to the cordon of plain-clothes men that he knew the commissioner had supplied.

He saw a smart looking launch beside the private wharf. It was small, but it had a cabin and its lines were built for speed. Off the wharf was Curran's auxiliary ketch. Her sails were reefed and under cover. It did not look as if she were going out that morning. It was now close to noon. But two men in whites stood on the wharf above the launch which they had evidently just lowered from davits.

There was no lodge or keeper as Manning drove into the grounds. Curran might be going out in the launch. It was possible and the first strategic move would be to head him off from the water.

He swung his car into a curving path that led to the garage, braked and jumped out as a man in chauffeur's livery presented himself and civilly but firmly asked what he wanted. A polite man, but one who could be hard upon occasion. More like a gangster's bodyguard than an ordinary driver. Manning put his question as to Curran's whereabouts.

"He don't see visitors without appointment," said the man who was clearly suspicious, inclined to be belligerent. "Were you expected?"

Manning saw the well-known figure of Curran emerge from the boathouse. If he was going out in that tender, Manning was going with him. The man opposed him for a moment and then subsided, as Manning, having no time for arguments, dropped him with a right to the jaw, leaped a low hedge and raced across a stretch of lawn to the head of the stone steps leading to the wharf. There he waved his cap and *halloo'd* to Curran, calling him by name. He ran down the steps so that Curran might recognize him, which he did. It was a performance out of character for Manning, but he had no time to waste, if his hunch was right.

CURRAN'S GREETING was cordial. He showed no surprise, beyond a transient gleam in his keen eyes. "I happened to be near here," Manning explained, a little breathlessly, "and I remembered your invitation to see your roses. But I see you are going out in the launch. Don't let me detain you."

"Good man!" said Curran heartily. "Fine! It is not just the best time of the year to see the roses, but we have a few late blooms." Manning fancied that Curran's shrewd gaze regarded him for a moment, speculatively, as if he wondered whether Manning did not know enough about roses to make an inspection trip at such a time of year. But he went on, reacting as Manning had felt sure he would. "In a hurry?"

"Not especially, for once."

"Then you'll come out in the tender for a trial run with me. It just arrived yesterday, specially built, fast, good enough for dirty weather, and the engine is powerful enough to tow the ketch if its own engine should break down; which, as a matter of fact, it has, or I would be cruising in her this minute. Glad I'm not, since you came. We'll be out about an hour, then you must lunch with me, and then we'll look at the roses."

They stepped into the well-appointed tender and Curran

made ready to start the engine before casting off. Manning stopped him.

"Mind if I do that?" he asked. "I'm interested in engines."

"Of course not, my boy," the other answered and sat in the awninged cockpit, staring quizzically while Manning went over the enclosed engine with scrupulous care. He inspected the self-starter, all connections, for some hidden gadget that would explode as soon as any one attempted to function the machinery. There was nothing and he got his spark, fed gas while the judge cast off and then surrendered the wheel to the owner as they sped from the wharf towards the harbor.

For its type, the launch was unusually fast. It was warranted to make better than thirty knots after its engine had become adjusted and got to know itself.

Manning noted that some of the fishing craft had taken up anchor and were making towards the harbor mouth, falling in behind the speedier launch. Also, two other launches had gone ahead. They had plenty of speed, too. While it seemed that only one or two people were aboard either of them, Manning did not doubt that there were more, cabined, armed with rifles, with machine guns or quick-firers.

Overhead, an amphibian plane was air cruising. It was a common enough sight.

"Then it was *not* just the roses," said Curran quietly when he had sped up his engine to the limit he wanted.

"No," said Manning. "Not just the roses. You may think me unwarranted, judge, but this is the copy of a letter I received yesterday. I don't like it."

Big Joe read the warning—or the threat—calmly, refolded the crisp, bond paper and handed it back to Manning.

"You seem to have taken this seriously enough to give me your personal protection, for which I am grateful," he said. "I imagine," he added a shade less cordially, "that the police is also taking it seriously. Some of these boats—all of which are strangers to the port—are acting curiously. It would seem," he added with a humorous quirk of his mobile mouth, "that the average detective methods are lacking in subtlety on water as well as on land. Both my men on the wharf, for example, have been wondering about them. On this tide none but a profound optimist would try fishing."

"It would not be wise *not* to take it seriously, sir," said Manning. "The country cannot afford to run any risks concerning your welfare."

"I am sixty-three, Manning," said Curran. "At least the last twenty-three years of my life have been punctuated with threats. I have yet to take any of them seriously. We'll take our police convoy along for a short cruise, then you and I will enjoy—I hope—our luncheon; and then we will consider roses. If you still attach importance to the limit set by this nameless correspondent, who may, or may not, be a 'well wisher,' I shall be only too delighted to have you as my guest."

"I shall be very glad to stay," Manning replied.

THEY WERE passing through the entrance to the harbor. On one side gulls were wheeling and dipping about the white lighthouse on Kidd's Neck. The blue water was ruffled by a freshening breeze. The blue sky was set with snowy, marestail cloud. Green shores smiled. Yachts showed their slanting canvas, launches clipped the water. Overhead an amphibian plane made a great circle and was coming back against the wind. The varying rhythm of her engines came down strongly, but she looked as if suspended in the air, rather than beating her way into the breeze.

Manning saw the boats he believed to be manned by the metropolitan police, form an obtrusive and irregular, but powerful escort to their own launch. The commissioner had been wise. The boats, at least, were not ostensibly those used by authorities. They had been borrowed, or perhaps impounded from captured rum-running craft. He did not know enough about the scanty air fleet attached to the force, and hardly yet a distinctive branch, to be sure if there were any amphibians attached to it. He rather fancied not. He kept his eye on the plane. If it was hostile it would be hard to deal with. They would be as helpless as a crippled teal opposed to a hungry tern, if it attacked. Yet he could not believe that the commissioner had neglected the air as a source of danger.

From behind Kidd's Neck a long, low-hulled, low-cabined launch shot into the deeper waters of the Sound like a projectile. The hull was polished mahogany that gave off camouflaged flashes; the cabin was tan. There was a glitter of brass and glass. Two figures showed astern, one steering, the other reclining aft, shaded by fluttering awnings.

A small flag waved at the taffrail—red, white and blue. There was a short mast with radio aërial spreaders. Here, also, a pennant showed membership in the Power Squadron. Both men were in whites with white caps, visored, braided, set with yachting emblems of ownership and authority.

Manning's gaze was swiftly on the craft. He used the powerful binoculars that hung in the cabin. Curran surveyed him with the same quizzical, half amused regard. A look that had made Manning wonder whether Big Joe was not, personally, a good deal of a fatalist.

The man astern wore colored glasses and a black beard. It was trimmed in the fashion of Commodore Vanderbilt, a mode not unusual, especially among yachtsmen. The dark glasses were quite an ordinary precaution with many men. But Manning did not like beard nor glasses. They were devices that might be used for disguise. He was suspicious of anything not open and aboveboard on this occasion. He glanced about the cabin. The launch was equipped, as required by law, with various paraphernalia, including life preservers and fire extinguishers.

There was no sign of any weapon. There *was* no weapon aboard, but his own shoulder-holstered gun. He might never have a chance to use that. In the jungle a repeating pistol or rifle is scant use against a horde of savages attacking unseen, unheard, unexpectedly. There might be the same conditions here, with a stranger, more ravening beast than even the jungle bred, stalking them.

He came into the cockpit and casually asked to take the wheel.

"You might like to watch the engine," he suggested. "It's smooth, but it has a tendency to heat up while running."

Curran made no spoken comment as he obeyed, but Manning again caught his humorous glance, the slightest shrug of Curran's shoulders.

The mahogany-hulled launch had developed trouble of its own. Its bow wave lowered, its speed faltered and it dropped back. The convoy of four boats had not overlooked it. They now held a diamond formation, one ahead of the Curran launch, one astern, and one each to starboard and port, practically abeam.

Manning glanced upwards. The amphibian was too close, it seemed, to evince too much interest. It might be police, of course. Police planes were generally confined to going after offenders who flew below the civic sky limits or were otherwise nuisances, and to prevent escapes of "wanted" men over the State Line.

The commissioner might have hired or borrowed an amphibian as he had got the launches. Still....

Manning did not like it. His hunch made protest. Something in him, seated perhaps in his pineal gland, that least known of seemingly useless relics of evolution, acted like a coherer. A message thrilled in it.

Danger!

It came. Instantly, like bolts from a summer sky. A daring maneuver, perfectly conceived, and had unerringly been executed. Nothing could balk its swift, concerted attack.

The plane came hurtling down in an abrupt dive, twisting, as if it were going into a tailspin. It looked as if the pilot had suddenly lost control, but the moment and place of his disability was too pat to be coincidental.

THE FLIER was skillful. Manning saw his helmeted head peering and wished he had a rifle. His inner voice told him to shoot this man, to kill to prevent murder. His pistol was useless at that range. His voice could not carry above the roar of the plane, which barely straightened out before it lunged into the water, sending up spray, lurching with a seeming clumsiness that Manning believed an excellently timed and deliberate movement.

It sideswiped the police boat to port with its starboard, metal pontoon and capsized it, left it sinking, while its crew struggled in the water.

With prop revving furiously, the amphibian appeared to blunder between Curran's tender and the police launch directly ahead. It screened the latter from view. Those on it could not see what might be happening to Big Joe's craft. They were anxious to help their comrades, thinking the amphibian's acts accidental. A crash had seemed inevitable, and fatal. Water is as hard to smash on as land, scarcely more elastic.

Manning had reflexly drawn his gun.

He saw the mahogany-hulled launch suddenly abandon all signs of trouble. It came tearing up astern at tremendous speed. It was making sixty, seventy, miles an hour. Its bow lifted to the pace and showed its racing "step" as it caught up with the police boat as if the latter were a scow.

Manning saw several men swarming in its cockpit.

It was abeam of the police launch for only a second or so, but it left it a sinking shambles. Manning saw pale flame vomit from the cockpit. Shrapnel, sprayed by trained gunners, perfectly calculating speed and range, belched from a quick-firer. It spattered the cabin glass and shattered the upper-works of the official craft. The trajectory shifted and tore through the hull at waterline. The police who had swarmed out of their hiding place were mowed down, and the murder-boat rushed on.

The police boat to starboard started to swerve in to the rescue.

A lame leveret might as well have tried to outrun a whippet. The swift cruiser let out another link of speed and seemed to leap clear of the water like a thrasher whale. Its quickfirer was now silent.

Manning watched it come as a man in a kayak might watch a charging narwhal. This attack was not the affair of some lone, insignificant crank. Its conception came from a subtle brain; one backed by resources.

He had no time to follow up that thought. He poised his gun and fired—once—as the cruiser surged alongside, and was gone.

He saw one man fall back. He dimly glimpsed another hurl two objects, as a pitcher with perfect control might pitch two balls in swift succession.

They crashed aboard the tender. There was a tremendous, deafening explosion that sent Manning staggering from its impact, his arm across his face. The launch seemed to fairly split apart and dissolve into flying fragments in a cloud of black, suffocating vapor that came from the second bomb.

Manning was flung to the disintegrating floor of the cockpit and, without trying to stand, he shuffled through into the cabin which was filled with ignited gas and rushing flame. He dimly saw the huddled figure of Curran by the broken engine and clutched for him, his own flesh seared, his hair and clothes singed. He held his breath against the fiery blast that would annihilate his existence if it reached his lungs and dragged Curran outside, if the wrecked hull could be said to have exterior or interior left. Half blind, Manning managed to topple overboard with the man he had tried to save.

He slumped into the water, near the stern, striking out, grasping the stilled propeller, supporting the helpless body of Big Joe.

The police boats would come to the rescue. Manning's blurred gaze, looking upwards, saw a second plane coming from the land, saw the amphibian in flight, its decoy trick of being damaged successfully played.

The mahogany-hulled cruiser was coming back again, literally running rings about the police craft. The mahogany hull was veneered steel, so were the tan sides of the cabin. The glass was bulletproof. It swept once more close to the remnants of the launch, now burning like a pitchpine torch. From it leaned the bearded man.

He had taken off his glasses. His eyes gleamed above his prow-like nose. They seemed to radiate a devilish satisfaction. He poised an automatic as his boat passed the stern where Manning clung with his limp burden.

Deliberately he fired two shots. His eyes centered with deadly aim. The first sent a slug fairly between the brows of Big Joe Curran, already almost drowned, if not burned, to death.

The second shot flung its missile as Manning sank under water, still holding the propeller—still clinging to the body of Big Joe. If the bearded man had fired at him first he would have been killed instantly. As it was, the bullet struck the water at an acute angle and ricocheted harmlessly as the cruiser rushed on, thinking its mission complete.

A police boat came up. Manning and the dead man were hauled aboard. Far north, twin specks in the sky, soared the planes. East, throwing spray, javelining for the open sea, where it might turn north or south and dodge into a thousand hiding places, rushed the cruiser with the mahogany hull.

Manning's face was set and grim as they landed him on the private wharf that had belonged to Big Joe Curran who now lay shrouded under a spare sail from the boathouse. One more "imperial Caesar turned to clay."

MANNING LOOKED like a scarecrow, with the clothes half burned off him, his face and hands blistered or raw, eyebrows, eyelashes and hair singed. He paid no attention to his hurts. They could wait.

He cursed eloquently in Malay as he saw the police plane

following the amphibian, once more acting as decoy. The mahogany-hulled cruiser was speeding like a ball-carrier in a
broken field. Even if any other boats, now heading for the scene,
tried to intercept her, she could dodge them or riddle them.
The men aboard would stop at nothing.

Who were they?

Like lightning on a dark night there flashed a solution into
Manning's brain.

The Griffin might be in this! He was a prisoner, barely out
of hospital, reported broken in mind and body, not liable to live
long. The last word from a visiting committee, including prominent alienists and psychiatrists, was that his fits of depressive
dementia were becoming chronic, his cerebral cortices breaking
down. They thought there was an abscess in his brilliant, but
always abnormal, brain and a lesion might occur at any moment.
He showed no interest in anything and was a victim of profound
melancholia.

But—there might have been a final flash that linked up his
once superb, though warped, mentality. And he might well have
had a grudge against Big Joe Curran. It was quite conceivable
that he might have made a plea, through his attorneys, for re-
examination, hoping that if he could be proven sane, the law
would find that his madness at the time he committed his
hideous crimes palliated them, and would set him free.

That was a fallacy, of course. His attorneys would know that
the Griffin would never be turned loose again. The whole press
of the nation would denounce such a move. He was a monster.

But, in his increasing madness, he might have held that
insane idea. His reaction to failure would be revenge. Even if
he was a life captive his cunning might have devised some
means of discovering, of making a leak, even through the stern
rule of Dannemora. His aerie had been destroyed with his
organization, but he might still have resources hidden away.

The idea hammered on Manning's brain like a striker on a
gong. His hunch held that hammer. It was not to be overlooked.

Clews to the crime just accomplished might be unearthed at the penitentiary.

He climbed into his car and raced to the nearest village. He got through long-distance to the commissioner and told him what had happened; breaking through the Commissioner's shocked comment.

"I'm meeting you at Dannemora," he said. "Phone the warden!"

He added his hunch, his supreme belief, that the Griffin, for all his weakness, had contrived outside communication with agents who were still faithful to him—faithful, at least, to the Griffin's hidden gold.

"I'll take a plane," said the commissioner. "How will you get there? Shall I pick you up?"

"I'm driving," said Manning. "I'll be halfway there by the time you step into your plane."

Manning's commissions given him by the New York Police Department and the governor were still in effect. He was one of a very chosen few given the privilege of a police siren, a special license plate and permit.

He changed plates, switched from his usual Klaxon horn and went screaming along the highways—from Long Island to the mainland of New York State, speeding north to Dannemora.

The commissioner, barely ahead of him, was waiting, with the warden, both their faces grave. The commissioner had been warned, he had taken what he deemed adequate precautions, and still the death of the most prominent man in the State, so far as politics and police were concerned, would be laid at his door. He had lost two members of his force, killed outright. Five more were desperately wounded. For once he trusted that Manning's hunch was not entirely true.

The warden held the same desire, though he was confident the Griffin could not have contrived to escape. He was almost moribund; he had been well guarded.

"I suppose you want to see him," said the commissioner. "I

did, just now. I think you're wrong, Manning. He couldn't have managed this."

Manning was inclined to agree with him when he looked through the grating of the door of the Griffin's cell. He saw a huddled figure that looked like a bundle of rags, inert. But he knew that supreme madman. He had seen a shark's heart beat twelve hours after it had been taken from its body and laid on a ship's rail. There might have been a flash of satanic intelligence, now vanished, that had devised this supreme and final crime, even though there was no longer cerebration to realize he had triumphed once again.

"I'll go in," said Manning. "Alone."

The warden demurred.

"He might be dangerous," he said. "He attacked the last man who talked with him. An alienist from Vienna. The Griffin resented his examination—scratched him up before the guard overpowered him."

"I handled the Griffin once," said Manning. "Unlock the door. I'm armed, if it's necessary."

It did not seem so. The huddled figure did not move. It hunkered in a corner of the cell, arms limp, head on its knees. The once burning eyes looked like grapes from which the bloom is rubbed. The ravages of physical illness, added to the disease rampant in the brain, showed the effects of his downfall and incarceration.

HE LOOKED without recognition at the man who had run him down, defeated him. The flaming spirit had dissolved. Only once, as Manning ordered him to stand up, he seemed to snarl, as a stricken tiger might, showing tusks that could no longer rend. He got slowly to his feet and stood in the corner.

His shoulders were bowed, his mouth sagged. These were the features of the Griffin, the monster who had boastingly destroyed almost a dozen prominent and outstandingly useful citizens out of a mad wantonness that seemed bred of the very heat of hell. It seemed to Manning as if that face, proud as

Lucifer's was now like a mask of wax that was in dissolution, blurred, hardly animate.

Surely this derelict could not have....

A terrible thought smote him as he gazed. Smote like the chiming of a brazen gong.

He gripped the Griffin by his shoulders. The other struggled with unexpected strength and Manning shifted his hold. He surged forward, pinning his man in the angle of the cell's steel walls, his forearm across the captive's throat, compressing his windpipe. He called to the others to come in; a summons not needed.

Manning lifted the prisoner's long hair as the guard and the warden pinioned him.

"This is not the Griffin!" cried Manning. "Look at his ears! I have seen the Griffin's ears when we fought together. Pointed, feral, like a satyr's ears. Tufted with hair. This man is an impostor, a substitute. The Griffin has escaped!"

They stood as if stunned. Only Manning ruled.

"You. Who are you?" he challenged.

The pseudo Griffin was suddenly docile. Intelligence came into his eyes. They showed cunning.

"Okay," he said. "You win. You're Manning, I suppose? I figured this might happen, but I took the chance of being discovered."

"For money?"

"Sure. For *big* money. I needed it. For my wife and kids. I was broke. It looked like a dive out of a top floor for me. The Griffin said he'd see I got out, same way he did. With money. Now I'll take the rap, but my folks are fixed, anyway."

"What's your name?" demanded the warden. The man jeered.

"Wouldn't you like to know, so you could hound down my family, take away the jack that I've earned. Try and find out, if you can. I'll stand the gaff."

"H E ' S   A N actor, of course," said Manning as he and the

Commissioner sat with the warden in the latter's private quarters. "Selected because he looked like the Griffin. Some character actor out of work. Plenty of them released these days by the stage and the film companies. Now, let's find out how he got in—and the Griffin got out."

The warden looked uncomfortable, but he was resigned. This man Gordon Manning was a genius.

"It's beyond me," he feebly parried. "Go ahead."

"Did the Griffin have any visitors, aside from the regulation visit of the Penology Board?" asked Manning. "How about that alienist he attacked? The doctor from Vienna?"

"He was the only one," answered the warden. "We do not even allow the Griffin yard exercise, though he asked for it. He seemed in pretty bad shape, although he may have faked it. But we took no chances. He claimed that the shock of his arrest, in which he suffered great physical injury, caused by you, Mr. Manning, I believe, had cleared his brain. He demanded a re-examination."

"For the first time?" asked Manning.

"So far as I know."

Manning said nothing. He knew that the Griffin must have smuggled out a letter to Curran. When that failed he evolved another scheme that included revenge on Curran. They could dig that up. Right now he was interested in the alienist from Vienna.

"He named a Dr. Genthe, of Vienna," the warden went on. "Claimed Genthe would be glad to visit him. A man who had written treatises and books on mental cases, delivered lectures, a master authority on criminal mania. He wanted us to write him."

"Didn't try to pass a letter out?" suggested Manning.

"He knew that was impossible."

Again Manning said nothing, but he held his own opinion in the matter. If the Griffin had asked for the letter to pass through prison channels, he had his reason for it.

"I sent it," said the warden, "because I did not believe there was any such person. I wanted to prove that to the Griffin. To get his reaction to it. But we got an answer."

"Have you got that answer handy?" asked Manning.

"Of course. In the files. We got a letter, and a book, in German, by Dr. Genthe, treating of criminal psychiatrics. I don't read German, but I gave it to a physician, who said it was sound, but did not advance any new ideas. Dr. Genthe said in his letter that he had read about the case and was interested in it, but not to the extent of making a special trip to the United States. He added frankly that, if a big enough fee was forthcoming, he might be tempted. Also that there was a slight possibility of his making a visit here, to the Psychiatric Congress, in which case he would like to see the Griffin, though he was sure there had not been, and could not be any recovery."

MANNING GRUNTED. His burns were beginning to sting badly, but he hardly heeded them. His mind was in action.

"So, when he did arrive, this Dr. Genthe, you gave him an interview with the Griffin and the Griffin flew into a rage? Was there a guard present?" he demanded.

"Certainly." The warden seemed slightly nettled. "The doctor was given professional privileges, but we did not let him see the Griffin alone."

"Sure of that?"

"I've just told you there was a guard."

"The interview was in his cell?"

"No. In one of the hospital rooms. Dr. Genthe wanted to observe certain eye and nerve reactions. It was that that threw the Griffin into his tantrum. He was convinced nothing was wrong with him."

"So Genthe got scratched up? Get treated for his hurts?"

"No. The guard separated them. They had to put a jacket on the Griffin. Dr. Genthe made light of it. Said the Griffin was incurably mad, but was still an interesting case."

"May I talk with that guard?" asked Manning.

"Not now, at any rate."

"Quit?" asked Manning grimly.

"Yes. He went out West to take up an inheritance."

"He would," said Manning, mentally resolving to have the man found. It must have been he who had mailed a letter to Curran.

"There is no Dr. Genthe of Vienna, never was, unless I myself have gone crazy," Manning went on. "There also has been no recent Psychiatric Congress. It was nicely done. Someone planted in Vienna at the given address to answer the letter of inquiry in a manner calculated to nicely erase any suggestion of sympathy. The book was sound, but held nothing new. Not hard to have a work on that subject translated into German, printed—in a limited edition—sent over here, with a portrait of Dr. Genthe, as he appeared to the warden, for a frontispiece. Neither hard, nor remarkable, for a man of the Griffin's peculiar genius. And very disarming.

"The rest was easy. The Griffin has acted a part here, ever since he began to recover. He had two accomplices. The pseudo Dr. Genthe and the guard. A Dr. Genthe came in, and a Dr. Genthe went out, with a scratched face, half concealing it with a handkerchief, no doubt; though he was still disguised with wig and flowing beard, with the clothes that suggested the eminent Viennese psychiatrist. Worn by the man, chosen by the agent with whom the bribed guard had already communicated, picking a man from the thousands of unemployed actors who was a fair double for the Griffin. With miming ability, with the right background, he had only to be moody and maintain the deception while the Griffin walked out free in the clothes, the make-up, and the manner of Dr. Genthe of Vienna—and parts unknown."

The commissioner and the warden were silent, holding no doubt that Manning had spoken the truth.

The Griffin was free! The inhuman monster had been loosed

again upon the society it hated, its murderous fury inflamed with a desire to be revenged.

The news could not be kept secret. The Griffin himself would see to that. He would surely again use the press to publish his taunting messages. He would strike again—and soon.

"You coped with him before, Manning," said the commissioner. "I pray God you can do it again!"

There was real reverence in his apostrophe to the Deity. For both himself and the warden, the handwriting was already shining on the wall. They needed no Daniel to translate its message of their downfall.

Manning said nothing. He was consumed with a fire that ate at his very vitals, the flame of a spirit pledged to battle with evil. Evil personified in the Griffin who, it seemed, had hoarded resources and was once more free to use them for his hellish purposes.

Closeted Behind Guarded Doors with Judge
Carruthers, Gordon Manning Waits for the
Diabolical Griffin to Spring his Death Trap

G ORDON MANNING was on his way, afoot, to his Wall Street office from the down town gymnasium where he kept himself physically fit. His lean, long body strode along replete with vitality and purpose; his eyes were clear and keen as he acknowledged the greetings of those who knew him and others who did not possess that distinction, but recognized him from the publicity that had once again environed him.

It was publicity he was never eager to have thrust upon him, although the reluctance had nothing to do with the fact that the columns, topped with flash lines, carrying pictures of Manning, of the victim and scene of the latest tragedy that had shocked Manhattan and all the nation bore the news that Manning had lost in his first encounter with the maniacal monster known as the Griffin, recently escaped from Dannemora.

It was Manning who had sent him there after a series of desperate encounters; after the police had despaired in the quest and Manning had been called in by the police commissioner to cope with the fiendish madman whose devilish genius had murdered one after another of the country's most brilliant and useful men.

Achievement, progress, benevolence, all seemed to arouse the Griffin to an insane fury, as if he was indeed the fallen Lucifer, Son of the Morning, who now hated all that was honorable and noble, all that was good; with a brain inflamed, but of incalculable ingenuity, coupled with the venom of serpents spawned in the foulest spot in Hades.

There was trouble in Manning's eyes, there were lines in his deeply tanned, hawklike face, that had not quite been erased since the Griffin had been sent to the State Hospital for the Criminally Insane at Dannemora, Clinton County.

Now the Griffin was free; the monster was loose again—a creature of infinite evil—loose to plan and perpetrate his frightful purposes. Already "It" had struck and killed, despite the efforts of the police, warned by Manning; despite the last hour attempt of Manning himself to save the victim. It was Manning's intuition that had uncovered the substitute left by the Griffin in his cell while he made good his escape; a substitute excellent enough to deceive the prison authorities.

That availed nothing. The Griffin was out and he would strike again, with scanty and mocking warning. Until the Griffin should be heard from again, Manning's hands were tied. Every effort to trace clews in the last crime—the one in which the most powerful controller of politics in the State had been sent to a horrible death because the Griffin believed he had blocked his release from Dannemora—had utterly failed, vanished in thin air.

Traffic halted Manning on a corner where he stood until the light changed, gazing without especial interest into the window of a store that specialized in automobile accessories. The window was arrayed with devices for radiator caps, emblems suggesting flight and speed. They had, most of them, been designed by excellent artists. Here were eagles, Mercurys, greyhounds, figures of men and beasts in headlong career. Some were ultra modern and symbolical, zigzags of shining lightning, a poised arrow.

The latest design of all held the center of the display. A beam of light fell upon it, distinguishing it from the rest. It was made of golden bronze and it was exquisitely fashioned.

It was a Griffin, sometimes called griffon, or gryphon—the

*Mr. Silbi (The Griffin) entered, closing
the door carefully behind him.*

rapacious creature with four legs, wings and a beak, the fore
part resembling an eagle, the after part a lion. Portrayed by the
Greeks and Syrians and Romans, shown in the cathedrals of
France and Italy, in the temple of Antoninus. Herodotus
claimed that the one-eyed Arimaspi waged constant war with
them. Sir John de Mandeville described them as eight times
larger than a lion.

Terrible beasts that could crouch for leap or flight; tear with
talons and beak—supposed inhabitants of Asiatic Scythia—
emblems of cruelty and death. Fit emblem of the inhuman
monster who had adopted them for his title.

The device seemed alive in the ray of light. The sculptor who
had first modeled it in clay had achieved a masterpiece. It embodied force and swiftness, the ruthlessness of perfect coördination. It hardly seemed adapted for an ordinary car ornament.
It might have fitted a racing machine, or a tank of war. It was
beautiful, but terrible.

MANNING FELT a clammy finger tracing his spine,

offset by a swift tingling of his blood, as he regarded it. It was to him a symbol that challenged all of his manhood. It summoned up a vision of the Griffin from his brain, where it always lived, never entirely dormant.

He was not a man who suffered from nerves or he would long ago have perished; explorer, scientist, adventurer, ex-major of the Military Intelligence Department, survivor of a thousand hazards on the field, in the jungle, by sea and land.

That varying tremor that went through him was a hunch, a warning from his subconscious mind where he automatically filed his observations, where the leaven of his experience waited for release.

He was going to hear from the Griffin. Once again he would be challenged; hear the mocking voice or read the high-flown message, tinged with the exaggeration of a grandiose dementia, that announced the Griffin's next fateful enterprise.

It was no surprise to him to see among the letters his secretary set in front of him an envelope of heavy, gray, handmade paper, the address inscribed with purple ink in a bold hand that, analyzed, showed the writer to be arrogant, forceful and abnormal.

Manning did not immediately open it. He took the letter and looked out of the window of his private office at the lofting spires and towers of the world's greatest city—at the spidery stretch of a bridge that was a web of human genius.

The envelope was sealed with scarlet wax in which was imprinted the upper part of a griffin's body, rampant.

The Griffin's resources were being reassembled. His old aerie with its corps of experts in science and mechanics, held under the Griffin's thrall by his knowledge of their lapses against the law, had been destroyed. But the Griffin had proved that he still had followers, that he still possessed the master-key to power, money. Here was the old, too familiar, style of correspondence. The letter seemed to fairly quiver with hidden menace, as if it diffused a deadly odor.

It took a stout heart to break that seal, a stouter one to read the communication. But Manning did not falter though the lines in his face deepened and a white streak showed where his jaw was set. The look in his eyes was grim.

> DEAR MANNING:
>
> We have met once since my, shall we call it emancipation?—and we shall meet again. It cheers me to realize that you still have sufficient resource and enterprise to render you an interesting and rather amusing opponent in this game of ours, resumed after several months of idleness on my part. Idleness and recuperation, my dear Manning.
>
> It somewhat lengthens the scores against you, but I shall delay that reckoning. Without you there would be no opposition whatever to my plans. They would be but tedious means to my ultimate end. What that is, in detail, I may tell you some day, but not at present.
>
> Some day I shall eliminate you, Manning, when you cease to interest me. Meanwhile I have certain items to be balanced on my book of life. One of these I have checked off. You may be interested in the next.
>
> I find that by horology and hepatoscopy....

Manning lowered the letter. Hepatoscopy! Divination of the liver. That meant that this half-crazed, but eminently dangerous being was still practicing unhallowed rites, endeavoring, perhaps, to justify his crimes to himself by consulting the stars and the livers taken, smoking, from still living bodies. They might even be human bodies, Manning considered. The incarceration at Dannemora had not alleviated, but aggravated his madness.

The Griffin invariably cast the horoscope of his intended victim, deciding when the protection of the planets was weakest and their maleficence greatest. In these rituals he doubtless catered to his conviction that he was an agent of Destiny, so appointed by a supreme power.

Again Manning gazed out at the lower end of Manhattan, the mighty city that the terror of one man had once held in thrall and might so again. There had been times when dread of the Griffin, results of his crimes, had not only shattered the peace of society, but had rocked the foundations of the civic and financial worlds. He could do it again. His evil fame, his fearfulness, had been trebled by his escape. And they were looking to Gordon Manning to once again enchain this monster, to destroy him.

He should have been destroyed, Manning told himself. The Griffin was as inhuman as the creature Frankenstein created from the grisly relics of graveyard and dissecting room and endowed with vitality. The Griffin's mind was a charnel house. The judge who had sentenced him, much against his will, had told Manning that he lamented the law.

"He should be put to death," said the distinguished jurist, Bernard Carruthers. "There is no virtue in his living. He is of no use, save as an examination of his brain may teach scientists something. He should be put out of the way, painlessly and peacefully—perhaps without any preparation, anaesthetized out of existence, as one would chloroform a mad dog. Jurisprudence and science have yet to unite in a thoroughly modern code. Meantime we must uphold the present statutes. So long as he lives that man is a menace."

Carruthers had not spoken publicly, but Manning wondered what he thought now, with the Griffin out. Manning resumed the letter.

I find by horology and hepatoscopy that the propitious moment in which he will be eliminated is close at hand. His hour has struck.

In ancient lore, as doubtless you are aware, but may have forgotten, griffins were consecrated to the Sun. They not only were held to have drawn the chariots of Helios and Jupiter, but also the car of Nemesis. You will see the allusion.

There is a man to whom I am directly indebted for long weeks of suffering, a man who poses as an upright judge, one who tempers justice with mercy, who clamors for the establishment of new prisons which shall be humane, sanitary, and upbuilding....

The bold writing had now covered three pages. Manning turned the fourth. The "allusion" was very clear. He knew the name he would read.

Carruthers!

> Therefore this man, who so ruthlessly and arrogantly sentenced me, Bernard Carruthers, is now sentenced in turn. He shall shuffle off this mortal coil between dawn on Friday, the seventeenth, and dawn on Saturday, the eighteenth. He shall no more see the sun, nor the light of day.
>
> Not even your vigilance and ingenuity, Manning, may avert this reprisal. It will be amusing to watch your efforts. In the meantime you should be glad to know that my scattered organization is being reassembled. I shall again prove a scourge to the unworthy. I, the Appointed One!

In place of a signature there was an *affiche* of thick scarlet paper in the shape of an oval, embossed by the signet of the Griffin. Thus:

T H E   B I G   studio on the top floor of the building was silent and dark. Some light filtered in through the great north-light and dimly revealed its furnishings. Carved chests and chairs, a big refectory table. A yawning fireplace. A deep lounge, many cushioned. Faint glitter of arms on the walls, a suit of armor, vessels of polished bronze and copper. Rugs and draperies and screens. The typical studio of a successful artist.

The whole building above the ground floor was given over to artists; few of them successful, most of them commercial. It was an old edifice, but it stood in the commercial heart of the city on the corner of a main avenue and a one-way side street. That gave it two entrances. There was one elevator, but it did not run after ten o'clock at night. Nobody actually lived there except the new tenant on the top floor.

The original tenant, one of the family that owned the building, had been killed in a car accident in Europe. The studio had been left vacant, untouched. Depression came, the artist's relatives lost their funds. They were glad to let the place to the Mr. Silbi who took a lease, paid a good price for the furnishings and moved in promptly.

He was not often seen. Sometimes the janitor would see him gliding down the stairs after the elevator ceased running, a somber figure in a long cape with its collar well turned up and almost meeting the rim of a black slouch hat. His shadow looked like that of some great bird of prey, swooping on.

A beaked nose, dark, piercing eyes, a mustache and vandyke beard with hair untrimmed. The typical artist, eccentric, inclined to be theatrical, but generous with rent and a regular tip to the janitor, to whom he explained that an old servant of his would clean his studio.

Sometimes there were men—always men—who hurried up the stairs and knocked at the studio door; emerging late in the night. The janitor listened now and then, a little fearfully, but there was a heavy drape inside the door and he heard nothing except murmurs, faint sounds of music.

The door opened now, with the key in the hand of the tenant, Mr. Silbi. He entered, closing the door carefully behind him, sliding additional bolts he had installed. He turned a switch and lights came on in oriental lanterns of brass filigree that hung in chains from the high ceiling, their glow ruby and amber through the glass insets. The stars winked out above the big skylight, it became only a blank of blackness.

Silbi touched a button and music sounded, softly—curious, exotic strains. They suggested barbarian encampments, music and marches, dirges and triumphal chants. He touched off the kindling beneath the cannel coal in a large brazier in the fireplace and held his hands to the gathering flames for a moment as if he were cold, though it was only late summer.

Then he tossed off his cloak and hat; he shed the mustache

and beard and wig, all masterpieces of deceptive craft, and sank into a deep chair in front of the hearth.

It was the Griffin. He had found sanctuary here, a place in which to recoup lost prestige, to foster revenge, to plot evil machinations and arrange a fresh organization. His face showed the hollows, the emaciation of suffering, of physical and mental stress. But vigor still emanated from him. He was dynamic, capable of storing energy and discharging it. The memory of his misfortunes stimulated his inflamed brain, increased its phantasmagoria. His conceit was still colossal.

His face was far from pleasant as he warmed his hands once more. It might have been that of Iblis, Prince of Darkness, the fallen angel of the Moslems, smitten by the curse of God for refusing to prostrate himself before Adam. Iblis, smitten but defiant, brooding in hell while its flames cheered him. Nor was it all coincidence that Silbi, (spelled backwards) was Iblis. There was no name on the door or in the hall, but the Griffin had signed his lease with that title in one of his characteristic moods of subtle irony.

Presently he filled the bowl of a Turkish pipe with tobacco that was finely cut and contained a blend of hasheesh. He lit it and held the tube of the hubble-bubble in one hand as the smoke came through the rose-scented water, sweet and soothing.

WITH HIS other hand he picked up an object he had bought recently, the same radiator cap ornament that Manning had noticed. It appealed to the Griffin, but he frowned as he remembered the golden griffin that had once mounted an onyx base on the desk of his now destroyed aerie. The recollection of all came back, the circular steel chamber, the underground laboratories, the mute Haitian dwarf who had been his bodyguard, the serfs laboring to carry out his commands.

Manning had demolished all that. There would be a reckoning with him some day; meantime the Griffin would use him as the antagonist, without whom the game would lack interest.

He still possessed his hidden sources of tremendous, incalculable wealth. He had been free only a few weeks, but already he had exterminated one against whom he held a grudge—the man who might have freed him—or, so the Griffin had imagined in his grandiose dementia. He had already located some of his old slaves who had imagined themselves free men once again; brought them again under his thrall, forced to do his bidding because of the Griffin's knowledge of their lapses against the law; men trying to go straight, but caught again in his infernal net. Through them he would get others.

In forty-eight hours the judge who had sentenced him would cease to live. His death would prove that the Griffin was again regnant. Thousands would cower, millions shudder at the news.

He chuckled suddenly, a deep, ghoulish chuckle. Michael, the Archangel, had flung Lucifer, Son of the Morning, into Hades, but Lucifer had risen, a mighty insurgent, a power for evil. So would he.

He touched another switch and a board became illumined. Tiny globes showed constellations. The signs of the zodiac glowed. An inset wheel spun, slowed down, clicking. Again the Griffin chuckled.

"It is so ordained," he muttered. "The stars in their courses fight for me and against thee."

There was a steel cage behind a screen, blanketed, set on a stand. The Griffin moved the covering, opened the door and a white monkey, little smaller than a chimpanzee, but infinitely more graceful and agile, sprang out, clung to his shoulder, chittering before it leaped to the floor and ran and crouched before the hearth, warming its paws, looking at the fire with eyes sad and curious, with gestures almost human.

"Alfar," said the Griffin. "To-night I sacrifice you to the Cause. It will be a swift passing, if my genius has not forsaken me."

The white monkey turned and gabbled something. The Griffin went into another room. Here was his kitchen and his laboratory. Off that, his bedroom and bathroom. He put on a long garment of black silk brocade weft with a design in gold. The pattern was that of chimaeras, the griffins of China, whose images were set to guard the tombs of kings.

Next he unlocked a tall, shelved steel cabinet. With a metal spatula he took yellowish crystals from a glass vessel and smeared them on the surface of a banana he peeled and tipped. The crystals instantly dissolved in the juice of the fruit.

The monkey cried for the banana, reaching eagerly. The Griffin watched as the quadruman took one bite and almost instantly collapsed, curled up with its topaz eyes glazing before the fire they no longer reflected. It shivered once and lay still.

The Griffin chuckled again.

"I thank you, Alfar," he said. "Who knows but what, in your next incarnation, you may be a man and thank me for your evolution."

He tossed the rest of the fruit on the fire, put the carcass of the monkey temporarily back in its cage. Then he resumed his nargileh pipe and sat brooding while the flames cast lights and shadows upon his face, vulturish, like the features of some ancient High Priest of Egypt, the mystic power behind the throne of Pharaoh.

MANNING HAD talked more than once with Judge Carruthers in the latter's chambers during the trial of the Griffin when the Law, rather than the Judge, let him escape the death penalty because of insanity. He found no difficulty in securing a private interview and close attention when he disclosed the reason for his call.

The distinguished jurist was a man in his early sixties, florid, not unlike the portraits of Washington, save for the thinning gray hair on the nobly proportioned head. He was slightly portly, eminently dignified.

He had been recently proffered, and had accepted, the highest honor in the gift of the nation—a seat on the Supreme Court of the United States. He had contributed much to the cause of moulding old Common Law to modern conditions and to create a universal Code for the Union rather than the wide differences now existing between the States. He was strong in his condemnation of the prevailing prison system, with its unsanitary cells, the hard labor given entering convicts, largely young, with a big percentage of them high school and college-bred. He declaimed the word "penitentiary" a ghastly sarcasm. Judge though he was, he tried to temper justice with mercy, he was a supreme and constructive humanitarian.

That such a man should be swept out of existence at the peak of his career, the prime of his achievement, was a suggestion so colossally iniquitous that only a madman could have conceived the idea.

"I have not been altogether unexpectant of some such threat," said the judge, "ever since I learned of the Griffin's escape and his first murder of revenge. My hands were tied. It was another instance of where the Law is blind. Some day, medical jurisprudence will be both ethical and logical.

"The Griffin is a biological failure. Abnormal. He should have been destroyed, as a surgeon cuts out a cyst. What do you want me to do? I hardly think, with ordinary precautions, that the Griffin can reach me here. The apartment house is well run, with night and day protection against annoyance. I have my own servants, who sleep out. I eat meals prepared by my own cook. Couple these facts with whatever bolstering you propose, Manning, and I see no cause to worry. I place myself in your hands."

Manning made an examination of the premises, looked into the running of the Highland Apartments and the judge's own private menage. He found little in the way of upsetting Carruthers' idea of security. Little that was logical. But the Griffin was *not* logical. His schemes might be those of a maniac, but it was hard for a normal man to predict them, to fathom their infinite and fiendish cunning.

On the face of things the suite could be made a hundred per

cent proof. The apartment house was modern in its appoint-
ments and service, but not so much so in its architecture. There
were no stepbacks to its floors. The walls rose sheer. The judge's
suite was twelve stories from the ground, five down from the
roof. It had neither balconies nor fire escapes. The building was
fireproof.

"I want," said Manning, "to stay here from midnight between
the sixteenth and seventeenth until well after dawn on the
eighteenth. Dawn comes about five at this time of year. I shall
have the place surrounded, under cover, by detectives. They will
be outside in the lobby, on this floor, on the roof. Your servants,
when they leave for the night, will not be molested though they
may be trailed."

"They are good servants," said Carruthers. "I should not like
to have them annoyed...."

"I understand," said Manning. "I shall be here myself on the
inside. I am going to taste every mouthful before you do, meat
or drink, merely as a matter of precaution. And I am going to
be sure of the source of supply. That may seem superfluous to
you, but not to me. No need to do it ostentatiously, of course."

"I'm under your orders," said Carruthers. "I wouldn't mind
being bait for the Griffin if I could be sure of his capture. Such
a monster demoralizes the nation. They will take better care of
him next time."

"NEXT TIME," said Manning. "If he gives us a chance
to get to actual grips the only man who will have to take care
of the Griffin is the keeper of the Morgue. That's the way the
whole Force feels about it. So do I, an unofficial member. As
for your being the bait, you are the goat tied under the tree, if
you'll excuse the simile, judge; waiting for the tiger."

"And you," said Carruthers, "the chap in the machan; the
man up the tree. I trust you'll shoot in time to save the goat."

"I hope so," said Manning gravely, "if it comes to shooting."

It was late that night when Manning reached his own house
in Pelham Manor. He had been closeted with the police com-

missioner whose position and reputation was at stake already with the Griffin's last crime. Another successful attempt, aside from the sheer shock of failure, would mean a new commissioner.

Manning's commissions, both from New York City and the Governor of the State, were still in effect. The police as well as the public pinned their faith on his ability to once more cope with this cunning fiend. The commissioner had promised him entire coöperation. Fifty men were detailed, picked from the squads. The manager of the Highland Apartments was enlisted. His first reaction was to insist that Judge Carruthers leave, but they persuaded him not to do it.

"I wanted the judge to promise to spend the day at Centre Street," said the commissioner. "You might as well ask Fighting Bob Evans to come off the bridge at the battle of Manila. His Honor was offended. He's a bit touchy about his dignity and his duty. We can take care of him, if you'll help us. It won't do you any harm if we land the Griffin. Let us put our own operators on your elevators, on your telephone board, and in your lobby."

The manager capitulated. He pointed out that there was a vacant apartment across from Carruthers' suite, which made their arrangements perfect. Aside from the servants, no one was to be allowed to leave the judge's quarters and even they would be shadowed. No one was to be permitted in on any pretext. Provisions would come up in the dumb-waiter and be inspected by Manning.

He realized that merely tasting the food might not be protection. A slow-acting poison might get him, as well as the judge, which would suit the Griffin just as well. The Griffin had always been fond of suggesting that Manning ran equal risks. Now, more than ever, Manning knew that the Griffin hated him with deadly enmity, that his maniacal mind might suddenly decide to include him in the murder. He intended to take along an analysis kit.

He was served a perfect meal by his Japanese servants. Afterwards he read and smoked, trying to relax enough to get some sleep. But the same prescience of oncoming disaster, ever coming closer and closer, like a hungry beast stalking its quarry—the warning hunch that had come to him on lonely jungle trails—possessed him now.

He overhauled his analytical apparatus in his private laboratory, made some delicate experiments, but when he sought sleep it would not come to him.

He lay at last on a leather couch, in pajamas, a fan blowing air from a refrigerating atmospheric adjuster. The night was hot and muggy. Indian summer had come to the city.

At two in the morning the telephone rang sharply. He knew who it was. His spirit was tuned up, vibrant to that evil sending. He knew the mocking voice, deep, confident; but with a strident note that betrayed the abnormal. He heard once more the strains of exotic music.

"Manning?" asked the Griffin. "I have not as yet reconstructed all my methods, but the dialing system makes precaution unnecessary. I am close by. I am slowly getting reëstablished, Manning. The next time you pay me a visit I shall be better prepared to really welcome you, as a permanent guest, I hope.

"Your precautions are excellent, no doubt. It makes the game better worth winning. Only—you do not know my opening move, the fatal move, Manning." The voice broke off into low, diabolical chuckling through which the music sounded. "I trust the judge, as a lawyer, has made his will. If not, tell him to do so, Manning. Ha-ha-ha! Ho-ho-ho-ho!"

The mocking laughter ceased, the music died while Manning, still holding the receiver to his ear, sat with his face setting into a mask of grim resolve that, this time, the Griffin should not score. But still that inner tremor, as of an alarm, persisted.

AT ELEVEN o'clock on the night of the sixteenth Manning was admitted to Judge Carruthers' suite by the latter's butler, Roberts. Manning had already inspected the hidden guards, given final instructions. The protection seemed perfect, impassable.

"The judge is expecting you in the library, sir," said Roberts respectfully.

"Shall I show you to your room first?"

Roberts was the perfect servant. A tall man, partly bald, in regulation black trousers and jacket with a vest cut high and banded with narrow wasp-stripes of black and yellow. Silent and deft. He looked pretty muscular. He might, Manning speculated, be handy for defense.

The butler hovered in the well appointed guest room with its private bath, unpacking Manning's bag—though not the locked case that held the analytical kit—laying out pajamas, hanging up dressing gown and extra clothes, disposing of toilet articles with trained dexterity. Then he left.

Manning opened the window of his bedroom and gazed out. There was a car drawn up to the curb, opposite, another close by. They held plain-clothes men ready to spring to action. The protection force also included a police surgeon.

Roberts came out of the pantry as Manning entered the dining room, and ushered him through the big living room—off which was the judge's bedroom and bathroom—to the library. He knocked on the door and a dog barked.

"I didn't know we had a dog," said Manning to Roberts.

"No, sir. We didn't, sir. Not till yesterday, sir. It seems a car bumped 'im, down town, just ahead of the judge's car, sir. It didn't hurt 'im much though he was a bit paralyzed, as it were, sir. The judge took 'im to the dog 'ospital and they found no bones broken. He 'ad a collar, but no tag. So the judge advertised 'im and brought 'im 'ome, temporary."

The dog, a wire-haired terrier, still a trifle lame, leaped on Manning, who patted him as Carruthers rose to greet him. The judge proffered cigars, ordered Roberts to bring ice and charged water.

"I still have some authentic and licit liquor," said the judge, clipping the end of his cigar. Manning followed his example. The butler picked up the automatic table lighter and gave them lights before he went back to his pantry. "What do you think of my latest acquisition? I confess to a most irregular hope that my advertisement will not be answered."

Manning fondled the terrier behind its ears.

"Bathed it?" he asked.

"No. Seems tolerably clean. Thinking of fleas?"

"I knew a man in Africa," said Manning seriously, "who had a tame serval cat. Also an enemy. The cat prowled nights. One day it scratched the man and he died, nastily. The serval's claws had been enameled with venom. The terrier may be harmless, but it is an outside element. We don't want any outside elements here for at least thirty hours."

"You think the Griffin may have planted it in front of a car at precisely the moment my car came along, down town?" asked the judge with a smile.

"He would be quite capable of it," answered Manning. "I'm going to bathe it, particularly the claws."

Roberts helped him, found some creolin disinfectant, brought towels. The terrier sniffed a bit, but did not protest vigorously. Roberts was dismissed for the night. He would be trailed, but if he was in any way mixed up with the Griffin that trail would prove a blind one, Manning knew.

Meanwhile he was possessed with the idea that the dog's presence was not entirely accidental. He made a final interior investigation. The judge was in the living room that looked out over the park. In the north the sky flashed sometimes violet, sometimes green. The low mutter of thunder sounded through the windows, slightly open for relief. The night was even hotter than the one before. When the lightning flared the trees in the park showed flat, like stage scenery.

The judge read a while, announced he would go to bed. The terrier followed him. Later Manning, inspecting, found him curled up at Carruthers' feet, with a beady and vigilant eye that opened and closed as it recognized Manning as a friend. The judge slept peacefully.

Gordon Manning envied him; he knew there would be no sleep for himself until the dawn had come and a new one followed it.

The first dawn arrived with a quivering of the purple sky, a fluttering of the stars.

Then the lifting sun colored pink the man-made cliffs of the high buildings on Central Park, West. Manning watched the trees get green, the derelicts crawling out from among the rock ledges, the early riders cantering along the bridle paths.

He stripped and took a shower, dressed and assured himself the men from Centre Street were on the job. Roberts had returned when he got back to the suite. The dog was friskily on hand. The cook and maid arrived. Breakfast was served with the judge unruffled.

Carruthers had work to do, he told Manning, who was content to have the judge closeted in his library. He was expecting to move to Washington at the end of the month and was getting ready to render certain opinions to close his New York calendar.

THE HOURS dragged. Through all the sultry day Manning felt some unseen, inexorable danger waiting for its moment to pounce, to kill. Manning received hourly reports from the police, but he felt sure that the peril was already planted. It was like a bomb whose fuse was lit, the spark eating steadily towards the explosion. He could not believe otherwise that it must come from within and he could not place it.

The cook was a cheery, stout Irishwoman, incapable of treachery. Carruthers' household was well ordered, but the servants might be unwitting agents. Manning frankly explained the menace to Mrs. Moriarty, and she, though gasping and crossing herself, stood by, welcoming his analysis of the food. The maid and Roberts proclaimed themselves anxious to coöperate.

"I've heard, of course, of the Griffin; also of you, sir," said the butler. "I only hope you get him."

The terrier panted on a rug. The temperature mounted to a record. Carruthers, reading decisions, annotating, seemed the coolest of them all, transferring all responsibility to Manning's shoulders. He took a nap after luncheon. Manning wondered if he was a fatalist. He himself was not, despite his travels in the mystic East. He did not believe in magic—save as a manifestation of knowledge over ignorance—in horoscopes or divinations. But he felt the pressure of the hidden menace.

Dinner was served. Carruthers talked on his favorite topic, the inadequacy of the current law to meet modern requirements. Roberts was the perfect servant. Neither ate much though the food was well chosen. The dog refused its meal.

"It looks as if it was working up for a bad storm," said the judge. "It may relieve conditions. Suppose we have coffee served in the living room? It's the coolest place."

Roberts brought coffee, also liqueurs. Manning refused to have the windows opened. Fans did their best to alleviate the heat. At last, with fresh cigars lighted, the butler brought ice cubes and charged water.

"Is there anything else, sir?" he asked.

"I think not," said Carruthers. "Have Mrs. Moriarty and her niece left?"

"Yes, sir."

Manning watched Roberts go into Carruthers' bedroom to see that the bed was opened, all ready for his master's retiring. The butler bowed to the judge.

"I'll change my things, sir, with your leave, and go home," he said. "Unless you want me further?"

"I think not, Roberts, thank you."

There seemed nothing less than a few hours of vigil. But Manning knew that when all seemed most serene, the Griffin was most to be feared. He had exerted himself to the utmost.

He could see no flaw in the arrangements. Again he got reports from the police, vigilantly on duty.

Roberts left to change his clothes. It struck Manning as a little peculiar that the butler should have mentioned this ordinary function. It was only a small thing, but small things seemed to count, more and more as the time dwindled.

The terrier went to Carruthers, its tongue quivering.

"Thirsty," said the judge. "I'll get him a drink. Don't bother, Manning. There's a chilled-water faucet in my bathroom."

Manning had noticed the same convenience in his own quarters. He watched Carruthers pick up the dish that had been chosen for the dog and go into his bedroom. He returned immediately with the dish filled with water and set it back of a settee. The thirsty terrier lapped eagerly.

"Do you mind if I finish up these papers, Manning?" asked the judge.

"I'd rather you stayed right here, for a while," Manning replied.

THERE WAS a tension in his voice that made Carruthers' eyebrows go up, but he said nothing as Manning passed quickly to the outer door of the suite and, opening it, saw the door of the opposite apartment open silently. He gave a brief order to the two men stationed there, and returned to the living room.

"Roberts generally say good night?" he asked.

The judge nodded.

Manning felt that the automatic in his shoulder sheath was loose. He took the same chair he had been using, from which he could see the dog behind the settee by the water dish. Roberts came in to make his regular formal farewell.

"Good night," said Carruthers.

"Good night, sir. You're sure you don't want me to stay 'ere to-night, sir? I'm willing, though it looks as if everything would be all right, with Mr. Manning 'ere and all."

The judge glanced at Manning, who shook his head.

"There's one thing you might do for me before you go, Roberts," he said.

"Yes, sir. Of course, sir."

"Get me a glass of cold water from Judge Carruthers' bathroom."

Roberts had a ruddy enough face, but it changed to the hue of chalk. His eyes became fixed, bulging. His voice was hoarse. He stared at Manning with his whole powerful body tense. Then he relaxed. Manning's voice had been perfectly casual, the request ordinary.

"I'll get you some from the pantry, sir, with ice," he said.

"I prefer it chilled, without ice, from the house service," said Manning evenly.

The butler's thin lips stretched, parted, showing his teeth in what might be meant for a grin. His eyes shone maliciously.

"Very good, sir," he said, and marched into the bedroom.

Manning made a warning gesture to the judge. The butler came back with a filled glass. He offered it to Manning.

"'Ere you are, sir," he said with his eyes baleful.

"It's for you, Roberts," said Manning. "*You* drink it. You understand?"

Again the blood receded from the butler's face. It rushed back again. His eyes narrowed. He took a step towards the door.

"That will do you no good, Roberts," said Manning. "They are waiting for you to come out. How did the Griffin manage to plant you here? You'll get off easier if you confess. You didn't kill the judge, you see."

Roberts' features were convulsed with fury.

"Damn you!" he cried. "Clever, but not clever enough, Mr. Manning."

He flung the glass, contents and all, at Manning's face and whipped out a flat gun from his hip pocket with the precision of long practice. He fired at Carruthers in his easy chair. The weapon had a silencer, it made no more sound than the popping of a cork.

The roar of Manning's service gun drowned it entirely. The water had checked him for a split pulse-beat. He did not know whether or not that hesitation in his own draw had been fatal to Carruthers. His bullet struck Roberts in the shoulder and spoiled the butler's second shot, this time at Manning.

The impact sent Roberts staggering back to the wall, one hand behind him to steady him. Manning wanted to cripple, not to kill him.

"Drop your gun," he ordered sharply. The men from across the hall had heard the report of Manning's weapon and they were at the outer door, hurrying to the scene when the lights went out and the room was plunged into darkness, only relieved by the vague light that came through the windows. Roberts' groping hand had thrown the switch he knew where to locate.

He and Manning fired simultaneously. A bullet zipped over the latter's head as he crouched, expecting the attack, trying to get the butler against the window. He knew he had scored. He heard a curse and the fall of Roberts' gun. He had got him in hand or arm.

Then he saw him staggering, swiftly making for the big window. He fancied he meant to leap through it, glass and all. Once more Manning fired and the butler toppled just as the plain-clothes men broke in and blazed at the fugitive before Manning could stop them.

Manning found the switch and put on the lights, infinitely relieved to see Carruthers alive. The bullet had gone into the padded arm of the wing-chair, missing the judge by inches. Manning's lead had scored first, spoiled the assassin's aim.

Roberts was dead, riddled. The detectives put a rug over him. Manning had hit him in shoulder, leg and the right wrist.

"Get the Medical Examiner up here," said Manning. "I'm sorry you killed him, though I think it would have been a tough job to make him talk."

"The commissioner is downstairs," said one of the detectives. "Sergeant Morgan told me so last time I rang the lobby to report."

Manning nodded. He turned back the rug part way, then replaced it. He fancied there had been other, swifter means of Roberts killing himself than by jumping out the window when he saw the game was up. The Griffin would never tolerate failure.

The lucky shot in the wrist had prevented him from trying to get it, preserved it for evidence. But Manning was a stickler for routine. He would not touch the body until the examining surgeon came.

"I T WA S a diabolically ingenious device," said Manning. "The Griffin boasted to me once that the way to murder a man was to study his habits and take advantage of them. No doubt he has done so in this case. He knew of the chilled water supplied by the building for all bathrooms. No one but the judge would use the faucet in his bathroom. And he always takes a little bicarbonate of soda in cold water before retiring.

"So Roberts, or whatever his name is, mixed some of those yellow crystals from that little box we found in his vest pocket with grease and lined the *inside* of the faucet. Probably with his finger. You may find traces under a nail."

"But how did you discover it, man?" asked Carruthers.

"I didn't," said Manning. "I was convinced this was to be an inside job. I sent the table cigar lighter down to headquarters some hours ago to see if they could find a record of Roberts' finger-prints, which were nicely registered on it. We should have results almost any minute. Of course Roberts would have been shadowed again. I had no intention of letting you out of my sight, judge, until dawn came. But there seemed no harm in your getting water for the dog. It was the dog that saved you, Judge Carruthers.

"You put his dish back of the settee. You could not see it, but I did. I saw the dog drink. I saw it die, instantaneously. Its body is back of the settee now though it looks as if it was asleep, poor little devil. I imagine most of the poison—whatever it turns out to be, undoubtedly some alkaloid—dissolved immediately and entirely. There was only enough grease to hold the crystals in place. Roberts, of course, did not know that the dog was dead. I wanted to confront him with discovery to force the truth out of him by surprise, but he was a resourceful beggar."

"You saved my life a second time," said Carruthers. "He did his best to shoot me. Do you imagine the Griffin will warn me a second time?"

"There won't be a second time if I know anything of him," said Manning. "Remember, he is insane. Failure breaks him. Don't forget that he actually believes in his star readings and divinations. They have betrayed him. He will be infuriated. He will be dangerous only to himself for a while. Then he will strike again if we have not found him beforehand, but not in the same place."

The telephone rang. Manning answered it, listening attentively for two or three minutes.

"All right," he said as he hung up and turned to the rest. "They have traced Roberts' prints," he said. "They had trouble doing so because they were not in the regular files. They were part of the batch of prints the Department made at the Griffin's aerie when we captured him. Some of those men he had working for him got away. This was one of them.

"The Griffin has been rounding them up. You told me you could guarantee your servants, judge," Manning went on severely. "He was a good butler, I grant. But where and when did you get him?"

Judge Carruthers looked almost sheepish.

"My man, whose name was also Roberts," he said, "had an accident six weeks ago. He was hit and badly hurt by a truck. As a matter of fact he never recovered consciousness after he was taken to the hospital. I was informed of it by this man. He telephoned me. He said he was with my Roberts and was his brother. He is about the same build and not unlike him in a general way. He told me that before his brother lapsed into his coma the main thing that troubled him was my being without a man. He offered to substitute. He showed me references, from abroad. The whole thing was so natural I never had the slightest misgiving. As you said, Manning, he was a good butler."

"Good also at observing your habits and reporting to the Griffin," said Manning. "You felt that it was unlikely that the dog might have been bumped by accident, and I agree with you. It was Fate and your own good fortune that it was hit where you saw it. But Roberts' injury and following death in the hospital was not an accident by any means. Thank God we found things out in time."

"Thank God, indeed," said the judge. "I might have taken a drink myself before I gave one to the dog. As a matter of fact I did think of it." He shivered. "I think a different sort of drink might do all of us good, gentlemen. How about it?"

They were in the library together. The police commissioner, Judge Carruthers and Gordon Manning. The grim procedure had been gone through. The body of the pseudo butler had been taken away. The plain-clothes men still kept the vigil that was nearly over.

Dawn was coming, graying the sky. Carruthers raised his glass.

"Give us a toast, Manning," he said. "I don't know whether we should drink to your health for preserving mine or to the failure of the Griffin."

Manning lifted his own highball.

"I suggest," he said, "that we drink to the dog."

DAY OF DOOM

It Seemed That Even the Griffin's Fiendish
Ingenuity Could Never Pierce the Vault of Steel to
Get Manning and the Man He Guarded, and Yet....

T HERE IS an hour when the world's greatest city, the city that never sleeps, drowses; when its din is hushed to inarticulate murmurs; the hour when both night and day seem reluctant to exchange their tasks; when the vitality of sleepers is lowest and they stir in uneasy dreams.

The hour of crime, of fugitive crooks and furtive murderers; of mysterious night prowlers, when the shadows are deepest and justice least alert.

Mists shroud the mighty towers and spires of Manhattan; the tide, in its twin rivers rolls strong and sullen under the veiled stars, past the frowning penitentiary at Ossining where convicts twist and moan in cells little larger than a kennel, or start awake with a shriek from horrid visions, dreading to hear the slow steps of the warden—and the priest—to know their last day dawning, all too soon.

A long black sedan with its headlights dimmed, gliding from south to north, from the all-night ferry to the slow-beating heart of the metropolis, swung off the main avenue to the one-way street. Just around the corner, it braked at the side entrance to an old building that still seemed to stand, stubborn and resentful, amid the modern edifices.

The driver sat like an automaton, in sable livery, the peak of his chauffeur's cap well down over his saturnine countenance. A man descended, cloaked from chin to knees, dressed all in black. Under the wide rim of his slouch hat features showed deathlike in their pallor and rigidity; black hair hung low inside the upturned velvet collar; black Spanish beard and mustachios, black eyes that glittered, and a nose like an eagle's beak.

He turned for a moment to speak in a strange, uncouth tongue to a passenger, then seemed to swoop into the dark recess of the doorway.

There was the click of a key and he entered a hallway with cracked floor mosaics, walls where the paint was dingy and the plaster falling. Stairs led upwards in the gloom. An elevator cage, closed for the night, was on his right.

He pressed the button of a bell beside a door next to the stairway. Its sharp ring below was like a spark in the night that burned and died.

Above the ground floor the building was rented in studios to struggling artists who worked there by day when there was work to be done. None lived there but this man, on the top floor in a studio suite that was exotically luxurious compared to the rest, furnished with the fantastic gleanings of a painter who had met swift tragedy abroad. The cloaked man had leased the dead painter's rooms, bought his furniture complete, adding to it certain possessions of his own.

The elevator ran only from eight in the morning until eight at night. The brother of its colored operator was the only person now in the building. Janitor and watchman in one, he styled himself superintendent.

Usually the cloaked man used the stairs. The other lessees did not see him, only the janitor who cleaned his studio and sometimes fearfully observed his somber shadow on the walls, swooping up or down like a great vulture, seeking corruption. Always between midnight and dawn.

THE JANITOR appeared from the cellarway, his eyes rolling, his manner humble.

"You been away, Mr. Silbi?"

The deep voice of the man who had signed the lease as Silbi, boomed and echoed in the shabby hallway.

"Yes. I've been away. But I'm back. I trust I shall find all as I left it. I have brought back somebody who will clean my studio and attend to my wants after this. You shall be no loser by it. I know your pay is small. I shall continue my addition to it. We will call it a gratuity, a tip. Here is what is owing you for the past weeks—since I have been away."

The janitor received the bills obsequiously.

"Anything I can do, suh?"

"Yes. This person I have brought is somewhat of a cripple. He cannot walk, at least upstairs. You can run the elevator for us?"

"Yes, suh. It's down below. I'll connect the current an' bring it up."

He dived down to his basement. The man called Silbi went to the doorway and whistled, as he might have whistled to a dog. The street lights gave him a sinister appearance, mysterious and unearthly. Spell his name backward and it became Iblis, Prince of Darkness, who was smitten of God for refusing to abase himself before God's creation, Adam.

Here indeed was a being who bowed to no man, who loved no man, and warred on all humanity; in whose abnormal brain brewed machinations as fiendish as any plotted in the council hall of Hades.

The chauffeur reached back to reopen the door. A creature swung from the car and scuttled with horrible agility across the sidewalk to its Master. It had the body of a man. On the chest and shoulders that might have belonged to a gorilla there was set a head little larger than that of an infant, that looked somewhat like the head of a monkey, something like that of a bulldog. It was unclad and entirely hairless.

The body ended at the hips. The creature propelled itself like an ape, on the knuckles of its hands. At every propulsion of its long and muscular arms the body swung clear, like a pendulum. If Iblis was its master, surely here was the familiar of that fallen angel, a thing misspawned in some fetid nook of hell.

"There is nothing to be afraid of,"
said Silbi. "He is human."

The janitor, stepping from the elevator he had brought to the level of the floor, stood aghast, his skin turned gray.

"There is nothing to be afraid of," said Silbi. "Speaking widely, he is human. A freak. But not dangerous, as a rule. What he has of body is tremendously developed. Nature has done her best to compensate. Not so strong of brain, but it has had little room to develop. Quite intelligent, far more so than a chimpanzee. And very useful. *Very useful.* He will not bother you so long as you do not bother him. He cannot understand what you say though he can speak, childishly and ungrammatically, in his own tongue."

Mr. Silbi spoke with a sort of pride, as if he had himself created this amorphous thing.

"He got a name?" asked the janitor, his curiosity bettering his awe. "He lose his legs in an accident?"

"A name? Hardly a christened one. His parents disowned him. His mother left him in a sack when he was a few hours old. I imagine she was too frightened to strangle him. You see, he was born without legs and that head of his must have been very small and rather alarming at that time. I rescued him from the ignominy of being exposed as a freak. I bought him from a sideshow."

"That mighty good of you, Mr. Silbi."

"Ah! Philanthropy is usually selfish at base. Suppose we call him Al. Not short for Alfred or Albert. Al was one of a very gruesome and impure group of demons in Persian mythology, found sitting in sandy places, plotting beastliness. I think Al is a very good name for him. Come, Al."

THE CREATURE half hopped, half swung into the elevator, squatting there, grotesque and obscene, as the lift ascended.

"I expect a visitor, soon," said Silbi. "You might let him use the elevator. He can walk downstairs," he added, and the sentence was a statement of fact rather than a suggestion.

Al followed his master into the vast studio, three high rooms made into one, others adjoining. His restless eyes took in the curious conglomeration of carved furniture, weapons, a suit of armor, lamps swung from the ceiling with amber and ruby lights, lounges, deep rugs. On a desk there was a globe of crystal. Low, weird music started to play as the lights went on. Incense rose. Stars shone golden on a field of black where the signs of the zodiac slowly circled, emblazoned in silver inlay.

The man whistled again and snapped his fingers. He preferred to communicate with Al by signs rather than promote his intelligence, if that were possible. He led the way to a tiled room that seemed part kitchen, part laboratory. There were locked steel cabinets against the walls. Next to the room was a closet with a high skylight.

"I'll get a cot for you, though you hardly need it," Silbi said aloud. "Rugs would be better, with a cushion or so."

He motioned for Al to stay there and the deformed creature fawned on him, stroking the hem of his cloak. Silbi locked him in, returning presently with a rug and a pillow. Al lay on his back, lumpish and inert. Silbi left him there.

In the main studio, Silbi stripped off his cloak, long-haired

wig and artificial beard and mustachios. He filled a Turkish
hubble-bubble and seated himself to smoke before the fire of
cannel coal. By its glow his face looked more than ever sinister,
Satanic.

There were signs of suffering there, and ever-snarling hate,
close to the surface.

It was the face of the incarnate fiend in human form known
as the Griffin, the being whose killings of distinguished men
had terrorized a continent, a monomaniac of murder.

He picked up a radiator ornament from a tabouret and
fondled it. It was a casting in golden bronze of the fabulous
creature whose name he had adopted; half eagle, half lion,
symbol of swiftness, rapaciousness, cruelty. He held it as a talisman, remembering bitterly the aerie he had built, where there
had lain a golden griffin as a paperweight upon a great table in
his circular room of steel.

He remembered his slaves who had worked for him in subterranean caverns, bound by his knowledge of their guilty pasts,
scientists, artisans and artists. He remembered endless days and
nights in Dannemora, crippled, celled. He remembered the
man who had shattered his organization, cast him into prison.
Gordon Manning.

His face grew more cruel, more like the profile of the sculp-
tured griffin radiator cap. Then, as he mused, a look of devilish
contentment supplanted wrath. His newest plans were matur-
ing. Soon he would challenge civilization again, challenge
Manning to a game of wits and action.

The tobacco in the bowl of the Turkish pipe was mostly ash,
the smoke bubbled slowly through the perfumed water, when
there came a knock upon the door.

II

THE GRIFFIN had refilled his hubble-bubble, deliberately, while his visitor waited, ill at ease, tall and gaunt,
a haunted look upon his sensitive Latin face.

"Ah, Raspetti," said the Griffin at last. "Guido, my good Guido, I am well pleased with you."

"*Signor,*" replied the man, speaking in Sicilian dialect. "That name is forgotten. I am Pietro Volenta."

"As you please. Let us trust the other name is forgotten. There is only one in this country, outside of your wife and perhaps your children, who knows of Guido Raspetti. Pietro, then; our little experiments have been very successful. Soon they will achieve their ultimate purpose."

"Dear God, *signor!* You have not—you will not...."

"Did you think I used your skill to kill a cat? You have well earned the money I promised you. I shall send it to your family. It is only for them you exist?"

"I will take it to them, *signor.* I..."

The Griffin checked him with a gesture.

"Pietro. You can never tell. Something might happen. I might have another errand to send you upon."

Raspetti stiffened, slumped to an attitude of desperate pleading.

"*Signor,* if I have done well, dismiss me. Ask no more. Always I have dreams. My head burns and spins. Sometimes I think I shall go mad."

"If I dismiss you, what would you do? Return to the position in which I found you, or rather refound you, after my—illness?"

"I do not know if they would take me back. But I can get another. I am an expert analyzing chemist. I...."

"Also an expert toxicologist. In medieval times the Borgias would have protected you—as I protect you—they would have proclaimed you the perfect poisoner. Even in their day such secrets were known, brought from the Orient by Marco Polo. Pietro, or Guido, if they knew in Rome that you were here, even my power could not save you. If you are going mad, how can I let you go? You have that fatal complaint, a conscience. Some night you will babble my secrets, you will confess them to your wife, or to a priest. And I do not trust either priests or women.

Your formula has been tested. It establishes your research, your wisdom. It answered to the day, aye, almost to the hour. You have killed again, by proxy. So...."

"Signor. I would not betray you...."

The Griffin's sensitive nostrils widened, his eyes were arrogant and luminous.

"No. I do not think you will betray me. You say your head spins. I have a cure for that. Behold this globe. Gaze on it, Guido. *Gaze!*"

The crystal orb clouded and then was shot with sudden fires. They whirled in spirals, changing like a kaleidoscope. Raspetti's look became a fixed stare. Again he stiffened in his chair, clutching it by its carven arms. Such a chair as Cesare Borgia himself might have occupied.

"So," said the Griffin, softly but with infinite force. "So, my Guido. I will cure your headache. Your brain holds too much. You shall not betray me. Relax, Guido, relax, and listen...."

The Griffin leaned forward, his look compelling.

"When you leave me, Guido, you will walk down the stairs, very quietly, very carefully. If you think anyone sees you you will pause and not go on until the way is clear. Thus to the street, thus to Fifth Avenue. The subway is running now. There will be few to enter or alight. You will look forward when you hear the rumble of the train, like a dragon in a cavern, its green eyes gleaming. So—you lean out, your foot slips, you *fall*, before the oncoming monster. And that, Guido mio, will be the end. The end! Now go."

The hypnotized man arose, moved like a sleepwalker to the door. The Griffin listened to his retiring footsteps, along the hall, softly down the stairs. Then he closed his portal and returned to his water pipe.

The coals flickered and made wavering, changing arabesques of light and shadow on the walls, the vapor from the herb bubbled through the rose-scented water; the incense, fragrant of amber, wisped about the great chamber while the exotic music rose and fell, swelled into a barbaric chant, dwindled to a desert lullaby.

The Griffin roused himself at last.

"He has gone into limbo," he muttered. "He was useful but he outlived his utility."

He moved to where the stars shone and the zodiacal belt gleamed, on the sable setting, turning the crisp leaves of parchment in a tome that was bound in heavy leather.

The Griffin was casting a horoscope, choosing a day for murder when the stars might be favorable to death.

GORDON MANNING, explorer, ex-Major in Army Intelligence, now, by avowed profession, consulting attorney, sat in the library of his own house at Pelham Manor. He had forced his mind to the solution of certain legal problems and he set aside the papers somewhat wearily.

He had been commissioned by the New York Police Commissioner and Governor of the State to combat the Griffin after the police had failed. It had been an arduous task to which he had often thrilled, of which he had sometimes despaired. He had unearthed the monster, had seen him sent to the State Institution for the Insane at Dannemora, when he should have been destroyed. Now the Griffin was loose again. Twice he had struck; once he had killed, once Manning had foiled him.

Manning's commissions were still in force, he was still the champion against the madman, a modern St. George, but it was an unequal combat, one that never let up. He fought against one whose brain, inflamed by insanity, was superhuman as a maniac's strength.

The Griffin chose to style it a game. In his conceit he named his victims and the day of their death, but only after he had made all his plans.

It was weeks since he had returned to his hidden lair, weeks in which his craft had plotted a killing which, this time, must be perfect. Failure would break him down, destroy his always excited coördination. Once before it had led him to collapse after strenuous encounters. But that had been at the end of tremendous stimulation. Since then, the Griffin had rested.

Soon, very soon, he would leap once more, winged, almost invincible.

In lonely places, where danger crouched, Manning had perfected his senses to super-reception. He was attuned to the vibrations of evil.

He reached for his pipe, for charged water, ice, and the decanter of good liquor set out by his Japanese butler. He mixed himself a long, cold drink, sipped it, raised a match to his pipe. Even before the sound was manifest to the outward ear, he knew the telephone was ringing; knew who it was on the wire at that hour of the night.

"MANNING? IT is the Griffin. Need I tell you? You scored in our last encounter but it was a fluke. This time there will be no flukes. I have done much in the past weeks, Manning. I have practically reorganized my corps. Even now, Manning, I am cutting in on your wire as I used to, so do not waste time in trying to trace me. On my part, I shall be brief, for it no longer amuses me to talk to you. I think, Manning, that you annoy me.

"If I decide so, I shall annihilate you also after I eliminate Haydn Shirley, on the twenty-fourth of this month. Twenty-four hours on that twenty-fourth day, Manning. In one of them he will cease to exist. You may accompany him across the Styx. Your horoscope does not indicate entirely his amount of peril, but the signs are sufficiently malignant to indicate that you may no longer furnish me with even a halfway satisfactory opponent.

"Until the twenty-fourth, then, five days from now, farewell! My only fear is that when you inform Haydn Shirley of his certain demise, he may disappoint me by a premature collapse. I trust not. I have designed and arranged a somewhat spectacular death for him. He has the instincts of a weasel but the heart of a mouse.

"He pretends to be a philanthropist and uses charity as a

cloak for his chicanery. Even you, Manning, can hardly defend him in your mind, though I trust you will endeavor to do so with your body.

"Good night—and pleasant dreams...."

The deep voice died away. The weird music that had been its background swelled suddenly like an organ. Then that subsided as Manning sat with the telephone arm still in his hand. There was a burst of mocking laughter and—silence.

Haydn Shirley! The multi-millionaire. He had endowed many institutions, he was ardent in the cause of prohibition, of the suppression of vice. He controlled the rubber industry. Haydn Shirley!

The untimely death of the man would complete the depression threatening the land. Securities would tumble, including the Shirley holdings. The foundations he had established would suffer. It would be a national disaster!

The Griffin might have been bitten by participation in Shirley corporations.

It did not matter. If Shirley died incontinently, hundreds of thousands, already harassed and impoverished, might find themselves destitute.

A hard man to reach. Surrounded with guards who might scoff at Manning's warning.

Manning called Centre Street and got an inspector. His name and reputation insured the connection he wanted. The home of the commissioner was equipped with special alarms. Soon the head of the police was on the phone.

"Haydn Shirley! Good God, man, you don't mean it! I don't know. The best thing to do is for me to come straight to you. Shirley is at Haydn Manor, on Long Island. We'll get through to him, somehow."

III

IT WAS no easy matter, getting through to the elderly plutocrat. The grounds of Haydn Manor were walled, the walls topped by spikes. There was a gatekeeper, and all of the men working on the gardens were part of his retainers intended primarily to preserve his privacy, rather than his life. There was a butler who was harder to convince than a king's sentry; secretaries who declined to transmit messages, who had blocked any attempt to reach Shirley by telephone.

The chief of these, when they had at last won to him, seemed frankly cynical of the suggestion that Haydn Shirley was in physical danger.

"We have our own precautions," he said. "They have proven eminently satisfactory so far. We do not care for the interference of the police authorities, nor do we need their protection."

His manner toward the police commissioner was condescending. He clearly regarded both him and Manning as unwarranted intruders whose persistence should be snubbed. Manning had advised the commissioner, who did the talking, not to mention the Griffin unless it became imperative to do so. The Griffin had got past defenses as adequate as these. He might have an agent now on the premises.

The secretary's manner got under his skin.

"You have been warned," he said. "I am Gordon Manning. If the Griffin should succeed in adding Mr. Shirley to the list of his victims, your attitude should entitle you to be cited as an accessory to the crime. We are not here to try and sell protection in any form nor to impress Mr. Shirley with the efficiency of the force. I tell you, my man, his blood be on your head!"

The secretary fell back a little. His face blanched slightly and his eyes widened at the name of dread.

"The Griffin?" he faltered. "Of course, Mr. Manning...."

Manning cut him short.

"The Griffin, following his usual habit," he said, "has notified me that he intends killing Haydn Shirley on the twenty-fourth of this month. It is true that I foiled his last effort, as you are doubtless informed through the press. It is equally true that I may not be able to prevent this attempt, which will surely be made. Sure also that the Griffin's plans are perfected. However, since you seem willing to accept the responsibility, there is nothing for us to do but leave."

The secretary stammered an apology, broken off by the querulous voice of an old man speaking from a gallery that ran across one end of the room where they had been at last given an audience.

It was Haydn Shirley. He was thin and bent, his face was lined. His eyes, deep-socketed, were his outstanding feature. He clasped the rail of the gallery balustrade with veined and corded hands and barked down at them. Manning detected fear in that bark. He fancied the trembling hands were not normally so palsied. Haydn Shirley was not a feeble man but Manning knew he was a frightened one.

"What's this? What's this I hear?" he snapped. "The Griffin! I'm coming down there. Richards, are you sure you know these two men?"

"Mr. Gordon Manning and the New York Police Commissioner, sir," said the secretary deferentially.

"Ha! I'm coming."

There was a wait while he disappeared and then entered the room. He was more than merely well dressed. His clothes suggested the dandy. Other men Manning had tried to protect had been courageous. Haydn Shirley wilted, physically and morally, as he listened. The light went out of his eyes, his skin seemed to dry, and though he thrust his hands deep in his pockets, he could not control nor conceal their shaking. His voice became a squeak.

"Kill me, on the twenty-fourth? It's incredible. Why, that's my birthday! Good God! They say the Griffin casts horoscopes to discover when a man is vulnerable. Why…? Look here, Manning, what do you propose to do? What can I do? I don't want to die. I can't die. I have much to do. Important things. Important for other people. The world can't afford to have me die yet, Manning! Mr. Commissioner! I want to live. I want to live!"

MANNING NOTICED the secretary, Richards, gazing at his employer with a peculiar expression. He was seeing the man he had almost defied exposed, stripped of dignity, whimpering like a child in a dark room, his quivering hands now clinging to Manning's arm. He had been hedged about with privacy but he had never feared assassination. Now his ego crumbled.

"The one thing to do, Mr. Shirley," said Manning, "is to secure your safety for the twenty-four hours in which your life is threatened. I am sure you are in no danger until midnight on the twenty-third, I do not believe you will be in any danger, if you are still alive, on midnight of the twenty-fourth."

Haydn Shirley cringed at the plain words—*if you are still alive*. His chin was trembling, his grip on Manning's sleeve became despairing, like the clutch of a drowning man.

"If we can foil the Griffin," Manning went on, "we shall convince him that he is fallible in his methods, we shall pierce the armor of his colossal conceit. He will not attack you again."

"Yes, yes," mumbled Shirley, his own morale destroyed. The potentate was only a puppet. "We must find some place where it is impossible for anyone to reach me. Not here." His uneasy glances darted about the place, rested with suspicion on the secretary. "Not here. The Griffin, as you say, may have made his plans already, to conform to my habits. He may have spies here. I may have traitors close to me. Why"—he sank his voice to a whistling whisper, waving his secretary to a distance—"if those close to me *knew* I was going to die on a certain date they could reap a fortune, a fortune! Think of some place, Manning, for me to stay—not alone. You with me. Some place utterly impregnable."

There was no courage in him, but there was cunning. The brain that had piled up millions was now, after the first shock, concentrating on this problem.

"I have it," he said. "Look you, Manning, Mr. Commissioner, see what you think of this. We have vaults in the Shirley Building, specially constructed. Burglar-proof, bomb-proof, fire-proof, even earthquake-proof. The last word of experts. There is a central room there where valuable papers may be shown and private matters discussed in secret and absolute safety. Access to it is guarded by the time-locks on the entrance to the vaults.

"There are guards outside. They can be doubled, tripled. The Treasury itself, the Mints, are not better protected. The twenty-fourth, my birthday, falls on Sunday. From Saturday until Monday, the time-locks hold the vaults inviolate. I will stay there, in the conference chamber—you with me, Manning. You will be armed, but there will be no need. I shall fast for those twenty-four hours. I will not touch food or drink of any sort. I will not smoke. The Griffin did not think of my vaults, gentlemen. He did not think of my vaults."

He had attained confidence, but it was not complete. He looked for assurance and the commissioner gave it to him.

"If the vaults are all you say, Mr. Shirley, we've got the Griffin stopped. And, as Mr. Manning points out, another failure might make a raving lunatic out of him again, instead of an insane genius. Will you consider Mr. Shirley's suggestion that you remain with him through the zero period, Manning?"

Manning nodded. He had not mentioned it, but he had not forgotten the Griffin's personal threat to him. And he did not think the Griffin had overlooked those vaults in the Shirley Building, invulnerable to attack as they might be.

"It sounds convincing," he said, "but there must be no mention, no suggestion, made of your purpose."

Haydn Shirley glanced again at his secretary. His narrow lips closed even more tightly.

"I will attend to that," he said grimly.

"And I will attend to matters on the outside," said the commissioner, "while Manning stays inside with you. There won't so much as a mouse get through the cordon I'll set round that building."

I V

THE CONFERENCE chamber, set as it was in the heart of metal even harder than chilled steel, was safer than the control room of a battleship. There were doors twenty inches thick containing twelve-inch plates of pure copper that conducted heat away too rapidly for the entire body to be raised to fusing point and rendered even oxy-acetylene torches inefficient while the ductility of the copper resisted explosives. There were walls of concrete reinforced by steel plates attached to the inner faces by rag-bolts. There were combination locks and four-movement time-locks, each combination known but to one man.

Attempts at unlawful entry released gases, flooded approaches. Invisible rays played sentry.

After minute inspection Manning was assured that the Griffin was absolutely baffled in any attempt to penetrate to the interior of this fortress where he and Haydn Shirley were to stand siege for the twenty-four hours between midnight of Saturday and midnight of Sunday. Actually they would be pent-up for a longer period—from six o'clock on Saturday night until nine on Monday morning.

The chamber was furnished with comfortable chairs and couches. There was excellent ventilation, outside communication through telephone; a lavatory. There was a buffet supplied with charged water, and stronger refreshments for privileged users, also a frigidaire. Additional comforts had been provided for the occasion in the shape of cots, bedding; and food for Manning.

Haydn Shirley persisted in his resolution to touch neither liquid nor solid nourishment, no matter how he might thirst or suffer hunger. Manning imagined he had little appetite. Certainly he had lost weight, little as he had to spare, in the past few days. He did not even propose to smoke. He would sleep, and read.

They could send out an alarm, but nothing could be done to reach them until the time-locks automatically released them. Only two employees knew that Shirley was passing the week-end in the vaults, with another unnamed man. These two assumed that this was some special conference, some vital discussion of a project that might shake the world's markets.

Nothing could reach them here. They were definitely and absolutely insulated from all danger from without, and Manning made certain there was none within. He knew his own life was threatened, but he did not go to Shirley's extremes of total abstinence. He had his service gun, though its possession seemed the sheerest folly.

Yet he was not content, though he simulated perfect assurance for Shirley's sake. An inner warning persisted as the hours passed, the hands of the electric clock registering the decreasing limit of the twenty-four. Haydn Shirley, on the contrary, seemed to absorb a confidence that Manning's logic told him he should share—but could not.

"Two hours more," said Shirley, as he looked at the clock. "Science has proven superior to a madman's dreams. The Griffin did not know my resources."

H E   W A S   almost jaunty, and rallied Manning upon the latter's gravity.

"It looks as if we had completely foiled him," Manning agreed. "Nothing living, no extraneous agency could hope to enter here. I will admit that I had some doubt as to the ventilation until I saw the ingenious device of merely renewing the freshness of the air contained here. But," he added, "I have made it a lifelong habit never to halloo until I was out of the wood."

Shirley grinned.

"You're a pessimist," he said. "I'm going to sleep."

Within five minutes he was slumbering while Manning

grimly watched the clock. There were still one hundred and fifteen minutes, still nearly seven thousand seconds....

He filled his pipe and smoked. At midnight he could end his vigil. The Griffin prided himself upon living up to his predictions. Accuracy was part and parcel of his scheming. The minute hand crept on. Ten-fifteen, ten-twenty, ten-twenty-five....

Haydn Shirley was writhing on his cot, twitching and jerking in supreme and fearful agony. It was a terrible thing to witness. He was in pajamas and the silken garments and the sheets beneath and above him—it was too warm for blankets—were blotched with sweat. His lips had cracked, his eyes had retreated in their deep sockets and were dull from pain as he flung himself about, arched from feet to the back of his skull; his spine bowed, rigid. His hands darted to his abdomen and then tossed high. There was foam on his lips.

He could not answer Manning. There was dreadful appeal in his faded eyes but he could not speak, he could barely moan in great gasps. Manning brought water, tried to give him whisky. It was useless. The man was dying. What reserves were in his aged frame were burning up, dissolved in torment.

Manning knew he was dying. He had seen men die like that before, from various hideous causes. He did not try now to diagnose this condition. Shirley was spent. His ghost was passing. In some manner that seemed supernatural the Griffin had scored, had passed all their defenses. Manning himself was not attacked, so far....

It looked like poison, frightfully and swiftly irritant. But Shirley had tasted nothing.

The foam on his lips was suddenly bloody. There was a rattle in his throat, last horrible convulsions. Shirley's body was racked, twisting like a man whose vitals were on fire.

Suddenly it was over.

Manning covered the collapsed form with a sheet. Haydn Shirley had ceased to exist. Manning might follow presently.

Only an autopsy could—or could not—tell what had killed the financier. But the Griffin had scored once again. It seemed to Manning that he could almost hear the mocking laughter of the fiend, echoing hollowly in the vaulted place. Ten hours still to pass. More than that. The clock marked the time at ten forty-eight. Shirley had been twenty-three minutes dying in increasing torture.

Manning did what he could. He used the telephone, reached the commissioner. Outside there was a cordon of police. The medical examiner would be on hand when the vaults opened automatically. But he would be too late. There would be men from Centre Street, camera men and reporters from the press, the tabloids, the newsreels. A horde of morbid people. Another national tragedy blazed in the headlines. Manning would be a leading but unheroic figure in the stories.

He had failed!

Those matters done, he prepared to take up his vigil with the body of the man he had hoped to protect. The conference chamber was now a mortuary.

Manning did not refill his pipe. He knew that its fumes would seem to gather into the semblance of the Griffin's triumphant, taunting face. He looked at the still outlines of the chilling corpse, trying to remember when he had seen a death like that before—and what had caused it.

So midnight came—and passed.

It brought no feeling of reprieve to Manning. The Griffin had hinted he would die, but the time limit had concerned only Haydn Shirley. The threat against Manning had been presaged as possible "after the elimination of Shirley."

The threat did not harass Manning. While he combated the Griffin, every breath he took might be his last. He wanted only to come to grips with the Griffin once again.

V

MANNING WAITED until the officially essential things were done before he attempted to leave the building. The medical examiner vaguely gave the cause of death as internal hemorrhage but reserved final decision until after an autopsy. Newspapermen swarmed, demanding details of the stirring and sensational story that would be flung upon the streets in extras. Already the news had spread; the market was reacting to the tragedy.

Manning's hunch warned him that the Griffin, knowing himself triumphant, might endeavor to make his victory all complete by ridding himself of the one man who had ever mastered him. Success might make him reckless.

At last Manning got clear and passed through the revolving door at the main entrance of the Shirley Building, courting fate.

A police sergeant saluted him. Other uniformed men handled the thick traffic.

Manning's own car was parked close by where it had stood since Saturday evening, immune from regulations by the number on the license plate. He moved towards it, alert, but with the problem of Haydn Shirley's death leavening in his brain. He thought he could answer that riddle. He wanted to get to his library, to his notebooks of travel, at Pelham Manor.

He saw a car in the congested traffic. The lights had shifted and it was speeding away. It was a black sedan with a long hood that suggested power. The morning sunlight glittered on the ornament that topped the radiator cap. A crouching griffin.

Manning glimpsed a driver in dark uniform, his face obscured by the peak of his cap. He saw another face, in the rear of the car, gazing through the glass.

The face of the Griffin, gloating, challenging, mocking!

And then the car had vanished. It was impossible to give chase in that crowded street.

Manning cursed, and then turned to his car. He had that premonition of danger. His roadster had stood in that spot through the nights of Saturday and Sunday. Patrols would not disturb it, under instructions, but they had not been constantly observing it. He opened the hood gingerly and his face became sharply set as he saw the infernal device that would have been set off at the first whirr of the starter's gear, would have made scrap-metal of his car, pulp of Gordon Manning.

I T   W A S   mid-afternoon when the medical examiner called Manning at his home.

"I am still at sea," he said. "The intestines seem to have been simultaneously perforated by foreign particles that have worked through the walls in scores of places. No trace in the stomach. I thought of powdered glass but…."

"The action would have been too swift," said Manning. "Look for traces of silica. Yes, silica. Or else setaceous animal matter. But I think silica."

"Setaceous? Bristles?" The surgeon's tone was bewildered.

"Yes," Manning answered a bit impatiently. "Haydn Shirley was killed by *guna guna*. That's Malay for magic. That means love philters, poisons. They get them from the dukon, the magician, who does his hocus-pocus and hands out the medicine. Or you can buy death charms in the native markets."

He realized that East was East and West was West. There were things in Oriental usages unknown to occidental pharmacopoeias.

Haydn Shirley had watched his diet since the day Manning had warned him. And, at that very moment, Manning believed, he had been a slowly dying man, incurable, unconscious of malady.

"Listen," Manning went on. "I've seen something of these things myself, but I've been checking up authorities. I'll quote you one. You may want to use it when you turn in your diagnosis. If you confirm it the papers will rise and call you blessed. This is by Hendrik de Leeuw in 'Cross Roads of the Java Sea.'

I'll just give you a paragraph. You can get the book. You'll find it illuminating. Here it is.

" 'But *guna guna* goes much further than this. Ground glass, tiger's whiskers, shredded bamboo fibre, and similar devices, are used to cause slow death, puncturing the internal organs. Such is the skill in the use of these that they can be administered unnoticed and may be timed to take just so long to produce the desired effect.'

"I could tell you curious tales about such cases," said Manning. "So does De Leeuw. Tiger's whiskers are not easy to get over here but bamboo is available. The outer cuticle is so siliceous it is used as a razor in the East, also as a whetstone. Tiny slivers of that cuticle make a hellish device for premeditated murder. I'm inclined to think I may have more confirmation, definite confirmation, before long. If I do I'll let you know. Meantime, test for silica."

He heard the medical examiner's shocked exclamation before he hung up.

Manning sat smoking, remembering the poisons, the "radjun," of Java and Sumatra and India. He saw again the medicine women of the market place in Djocja, Java, selling openly, and without fear, arsenic, pounded glass, shredded bamboo, tiger's whiskers, oil from glands of the seacow. Those old witches were said to be able to calculate to a nicety the effect of various lethal means of inducing an apparently innocent death.

The Griffin did not care for the aspect of innocence. He was inclined to boast of his satanic ingenuity. Manning had escaped death by a narrow margin, Shirley had met it. The Griffin's thoughts should be divided between triumph and chagrin. Though there was no telling how his disordered mind might work.

Manning was just finishing his dinner when the medical examiner called back.

"I found it," he said, "thanks to your tip. The shredded fibers showed up under the microscope. They'll make a big spread of it in the morning editions. The boys are waiting here now for my report. I'm giving you the credit, naturally."

"I don't want it," said Manning. "I merely tipped you off. It will be much more authoritative, coming from you, and it will show off the acumen of the police force, which won't do any harm. Leave me out of it."

His Japanese butler entered with coffee and liqueurs, passing through to the living room. Manning trailed the man. His nerves were tingling, vibrating like the aërial antennae of a radio. He knew he was about to hear from the Griffin.

Within the hour it came, delivered by telegraphic messenger service. Manning did not trouble to detain the uniformed lad. He was probably authentic. The sender could not be traced.

He broke the splotch of scarlet wax with the imprint of the Griffin's signet upon it, opened the double sheet of heavy, hand-made, gray paper, written on with purple ink in striking chirography. Three clippings were enclosed. Manning glanced them over.

THEY WERE brief. Accounts of inconspicuous persons who had been found dead, who had lived alone. One a trapper in Missouri; one a man who collected and sold to tourists mineral specimens in North Carolina; the third a fisherman dwelling on the marshy shores of Chesapeake Bay, selling clams, oysters, shad, and occasional ducks and shore birds.

Men, Manning gathered, who were missed but not lamented. Obscure, if useful beings, without relatives to question or be questioned. None of them living with women. The time of death was approximated by the various coroners after discovery of the bodies. In every case the cause was given as inflammation of the bowels, probably induced by drinking poisonous alcohol.

Manning put the clippings under a weight, read the Griffin's letter. It was characteristic.

> Since you are still alive, my dear Manning, I imagine you have guessed the cause of Haydn Shirley's well deserved death.

I watched you as your astuteness discovered the little contrivance I had placed in your car, which would have instantly solved all your earthly problems, including the one of my capture. I decided that you were still amusing. Therefore I shall again set the board before long, for another contest between your wits and my genius.

This time I took a leaf out of your own book, Manning. I used the methods of the Orient. Haydn Shirley was a coward and not so readily dealt with as a brave man. His habits, carefully studied, gave me my opportunity. I do not hesitate to give you details, since I never repeat myself. Shirley lunched every Thursday at the exclusive club known as The Financiers. I had my man there as waiter for the past seven weeks, catering to Haydn Shirley's idiosyncrasies. He learned just how to serve him.

Meanwhile, with the aid of another of my retainers, a really superb chemist, a specialist in poisons who unfortunately threw himself in front of a subway train quite recently, I conducted some personal experiments to check up his statements. As you will see by the clippings, I choose my subjects judiciously and the reactions were very satisfactory. My late servitor timed the use of Bambusa Vulgaris to a nicety.

In these preliminary experiments he gauged the reactions within an hour. He did not know that I was going to test his statements with actual subjects, though he may have surmised it.

There was some discrepancy with Haydn Shirley. I learn, however, through the obliging press, that he fasted during his retreat in the vaults he thought Death could not enter, though Death strode, step by step with him. The fasting delayed, to some extent, the intestinal constrictions. But not efficiently.

You escorted a dead man into those vaults, Manning. I thought you might like to give these details to the papers. When you do, tell them to expect another sensation shortly. Tell them the Griffin, like the phoenix, is immortal, arising from destruction. Tell them....

The characteristic writing trailed off into an indecisive, wavy sprawl. There was no signature.

Only the *affiche* of an oval of embossed paper, scarlet, bearing the embossed device of a griffin's head and upper body, rampant.

The Griffin had scored again. He was contemplating fresh deviltries.

"The Deed I Propose Shall Be Fitting in
Thine Eyes!" It Was the Griffin's Dread
Vow to the Four-Armed Ebon Goddess

FULL MOONLIGHT shone through the big skylight of the nearly dismantled studio and Al, the legless biological "sport," rested on his trunk, muscled and formed like that of a gladiator, torturing with a lighted cigarette a dozen blotched and bloated toads in a tray.

He was supposed to tend them, feed them with flies, but his malicious nature prompted him to torment. His nature was akin to his Master's, who had bought him from a traveling sideshow and now used him as slave and bodyguard. He was efficient enough, in spite of his missing limbs.

These toads were not ordinary species. They came from the interior of China and, when irritated, their glands produced a poison that, dried, produced Senso, allied to picrotoxin, causing spasmodic death. It was part of the fiendish experimentations of the monster known as the Griffin, murderer and maniac at large, killer of invaluable citizens, hater and envier of all that was worthy and progressive.

This studio, in mid-Manhattan, was a temporary aerie of the Griffin. Since his escape from Dannemora where he had been sent by the master-investigator, Gordon Manning, ex-Military Intelligence, explorer, adventurer and scientist, he had rehabilitated his organization, assembled his vast resources, and was once again ready to extend his career of satanic crime. He was established finally within fifty miles of New York in an old manor house in the midst of wild acres, whose uncertain title kept them from development and gave him isolation.

The city building from which he had not yet moved, was a survival, fifty years old, amid modern skyscrapers. It stood on the corner of a main avenue and a one-way street, and, above the ground floor, was leased to commercial artists. The studio suite on the top floor, laid out to suit one of the heirs of the estate, dead in Europe from an accident, had been rented to the Griffin, masquerading as Mr. Silbi. He had taken a long lease and bought the furnishings. The money meant little to him. He would still retain the place, unless Manning should discover it. In any event it had served his purpose.

Now his form, cloaked and sormbreroed, flitted up the stairs (the elevator was shut down at eight) like the form of a condor, a mysterious and sinister figure. His velvet collar was turned high. Long hair that was not his own, any more than the mustachios and Spanish forked beard that accentuated his saturnine features, strayed over the collar and made him appear a romantic figure, an eccentric artist or musician, a conspirator. Rasputin himself must have cast such a shadow.

There was a jeering twist to that name, Silbi. Spelled backwards, it was Iblis, the angel flung from heaven to become a devil because he would not give tribute to God's creation, Adam. Equally the Griffin hated mankind, in general and particular, and deemed himself appointed The Destroyer. The man was insane with grandiose dementia, but that inflamed brain of his was potent for evil. The sinful phantasmagoria it conjured up were colossal in their conception and execution.

HE WENT swiftly up the stairs beneath dim electric lights, and let himself into the studio. The main fixtures had been removed, but, as he set a switch, some lights shaded in violet and amber went on and gave mysterious light to the roomy place. A globe of crystal began to revolve, and within it showed whorls of colored smoke. Exotic music sounded and a censer

*"You shall open it.
I trust I have not
deceived you."*

automatically heated incense that gave off fumes like burning amber, intoxicating, sensuous.

Al came swinging forward on his arms, active as an ape, fawning like a dog, then hastening to set fire to the wood and cannel coal in a big firepot in the open hearth. The weather was warm, but the Griffin's blood was as cold as that of the squatting toads. He threw off his cloak and warmed his hands. Lines of suffering were graven in his vulturine features, the face with the beaked nose and the cruel eyes.

He poured a purple liquor from a decanter of Venetian glass into a small silver goblet and sipped it slowly, chuckling.

He was expecting a visitor. He had planned another coup, consulted the stars and found the time propitious, the house of his victim threatened, his own horoscope favorable.

The music gave out its strange phrases and barbaric rhythms. Al squatted in a dark corner, his eyes intent upon his Master, his fingers playing with the hilt of a straight dagger in a scabbard slung to chest and shoulder.

Presently the Griffin rose and pulled aside a curtain revealing a painting on Hindu muslin. The subject was not a pleasant one, but the Griffin gave it a sort of ironical obeisance.

It was the gigantic figure of a woman, a heathen goddess. Her skin was ebon, she was four-armed. Her palms and eyes were red, her tongue and breasts and face stained with blood, her hair was matted and her teeth like fangs. She wore a necklace of skulls, her earrings were corpses and she was girdled with snakes.

"O Kali-Mai, Dark Mother, wife of Siva the Destroyer! O Chamunda, Chhinnamastaka!" intoned the Griffin. "I bring to thee a devotee, a worshiper of thy cult. We are of one mind, thou and I, and the deed I propose shall be fitting in thine eyes. Lo, I have consecrated to you the pickax and made the sacrifice of sugar. I will kill a goat for thee in the dark of the moon and acquire thy favor. I shall divine its liver and know your sanction."

There was a knocking on the door of the studio and Al, following his Master's nod, swung to open it, one hand reaching to the latch, the other balancing his torso. Then, as the man entered, the freak, at another gesture, returned to his corner, hidden by a screen.

The visitor was of medium height and supple frame. His moves were feline, his whole manner furtive. He was of Hindu type, though he might have passed for an Arab, a Cuban, or a Sicilian.

His bow was formal, his voice toneless. Its placidity suggested a certain lack of soul well fitting to one employed by the Griffin.

"You are welcome, Phansigar," said the Griffin, using a jargon known as Ramasi, a cultural dialect, rather than a lingual one. "All is prepared. Here is the tale that you must study carefully in case there is delay. Here is the gold that is only a retainer for a fuller fee upon success. Meet me here three days from now at this hour and see you fail me not."

"I do not fail," was the answer, as the man prostrated himself before the painting of the goddess, thrice. He put away the gold and the papers and went, silent as a tiger, to the door. The Griffin watched him, chuckling silently.

He took a seat in front of the fire and picked up a gilt-bronze statuette designed for a radiator ornament, a well modeled figure of a griffin, half lion, half eagle, poised to leap or soar, to tear and claw, fit symbol of the monster who now caressed it.

Then he stood up and moved to a carven prie-dieu that held writing materials on its sloping shelf, heavy, gray, handmade paper and envelopes, purple ink, pen and sealing materials, scarlet wax and an intaglio on onyx of a demi-griffin.

He wrote in a bold hand, made, instead of signature, a crisp and clever drawing of his seal, set the missive in an envelope and sealed that with wax and signet before he inscribed it:

GORDON MANNING, ESQ.
KHORASSIN LODGE
PELHAM MANOR
N.Y.

He had his own means of delivery. To his beckoning, Al brought an oriental waterpipe, its bowl charged with tobacco blent with hashish, the water through which the cooling smoke must pass scented and flavored with attar of roses.

The Griffin ignited the weed and sat back, inhaling, contemplating the firelight that played fitfully upon his features. In that crimson glow he looked indeed like Iblis, plotting in Hades.

II

...THE STARS tell me that the seventeenth of this month, falling on Wednesday, is most favorable for my design. Some swift moment between midnight and midnight, Manning, Erle Crossleigh will be eliminated. May you be there to see. I shall not be far away.

This arrogant fool who presumes to establish my descent, and yours, my dear Manning, from the mouldering relics of arboreal apes, has lived too long.

The board is set. Prepare your defense. It may be I shall lose a pawn, but I have studied well my gambit. I shall win the game.

Gordon Manning was in his library, his pipe clenched between his teeth, his face grim. The tension of weeks was, in a measure, relieved. The Griffin, in his usual arrogance, had announced his purpose, the name of his victim, the date of death.

Erle Crossleigh, eminent anthropologist, the man who had gone farthest to establish the Descent of Man, was doomed, but the doom was not yet definite. The Griffin was positive of final triumph, Manning resolute to prevent it.

Most of all, he itched to come to handgrips with the monster, as he had once before. This time Manning would make no endeavor to capture the fiend alive, to deliver him to justice. The law, in its practice of medieval jurisprudence, had not condemned the Griffin to the chair, but had sent him to an institution for the criminal insane. He should be destroyed, utterly, and Manning meant to be the agent.

But, first, Crossleigh must be protected. It would not be an easy task, despite the aid of the police, of protective agencies.

The Griffin, of course, had prepared for weeks with infinite cunning, an exhaustive study of Crossleigh's mode of living. He had boasted more than once that a man's habits, properly comprehended, left him open to well planned attack. The Griffin was an evil genius. Rightly directed, his powers could have lifted him to a supreme height of advancement. Instead he reveled in diabolical intrigue, in plots that might have been hatched in hell.

Manning, in the brief time left him, must acquaint himself with Crossleigh's customs and environment, must pit his brains and fearlessness against that of the monster, anticipate the deadly stroke, not knowing from what source it might be delivered; handicapped by the Griffin's strategy of infinite pains and devilish inspiration.

He rested an elbow on the arm of his chair and cupped his left-hand fingers about the bowl of his briar, reflecting. A high window looked out into the sidewalk to his garden. The panes were leaded and the glass was bulletproof. Well locked gates barred intruders.

A gun, these days, was always close to his hand. The next instant he clutched it, almost squeezed trigger before he realized the two way purpose of that protective glazing. No ordinary missile might pass it, and his own would only star the diamonds through which leered a fiendish countenance with glittering eyes that looked like live coals, a beaked nose, mustachios, and twin peaks of beard under a high-crowned, black sombrero.

It was the Griffin! Manning's Airedale had not barked. His servants had heard nothing.

There was no trace of an invader when he searched the premises. Only the dog, lying dead, a little foam on its jaws, its limbs stiffening from convulsion.

Manning made the autopsy in his own laboratory. He found a titbit of undigested liver still impregnated with what his reactions showed to be an isolation of epinephrine, an alkaloid akin to the frog venom used by the Choco Indians of South America on their arrow tips, to the Senso drug of China and Japan, used for heart trouble and hemorrhages—also for poisons. Bufagin! Toads' venom, possessing the essential toxic features of digitalis.

CROSSLEIGH OWNED two houses on Central Park West. Hotels and big apartment houses hemmed him in, but the neighborhood suited him and he would not sell. Above all things, he disliked to be bothered with even the thought of removal. The houses were spacious and he had made them into one with well planned alterations. The two gardens had been used as space for his workshop, as he styled it, though it was more likely a museum dedicated to evolution.

The workshop was lit by skylights. High walls of surrounding buildings towered about it. It was professedly fire and burglar-proof. The skylights were reinforced by steel grids. The only entrance was from the duplex residence.

Crossleigh received Manning in his spacious library, where the higher halves of the lofty walls were practically covered above the shelves of books with paintings reconstructing primitive forms of life.

In the museum were their fossils, their bones, and perfect reproductions of existing animals with their skins fitted over plaster, arranged in backgrounds showing their native habitat.

There were reconstructions of man's more immediate ancestors, and also actual parts of their skeletons.

The library opened into the museum and Manning, asked to wait, examined the exhibits with absorbing interest. Here was the process of evolution made exceedingly plain. A child could understand it. One case showed the stages of the horse. There were primitive implements, of wood, of shell, flint, agate and quartz. There were hammerstones and lever-sticks used by baboons for breaking nuts and prying up rocks, even for striking blows.

Despite the ominous and imperative nature of his mission, Manning was fascinated. A man like Crossleigh, supreme anthropologist, student and revealer of the natural history of Man, was threatened by the mad Griffin because the latter considered his own swollen ego insulted by the suggestion that his ancestors had lived in trees.

Manning felt that Crossleigh would laugh at the Griffin's communication on one score. An exhibit, with its legend, proclaimed boldly that Man was not descended from the great arboreal apes, but that his immediate ancestors were extinct running-apes of the early Cainozoic period.

He heard a step behind him and turned to greet a man taller

than himself, athletic, tanned, vigorous, a fellow-explorer. Manning recognized in him a kindred spirit. Crossleigh's eyes were shining with the enthusiasm of a man who lives for but a single purpose.

He gripped Manning with a powerful hand. Here was a man who would give a good account of himself in any fair encounter, would win against odds. But not, perhaps, against the Griffin's guile.

The meeting had been arranged through a mutual friend, and the fact that they were both active members of the Explorers' Club. Crossleigh was cordial, apologizing for the delay in coming down.

"I knew you would understand," he said. "I was dictating something and I wanted to get it down while it was fresh in my mind. Slosson tells me you want to see me about something vitally important. I have seen you occasionally at the club and, of course, I know of some of your accomplishments, including your capture of the Griffin, though I have only just come back from Europe, from Aurignac, in France. They have made some more important finds there, you know. Most important. You are interested in these matters?" he added.

"Yes," answered Manning. "Right now, I am more interested in *you*."

Crossleigh looked at him sharply.

"You mean the Griffin?" he asked.

Manning nodded, handed him the letter he had received.

III

CROSSLEIGH READ it through without a tremor. His eyes were clear and courageous, and he gave the communication back without especial comment, not even about the arboreal apes.

"He does not furnish much warning," he said. "Not enough. I have a strong objection to dying at present. I am on the brink of an important thing, Manning. I doubt if I shall have the evidence I am expecting much before the seventeenth, and after the receipt of it there is much to be done. You have foiled the Griffin before this. I place myself in your hands, only asking to be allowed opportunity for work without interruption. I think you will do much for Science if you keep me alive for thirty days."

"If you are alive on the morning of the eighteenth," said Manning, "you will not have to worry any more about the Griffin. He studies the stars and makes divinations before he announces his proposed victim's name and the date of elimination. If he fails he wipes the thing out of his own mind. Contemplation of failure drove him beyond the safety line once before, and I think he recognizes that. His ego cannot bear to dwell on a mistake. Above all, he strives to save his face."

"Good!" said Crossleigh. "I will show you all over the premises, so you can make a fortress of them. You can go ahead and fill them with plain-clothes men, so long as I am not disturbed in my work. I get absorbed in it and probably would not notice you unless you forced me to it, but the knowledge of being overlooked would irritate me. I will go armed, if you prefer it and, of course, you will be my guest for as long as you please."

"I am afraid I shall have to be your shadow," said Manning. "At least for the twenty-four hours mentioned. But I shall try to be both silent and invisible."

"Fine! You see, Manning," the anthropologist said, "I have just had great news from Java. I have just heard from a man named Kumar Asit Gupta, once assistant curator in the Museum at Delhi, who has been investigating the ruins of the ancient Hindu temples at Boro-Boedoer. In excavating, he came across an upheaved stratum of the Pleistocene period, with two skulls, both complete, and other fossil bones that show development from the first Java men. He is now on the way with these relics that are enormously unique, quite invaluable. I cannot tell you all that it means, save that it ties up with my own pet theory of the origin of modern Man.

"I am sorry to have bored you," he ended with a change of tone. "I am an enthusiast, practically a fanatic. But these things are not mine, they belong to Science so, let us foil the Griffin, somehow."

"When do you expect this Gupta, Hindu, from his name?" asked Manning.

"I had a telegram from him saying he had landed and was leaving San Francisco. Here it is."

Manning read the message.

"This should bring him here on the sixteenth. We must try and have him met, see where he stays. If he sees you on the sixteenth I shall be better content than if he puts it off until the next day."

Crossleigh laughed.

"You would hardly associate a studious babu named Kumar Asit Gupta, come all the way from Magelang, with the Griffin's desire to murder me. Perhaps you don't know the type."

"I know the Griffin," said Manning grimly. "If you see Gupta on the seventeenth, I want to be present, if unseen."

For the moment Crossleigh seemed annoyed, then the frown left his face.

"Agreed," he said, "if it makes you feel any better. I speak Hindu and Malay. I should detect an impostor before he showed me anything."

"I am merely taking precautions. They are necessary. I shall want personally to supervise your food that day and to be continually with you. If Gupta comes, well and good, but he will be the only stranger to be admitted during those twenty-four hours. We can check him up pretty well."

"Do what you please, Manning, but don't delay the arrival of those fossil bones. Now, shall we look over the house?"

THERE SEEMED no doubt about the authenticity of Kumar Asit Gupta. He was discovered registered at the Plaza in the suite he had reserved by telegram from the Coast, sent the same time as his wire to Crossleigh.

A quiet and unobtrusive man, who spoke good English and, but for his signature, might have been one of a dozen nationalities with skins inclined to swarthiness.

He had not announced by which railroad he was traveling and the squadmen had failed to pick him up at depots or ferries, mainly because they had been imagining someone with a turban and an air of strangeness. According to the hotel management, Gupta was completely cosmopolitan. He had asked that a certain leather trunk, small enough to be carried, and which he had himself transported from his cab, should be placed in a vault. And he had ordered a modest but well chosen meal in his room without revealing any caste prejudices.

Later, he had telephoned Crossleigh and made an appointment for ten o'clock on the morning of the seventeenth.

All this Manning knew before he took charge of the Crossleigh premises, fortified by forty picked men, distributed strategically. In only one thing Crossleigh had proved difficult. He wanted to go to work immediately upon receipt of the relics, and insisted upon two of his assistants remaining. After all, this bid fair to crown the achievements of his lifetime, he considered it as vital as life itself, and he had placed the full responsibility of guarding that life upon Manning.

Manning found out that it was customary for Crossleigh to shut himself up for days at a time in his workshop with one or more assistants, or by himself, and that nobody dared disturb him. On these occasions he prepared his own meals, which he confessed to Manning were generally either inadequate or rather horrible messes, concocted on the gas burners he used in his experimental work.

Manning announced himself as the cook on this occasion. The two assistants seemed beyond suspicion, but their demeanor and their records did not eliminate them from Manning's scrutiny. The Griffin had practically bought himself out of Dannemora, combining bribery of a supposedly honest guard with a most ingenious method of departure. Even assiduous scientific assistants had sick wives, mortgages, and private troubles that a golden wand might make vanish. They were not too lavishly paid.

Crossleigh curbed his impatience with difficulty as ten o'clock approached. His two aides were at work in a dark room and a partitioned off space, respectively, ready to make photographs and casts of the expected fossils.

A house phone rang and Manning answered it.

"It's Gupta," he said. "I'll let him in here."

The babu had exchanged his traveling suit of blue serge for haircloth clothing, a long, close-fitting coat, trousers tied at the ankles, shoes of soft leather, and an elaborate turban.

He was excessively polite, without humility. He carried, not the small leather trunk, but a casket of black wood, bound with brass, inlaid with nacre. This he retained hold of, while making his obeisance, first to Manning and then to Crossleigh. He mistook the two, thinking Manning the anthropologist.

Manning explained and retired. He took a place behind two exhibit cases, using the glass side of one as a mirror. Crossleigh returned formal salutation, but he was plainly afire with expectation as Kumar Asit Gupta set down the casket on a small table and proceeded to unlock it.

An assistant came from the dark room but stopped, seeing the visitor.

The babu set the key in the lock then stepped back.

"You shall open it yourself," he said. "I trust I have not in any way deceived or disappointed you."

NOTHING COULD seem more harmless than the polite Oriental. His clothes were close and smooth-fitting as a skin, revealing no weapon, but Manning did not trust him. He did not trust anybody during these twenty-four hours, even Crossleigh. He knew the Oriental guile, and, even though there seemed no motive for the babu to harm Crossleigh, Manning was alert.

There might be a poisoned spring connected with that casket—he had not forgotten his dead dog—there might be a venomous snake, teased by electric cells.

He had made Crossleigh promise to open nothing, but now the anthropologist, with such a rich prize almost in hand, forgot everything else. Gupta had moved back, standing behind Crossleigh's shoulder, a slighter, shorter man, his smile slightly deprecating.

Manning called a warning to Crossleigh, but it was not heeded. The lid opened. Crossleigh gave a gasp and leaned forward, lifting a layer of cottonwool. Nothing happened.

But now it came, like a stroke of lightning from a clear sky. The action was too swift for eye to follow, but something came out of Gupta's sleeve, shaken out as a Hindu conjurer shakes the cobra in the mango trick. There was a glimmer of crimson and then Crossleigh was on his knees, his face darker than the silken scarf about his throat. Gupta's placid face transformed to that of a demon in some hideous ritual, twisted with fingers of steel.

It was Thuggee. The Hindu was one of the professional killers who laid down their lives for a cause. A noose-operator, a worshiper of Kali, the Dark Mother, an expert at murder, a hireling of elimination.

He was swiftly expert. Crossleigh's tongue protruded, with his eyes. A frightful wheezing came from his compressed windpipe. But Gupta was not swifter than Manning's bullet that smashed into one arm at the shoulder and plowed on through, paralyzing the strangler, shocking his nerves with the splintering of bone.

He staggered back and Crossleigh dropped to the floor, feebly clutching at the silk throttling-scarf, linked with a sewn-in coin at one end. He could barely breathe, was still conscious, though veins stood out on his forehead like cords.

The assistant came running forward, kneeling beside Crossleigh, using a penknife to cut the constricting scarf, as Manning called on Gupta to surrender, to throw up his hands. Crossleigh gasped with relief, sitting up and tenderly feeling his throat, bruised and swollen. It had been a close call.

The Hindu was badly hurt. His black mohair clothing was sodden with blood, but he recovered, like a sorely wounded tiger that fights as long as life lasts.

He tossed up his hands in a gesture and flung abroad a powder that blinded and strangled. Manning fired through the dust of it and the babu darted for the door, opened it, plunged on for the street entrance.

Manning followed, gasping, wiping scalding tears away. He yelled at two plain-clothesmen who appeared with leveled guns.

"Let him go!" he shouted. "Follow up, but let him go now."

Astounded, they withheld their fire. Manning was in supreme command by order of the police commissioner, as well as by virtue of his commission from the governor. Then, being experienced men, they caught his meaning.

The Hindu, wounded desperately, acting subconsciously, was, like a crippled beast, making for a lair, hoping for a getaway.

He dived out of the front door, dripping blood. Manning was hard on his heels, gun ready, eyes clearing a little.

His own car was parked, against ordinances, but privileged by its special license number, close by.

He saw a black sedan come gliding up. Its engine purred under the long hood that spoke of power. A curtain was half raised and a sinister face looked out of it for a moment before the blind was pulled down and the sedan swung out to the middle of the road, its speed accelerating, abandoning the wretch that now sprawled upon the sidewalk, splotching it with crimson, his turban unwound, his strength spent with his blood.

Manning leaped over Gupta's limp body, racing for his car. It was a roadster and should be as powerful as the black sedan now disappearing round the corner. He left the babu to the detectives. Crossleigh had been saved in time, but Manning had seen the gloating countenance of the Griffin, mustachioed and fork-bearded, with his hooked nose like a beak above the cruel mouth, between the glittering eyes.

MANNING'S STARTER whirred, his engine came to life. He cut out his ordinary signal horn and connected up the police siren to which he was entitled. He saw the sedan ahead speeding for Columbus Circle, sounding a similar alarm. Traffic made way. New York was used to the unusual. Theirs not to question why, when that shrill alarm proclaimed authority. Officers saluted, if a little doubtfully, as the black sedan and the cream-colored roadster sped past at even rates of speed, neither gaining or losing.

The black sedan selected Broadway. At Thirty-Fourth it swung east, careening on two wheels, Manning close behind. One block, and the sedan swerved south, down Fifth Avenue.

The radio cruisers would soon be closing in, Manning told himself, as they sped by crosstown traffic at Twenty-Third, held up by officers obedient to the ear-splitting clamor of the sirens.

At Washington Arch, the Avenue divided, but now it made a perfect speedway, with Manning beginning to gain a little.

Suddenly the sedan turned west. The one-way street was choked with cars and the sedan lunged up on the sidewalk, scattering foot-citizens like frightened fowl.

There was a report, like a backfire, or a shot, and the sedan came to a crashing halt, sideswiping a light truck. Manning threw on his protesting brakes as he saw a cloaked figure dart from the car and rush into a doorway.

Police cars were coming up, traffic officers and patrolmen were running. The truck driver was bleeding and cursing. The chauffeur of the black sedan was slumped over his wheel.

Manning glimpsed the face of the Griffin behind the gate of an elevator that slammed as the car shot upwards. His bullet struck the metal grille and glanced, whining. There was no return shot from the Griffin. For once, his face seemed desperate.

Manning imagined him holding his weapon on the elevator man. But he had traced the monster to his aerie. Crossleigh was all right, the would-be assassin was in custody, if he was not dead by now.

He took the stairs. The police were following. Manning was fast enough to be sure the elevator did not stop on the next floor, nor the next. As he gained the fourth, and top floor, it was going down.

He barely glimpsed the closing of a door at the far end of a passage. There was no name there, none on the two doors before it. But the Griffin had gone in.

A sergeant and a first-grade man came racing up, let out of the elevator.

"Guard those two doors," said Manning. "Stand by!"

He pressed a bell on the one through which he had half seen the Griffin disappear. There was no answer. Manning smashed the upper glass panel with his gun butt, reached through and sprung the lock.

The studio seemed empty. A fireplace to the left, a door to the right. Manning went through it to a room that seemed half kitchen, half laboratory. It was vacant, without a hiding place. There had been a screen in the studio and Manning had looked behind it and seen nothing but what looked like a stool, covered with a drape.

He thrust his way into the third room of the suite. It seemed to be a bedroom with a couch, a chair, a bureau and a washstand.

A man stood there at bay, his black cloak cast aside, snarling, gun in hand.

Lead seared Manning's collarbone, lead nicked his ribs, but the other toppled on his mustachioed and bearded face, shot through the heart.

MANNING STOOD over him, powder-gas streaking

from his gun. It seemed a tame ending for the Griffin. Too tame.

He stooped. He was hatless. Something like a white hot wire divided his hair, seared his scalp, and he saw a straight bladed knife embedded deep in the plaster of the wall. Then something attacked him savagely from the rear.

Hands, like claws, clutched him, clawed their way upwards with incredible fury as a living lump struck his spine. The claws gripped his throat, his windpipe was compressed.

He fought with the creature, casting his arms behind him, realizing that the thing had no legs. He hurled himself backwards and felt the figure squirm, muscular but formless, as wood and glass panels splintered and the police rushed in.

Manning saw an incredible figure that might have been evoked by his blood-flooded brain, thrust up a window with widespread hands and vault through the opening.

Uproar came from the street as Manning reeled forward. There was a burst of gunfire. It ceased and he looked upwards. There was nothing in sight.

"You see anything go out that window?" he asked an officer.

"I thought I did. I ain't sure. It didn't look human."

Manning ordered them to the roof and examined the body of the Griffin. He was beginning to feel a trifle groggy and he did not improve as he saw a wig awry, a mustache pushed out of place by a dying hand. Under the wig the hair was scanty, reddish.

Here was a masquerader, some actor out of work, desperate for money, cleverly made up to a semblance of the fiend who must even now be chuckling.

Not chuckling too emphatically. Crossleigh had been rescued. The Griffin had lost two pawns—this impoverished Thespian, and Gupta.

Of course there had been no discovery in Java. Now Manning understood. Gupta had never come from there, even from San Francisco. The Griffin had arranged the telegrams, hired the disciple of Thuggee. There were probably no relics in the casket, at best poor imitations. But the Griffin had failed. The chagrin of it would bite into his ego like acid.

This was his aerie. Manning gazed about the studio uncertainly. It looked as if the Griffin had been ready to desert the place. His wounds smarted, his hair was clogged with blood. He looked at the dead man, another victim of the Griffin, perhaps, primarily, of depression. Poor devil, disguising himself for a fatal fee.

The sergeant reëntered.

"The commissioner's on the way," he said. "Say, you look like you needed the surgeon yourself. He's coming."

"Okay!" said Manning. "How about that thing that went out the window?"

"They're searching the roofs. They saw something like an ape climbing up a fire shutter to the coping. But they can't find it."

Manning felt his throat tenderly. It was curious that both Crossleigh and he should have been attacked the same way, he thought. But the Griffin's ways were not ordinary ways.

Suddenly a voice sounded in the great studio.

There was no ordinary radio there. A bronze disk, like a gong, seemed to be vibrating.

"Manning, you score this game. Luck was largely with you. It may not be, next time. You have failed to be amusing. But I can still laugh, thinking of the future."

Chuckles sounded in the studio, growing fainter, lost in the sound of strange music. The sergeant seemed entranced.

"If that's the Griffin," he said, "I don't want anything more to do with him. I'll transfer to the loft squad first. That guy ain't human. Any more than that thing that went out of the window."

"They are both human enough, Sergeant, so far as they go," said Manning, a trifle wearily. "Is that the medical examiner?"

The sergeant nodded as the surgeon entered.

"Dead man in the other room, Doc," said Manning. "Better look me over first."

AL WAS squatting, not unlike an enormous toad, in a long disused water tank on an adjoining roof. It had been supplied with food for emergency and, with a faith worthy of a greater cause, he waited for his Master, the Griffin, to rescue him. It might take many dreary days, until the pursuit he heard scuttling on the leads died down, but he was certain that, ultimately, he would be released.